CHASING THE DEAD

Praise for Joel Goldman

"Exciting…"
Publishers Weekly on *Motion to Kill*

"Fast, furious and thoroughly enjoyable."
Jeffery Deaver on *The Last Witness*

"Joel Goldman is the real deal."
John Lescroart on *Cold Truth*

"Highly recommended."
Lee Child on *Deadlocked*

"A page turner of the highest caliber…I loved it."
Michael Connelly on *Final Judgment*

"Chillingly realistic…fast-paced, smartly plotted and gripping."
Linda Fairstein on *Shakedown*

"A masterful blend of rock-solid detecive work and escalating dread."
Robert Crais on *The Dead Man*

"A page turner that keeps going full speed until the very end."
Faye Kellerman on *No Way Out*

"Suspense at its very best."
Libby Fischer Hellmann on *Stone Cold and Chasing the Dead*

CHASING THE DEAD

AN ALEX STONE THRILLER

A NOVEL BY
JOEL GOLDMAN

This is a work of fiction.
Names, characters, places, and incidents either are the product of the author's imagination or are used fictitiously. Any resemblance to actual events or persons, living or dead, is entirely coincidental.
All rights reserved.
No part of this book may be reproduced or stored in a retrieval system or transmitted in any form or by any means, electronic, mechanical, photocopying, recording, or otherwise without the express written permission of the publisher.

Published by Character Flaw Press, LLC
12120 State Line Road, #253
Leawood, KS 66209

Copyright 2002 Joel Goldman
Copyright 2013 Character Flaw Press, LLC

ISBN: 0989859924
ISBN-13: 9780989859929

Books by Joel Goldman

Motion to Kill
The Last Witness
Cold Truth
Deadlocked
Final Judgment
Shakedown
The Dead Man
No Way Out
Stone Cold
Chasing The Dead
Freaks Must Die

For Gummy

ONE

The woman's nude body lay faceup on a narrow sandbar in Rock Creek. Her head and torso were cushioned in soft mud jutting out from the edge of the bank. September moonlight flattened against her pale skin, her sightless eyes open and as cold as the lunar gaze. Long black hair fanned out from her face. A gold crucifix was embedded flat against her skin just above the swell of her bruised left breast.

She looked like she'd fallen from the sky. Her arms were flung away from her body, forearms dangling like broken wings. Her legs were flared out from her waist, all four limbs resting in the shallow water on either side of the sandbar.

Jared Bell stared at her. She reminded him of Ali. He knelt and stroked her cheek, letting his hand find her breast, his fingertips curling around the crucifix, prying it loose as a diamondback snake slithered out of the water and across her belly, disappearing downstream.

His eyelids fluttered and closed and he saw Ali again. She was on her knees, hands bound behind her back, a gun pressed against the side of her face, the muzzle buried in her cheek. She looked up at him, her mouth forming a plea – *Jared, help me.* The gun fired and her head exploded. Jared squeezed his eyes until he saw stars and her ruined face melted away.

He shook his head and opened his eyes. The woman was still in the water. For an instant he didn't know how he'd gotten there. The recurring flash of uncertainty, of losing himself to another time and place, sent a terrifying jolt through him, as if he'd been struck by lightning. He flung himself backward and into the stream, clutching the crucifix. Breathless, he coughed creek water, wiped his chin, and stuffed the cross in his pocket.

Jared crawled back to the woman, cupping her face in his hands as he muttered apologies. He thought about closing her eyes but didn't because his grandfather, who had been a preacher, told him when his mother died that her eyes had stayed open so her soul could leave her body, and whatever else he'd done, he didn't want to risk trapping the woman's soul.

He climbed up the creek bank, slipping on the mud. He gave her a last look and walked back to his tent, changed out of his wet clothes, and put on jeans and a T-shirt. His sneakers were soaked but he couldn't do anything about that. They were the only pair of shoes he owned. He took them off, shook out the grit from the creek, and put them back on.

Kaleidoscopic images of the woman and Ali flooded his thoughts, disconnecting him from the here and now. He sat on the tent floor, cross-legged, head in his hands, until the moment passed and he felt anchored again.

Rock Creek was a low-water tributary of the Missouri River that bisected Liberty Park where Jared had pitched his tent. Half a dozen tents were spread out on his side of the creek, all of them dark and quiet, silhouetted in the moonlight, a cool midnight breeze rippling through the grounds. The week before, there had been eight tents. Next week there could be more. It all depended on how full the homeless shelters were, the overflow finding their way to the park.

His tent was closest to the water, the others scattered farther away among the beaten grass, rough brush, and thick woods, including one backing against a towering cliff carved out of a long-ago-excavated hillside.

East of the park were more hills, home to a hardscrabble neighborhood nicknamed Dogpatch, where people lived in flimsy trailers set on concrete blocks and dilapidated houses cockeyed with wood rot and tucked back from rough ribbons of narrow, poorly lit, winding asphalt. Warnings to keep out and beware of dogs were strung from one yard to the next.

I-435, the beltway encircling Kansas City, ran along the west side of the park, filling it with an unrelenting hum that rose to a roar whenever a convoy of eighteen-wheelers rumbled past.

Liberty Park wasn't a real park, not the kind with sheltered picnic tables, water fountains, and baseball diamonds. It was a hundred acres of forgotten ground on Kansas City's far eastern edge, wide in the center, tapered at each end. Someone had driven a fence post into the ground and topped it with a plywood rectangle, hand-drawn lettering giving the place its name.

Dry and dressed, Jared headed out of the park, keeping his distance from the other tents, careful not to disturb anyone. He walked a couple of miles until he reached a pay phone bolted to the wall of a shuttered convenience store, picked up the receiver, dialed 911, and waited for someone to answer.

"What's your emergency?" the dispatcher asked.

"I'd like to report a murder."

TWO

The first patrol car pulled into the convenience store parking lot at one a.m. on Tuesday, September 14, fifteen minutes after Jared's 911 call, the car's headlights framing Jared. Officer Ernie Schmitt kept his car door between them until he had a better feel for the situation.

"Are you the guy who made the 911 call about a murder?" Schmitt asked.

"Yes, sir. That was me. The body's in Rock Creek down in Liberty Park."

"What's your name?"

"Bell, sir. Jared Bell."

Ernie Schmitt was a big man, in good enough shape to subdue someone a head shorter and fifty pounds lighter like Jared, though he guessed Jared was a good fifteen, maybe twenty years younger and, with his scrawny frame, could outrun him and could sure as hell shoot him if he was armed.

That Jared had called 911 didn't eliminate him as a suspect or a threat. It was the middle of the night on a deserted strip of road. A Jackson County sheriff's deputy had been ambushed after responding to a similar call the year before, Schmitt's memory of the deputy's funeral still fresh. He unsnapped the holster of his service pistol, keeping a light grip on the butt. He radioed his dispatcher, advising that he had secured the caller and was waiting for backup and a detective.

"Sit tight, Mr. Bell," Schmitt said. "A detective will be here soon. You can tell him all about it."

Jared nodded, lowering himself to the pavement, sitting cross-legged and tapping his hands against his thighs.

By the time Detective Hank Rossi rolled up, the parking lot was filled with two more patrol cruisers and an ambulance. Rossi had been called out the night before, worked a full shift earlier that day, and gone home. Certain he had the night off, he had knocked back a bottle of wine with a rare steak, riding the buzz to bed, digging out of the fog when his phone rang. He braced his lean six-foot frame against the open car door, a dull ache throbbing between his eyes, and steadied himself, apologizing to his dead mother for not taking her advice and becoming a dentist, cursing the nightmares the booze couldn't subdue.

Rossi and Schmitt had forty-five years in the department between them, long enough for Schmitt to know that Rossi didn't want him asking Jared any questions other than to establish identity. Schmitt signaled to the other uniforms, Douglas and Lyle, to keep an eye on Jared and met Rossi at his car.

"He's the caller?" Rossi asked.

"That's what he says."

"Who is he?"

"Says his name is Jared Bell."

"Is that the name on his driver's license?"

Schmitt smiled. "Doesn't have one. Only ID he has is a VA card."

"Did you run him?"

"While you were still getting out of bed. He's twenty-eight. No priors. No warrants. Guy's not right, though—I can tell you that much."

"What do you mean?" Rossi asked.

"Look at him. He's on another planet: half the time he's a one-man band playing his knees like they're fucking bongos. The rest of the time, it's like he's somewhere else."

Jared was sitting cross-legged on the pavement, his face blank, staring into the darkness outside the circle of squad cars.

"Man's eccentric. Doesn't make him crazy. He volunteer anything?"

"Just that he's the one who made the 911 call about a body in Rock Creek where it runs through Liberty Park. Figured to let you ask the rest of the questions."

Rossi sighed, scratching the scruff on his chin. "Great. That's all I need: a midnight stroll among the dead and the deadbeats."

"Don't forget the pervs. Every time we make a sweep down there, we get a couple of sex offenders who forgot to register."

"Maybe they figure Liberty Park isn't much of an address."

"Could be worse. Could be Dogpatch instead. Start knocking on those doors in the middle of the night and you're just as likely to get shot as have a damn pit bull take a chunk out of your ass."

Rossi shook his head. "Can't be helped, since we'll have to canvass Dogpatch and find out if any of the neighborhood women have gone missing."

"Like they'd tell us. More likely they'd shoot us for trespassing."

"Call dispatch and ask for any detectives and uniforms they can send us. We'll need help with the campers in Liberty Park and the friendly folks in Dogpatch."

The officers guarding Jared stepped aside when Rossi approached. Jared jumped to his feet, holding his arms stiff at his sides, straining to stay still. Rossi thought he was trying not to salute, though the military impulse looked out of place with the rest of him. His hair was a ragged mop, his face was splotched with irregular patches of whiskers, and he reeked of sour sweat, missing only the boozy tang Rossi expected from someone living in Liberty Park.

"I'm Detective Rossi."

"Yes, sir," Jared said.

"Officer Schmitt tells me you were in the service."

"Army. Did a tour in Afghanistan."

"Mind if I have a look at your VA card?"

Jared handed it to him. It was one of the new cards, the ones that omitted social security numbers and dates of birth, limiting the information on the card to a name, photograph, and special eligibility indicators—Service Connected, Purple Heart, and Former POW—if applicable. Jared Bell had been awarded the Purple Heart.

Rossi returned the card. "Purple Heart, huh? How'd it happen?"

"I took a round in my gut."

Jared pulled up his T-shirt, showing Rossi a ridged, ropy scar running six inches across his belly, a field-surgery souvenir.

"I got my scar in the first Gulf War," Rossi said. Though he'd served, he hadn't been wounded, telling the lie to build trust and rapport. "Sniper nicked me in the ass, not bad enough for a medal. Did you get him?"

Jared shook his head. "Not yet, but I'll get him one day."

"How you going to do that? Reenlist?"

"No, sir. Just talk, I guess. I see him all the time in my dreams, that and a lot of other shit," he said, dragging both hands down the sides of his nose and over his mouth, then shaking his head. "Maybe I'll get him one of these nights. That's all. How about you, sir? Did you get yours?"

"I didn't, but some soldiers in a helicopter gunship took him out."

"Good for them, sir."

Rossi studied the face on the ID, wondering how long it had been since the photograph had been taken. The man in the picture had steady, confident eyes and a square jaw. The man who'd made the 911 call looked lost, his mouth open in a loose grin, jittery and shuffling his feet, dreaming about killing an enemy who was half a world away and probably dead by now anyway.

"So I'm guessing this body you found wasn't the first one you've ever seen."

"No, sir. I've seen a bunch."

"What can you tell me about this one?"

"Not much, sir. Just that she's in the creek and she's dead."

"How'd you happen to find her?"

"I was sleeping in my tent and got up to take a leak. I did my business and decided to walk a little bit cause I don't sleep so good. I was down along the creek when I seen her."

"Tell me what you saw."

"She was on her back, looking straight up at me; at least that's what it seemed like to me."

"What did you do?"

"Well, I was pretty sure she was dead, but I wanted to be sure—you know what I mean, just in case she wasn't. So I got down in the water and she was dead all right."

"What makes you think she was murdered?"

"There was marks all around her neck, like she was strangled."

"Anything else?"

"Well, sir, she wasn't wearing any clothes."

"I'd say those are pretty good reasons. Thanks for calling it in. Can you show us where you found her?"

Jared nodded. "That's why I called you. Nobody should be left like that."

THREE

They parked on the north end of Liberty Park, police and paramedics leaving their emergency flashers on to warn approaching cars—red, white, and blue streamers splitting the darkness as they formed a circle around Rossi, waiting for instructions.

"I want to get a look at the body, but we have to be careful with the people in those tents," Rossi said. "If they fit the homeless profile, some of them may be crazy, some of them may be armed, some of them may be wanted, and some of them may be all three. So be careful. Their first instinct may be to shoot or run, and their second will be to keep their mouths shut. We can't make them talk, but we can hold on to them long enough to give them a chance to tell us if they heard or saw something."

"No way to know how many people are down there or where they are. The woods are kind of thick in parts. How do you want to handle it?" Schmitt asked.

"You and the EMTs come with me. Everyone else, gather whoever is camping out. Keep them calm, don't let them talk to each other, and don't let them back in their tents until we figure out if we need to search them."

He shined a flashlight toward the park.

"Okay, Jared, show us how you found her, starting from your tent."

"My tent?"

"Yeah, I want to see things the way you saw them. You started out from your tent, so that's what we'll do."

Jared nodded, swallowing, jutting his chin out and in like a turtle poking its head in and out of its shell. "You got it, sir."

Rossi knew that Jared wouldn't be the first or last to kill someone and report the crime, enjoying the spotlight much as the arsonist who helps put out the fire. Letting Jared lead the way would give him the chance to show off and make a mistake that might expose him as the killer. Rossi and Schmitt flanked him as they entered the park, stopping at a dome-shaped tent.

"This is it, my tent," Jared said.

Rossi nodded at Schmitt, who took up station at the entrance, arms crossed.

"What's he doing?" Jared asked Rossi, pointing at Schmitt.

Rossi smiled, putting his arm across Jared's shoulders. "Making sure no one bothers your stuff while we're busy with this dead body of yours."

Jared wriggled away from Rossi, staring at Schmitt, mouth agape, eyes wild.

"Everything I got's in that tent. I don't want him or nobody else messin' with my stuff."

Rossi figured that by now Jared was sorry he'd called 911. People like him always were. Thinking they were doing the right thing or not thinking at all, and before they knew what hit them, they were caught in a trap they'd set for themselves without realizing it.

"Hey, don't worry," Rossi said. "Just do your duty, soldier."

Jared took a deep breath and pointed downstream.

"She's over there."

"Take the point," Rossi told him, motioning to the paramedics to fall in behind him. "We'll be right behind you."

Jared walked straight from his tent to the edge of the creek, turning north and taking a few steps downstream before Rossi stopped him.

"Is this the route you took? Right along the creek here?"

He didn't turn around. "Yes, sir."

"That's real helpful, Jared. How about we keep a little farther from the edge. You know this area but I don't, and it's dark. I don't want to take a chance I might slip and fall in the creek and you'd have to pull me out."

Rossi was a little unsure of his footing after drinking his way through his late dinner, but he had other reasons for cautioning Jared. He wanted Jared to believe that he was depending on him, giving Jared another reason to trust him. It was like telling a woman he'd just met in a bar that she was the best thing that had happened to him all day. And he wanted to make sure they didn't contaminate the scene by trampling the exact route Jared had taken.

Jared moved inland about ten feet. Rossi followed him, sweeping his flashlight along the edge of the creek. The grass was upright, dew glistening on each blade, none of it matted with Jared's footprints, as it would have been if he'd taken that route. He grunted, satisfied he'd caught Jared in his first lie. Rossi counted their steps, measuring each pace at three feet, until Jared stopped, close to seven hundred feet north of his tent.

"She's over there," Jared said, cocking his head toward the creek, keeping his distance.

Rossi scanned the landscape behind him, checking sight lines for possible witnesses. It was empty. The tents on the east side were behind them to the south. He shined his light across the water. Wherever the nearest tent on the west side was, it was beyond the reach of his flashlight.

"Stay here," Rossi said.

FOUR

Rossi walked to the creek bank and turned off his flashlight, wanting to see the body the same way Jared claimed to have seen it. It was an hour and a half since Jared had called 911, longer since he had found her. The moon was lower in the sky but still shining.

The body was five feet below him, faceup and eyes open, head resting near the bank, arms and legs splayed. He focused his light on her neck. The ligature marks Jared had described were easy to see, a purpled narrow band with a pattern he'd seen in other cases where the killer used an electrical extension cord to strangle the victim. There was a cross-shaped abrasion above her left breast as if something had been compressed into the skin, maybe a crucifix.

Scanning the rest of her body, he didn't see any obvious defensive wounds, though the water and his distance from the body made it impossible to rule out whether she had struggled against her killer.

From his vantage point above the body, it appeared that she hadn't been in the water very long. There was no evidence of decomposition, though he couldn't tell whether any rigor was present without getting a closer look. He aimed the flashlight at her legs, not finding any signs of lividity in the dependent areas of the body, knowing that the bluish discoloration took six to eight hours to become severe. The coroner was on the way and would give him a better approximation of time of death.

He took his time examining the bank directly above and to either side of the body, noting the partial footprints pressed into the mud, the rounded edges of shoes climbing the bank easy to pick out. He couldn't find tracks leading down the bank and into the creek, but the crime scene investigators would find them if they were there.

"Jared," Rossi said, "come over here."

"Yes, sir."

"Is there where you climbed down to the water?"

"Yes, sir. Right here."

Rossi let his flashlight play across Jared's muddy shoes.

"Those the shoes you were wearing?"

"Yes, sir."

Rossi examined the bank with his flashlight, not finding any evidence of descending footprints. He pointed his flashlight at the body, watching Jared's reaction.

"Look at her. Is that the way you found her?"

"Yes, sir. Just like that," he said.

"And then you got down in the water with her?"

"Just long enough to make sure she was dead."

"Did you touch her?"

He shook his head. "No, sir. No need. I could tell she was dead."

"You were right about that. Who is she?"

Jared pushed away from the creek, stood, and turned, his back to Rossi.

"I don't know her name."

Rossi fronted him. "But you do know her?"

"Seen her around."

"Here? At Liberty Park?"

"Some. In town too."

"Where?"

"Over in Northeast. I seen on her on Independence Avenue once or twice, on the street."

Independence Avenue was a favorite hangout for prostitutes. "You saying she was a hooker?"

Jared wrapped his arms tight around his middle, tossing his head from side to side. "I'm not saying that. I'm only saying that's where I seen her."

Rossi was feeling the bottle of wine he'd put away before he went to bed, his mouth cottony and his gut swimming in acid. All he wanted was to clear this case, put it on Jared if he was the killer, and go home.

Jared's facial muscles were quivering. He looked past Rossi, then at the ground, and then at the stars, repeating the rotation over and over. Rossi doubted Jared's story about how he'd found the woman, and his body language screamed *Crazy—Guilty—Crazy—Guilty,* like a flashing neon sign. But none of that was proof.

He sighed. "What did you do after you found the body?"

"Went back to my tent and got out of my wet clothes. Then I walked to the pay phone and called 911."

"The water isn't more than a foot deep. How'd you get wet?"

"Slipped and fell, I guess."

Rossi told the paramedics to remain with the body until the crime scene investigators showed up, then motioned to Jared.

"Let's go back to your tent, same way we came."

Officer Schmitt was still standing outside Jared's tent.

"We've corralled the campers on both sides of the creek. You can question them soon as you're ready," Schmitt said.

"Is that it? Can I go now?" Jared asked, shifting his feet and glancing in all directions.

"Take it easy, Jared. I'm talking to Officer Schmitt," Rossi said.

"Well, I'm not waitin' out here. I don't like all this commotion."

He ducked into his tent. Rossi and Schmitt followed him, Schmitt banging his head on a lantern hanging from a hook in the center of the tent ceiling, spraying shadows against the walls.

There was a sleeping bag on the floor and a coffee can resting on a soiled pillow. Thirty-gallon black trash bags filled to capacity with cans and bottles and tied off at the top lined one side of the tent. A damp pair of shorts and a T-shirt hung from another hook dangling on a sidewall.

"Why you rushing off?" Rossi asked.

Jared whirled around. "I showed you the body. Nothing else for me to do. And I don't like people barging in on me."

"Just a couple more questions," Rossi said, "and we'll be on our way. You don't mind, do you?"

Jared didn't answer, his Adam's apple bobbing up down.

"What's in those bags? Cans or bottles?"

Jared swallowed. "Some of both."

"You get much for them?"

He shrugged. "Enough."

Rossi pulled the wet shorts off the hook. "This what you were wearing when you found the body?"

Jared nodded and stepped back, knocking the coffee can over, watches, rings, bracelets, and other jewelry spilling onto the floor. He dropped to his knees, scrambling to shove them back into the can.

"You have receipts for that stuff?" Rossi asked, taking a step closer, still holding on to the wet shorts.

Jared sat on his haunches, clutching the can to his chest. "This is my stuff. I found it."

Rossi slipped on a pair of latex gloves and crouched on the floor of the tent, eye level with Jared. He felt the outside of the wet shorts he'd removed from the hook, stopping when his fingers pressed against something hard in one of the pockets. When he turned the pocket inside out, a gold cross fell into his palm. Rossi held it up by the corners, seeing at once the similarity with the wound on the victim's chest.

"Hey, Jared, where did you find this?"

FIVE

"Anything else, Ms. Stone?" Judge William West asked from the bench.

Alex Stone thumbed through several pages of notes she'd scribbled on her legal pad.

"As I said, Your Honor, the police did not have probable cause for entering my client's home without a search warrant, and therefore any evidence they obtained from that illegal search must be suppressed."

Judge West stared at her, his hooded eyes half-hidden, his hands clasped across his broad belly.

"And as I said, Counsel, do you have anything else that I haven't heard you repeat three times over the last hour?"

Alex pursed her lips, fighting the urge to shout, *"What difference would it make? We both know that you made up your mind before I said it the first time."* But she couldn't say a word, not after agreeing to serve her clients up to him for maximum sentences, a deal she'd made in the aftermath of a tragedy for which she took the blame. Now she longed for a way out of a bargain that had come back to haunt her. She turned her head toward her counsel table, where her client, John Atwell, was sitting, wondering if this would be the moment when she found the courage she'd been lacking. When he shook his head, Alex looked back at Judge West.

"No, Your Honor."

"If I may," Kalena Greene said.

"You may not," Judge West answered. "I understand the state's position. I'll take the defendant's motion to suppress under advisement. We're adjourned."

After the judge and his court reporter left, Atwell rose, briefly leaning in close, whispering to Alex before a sheriff's deputy took him back to his cell, leaving Alex and Kalena alone.

"Your client should take the deal we offered him last week," she told Alex.

"Why?"

"Because Atwell is guilty and this is the best deal he's going to get."

"Fifteen years? For a jewelry-store stickup? That's not much of a deal."

"It's a Class A felony. He could get thirty years or life. And we'll drop the armed criminal action count. We both know Judge West loves using that to double the sentence. So fifteen years is a bargain."

"Fifty percent off," Alex said. "You must be worried about my motion."

"I'm not. We want your guy off the street before he sticks up another jewelry store or assaults another old woman who pisses him off."

"The assault happened a year before the jewelry store, but you didn't charge him. If you had, he wouldn't have done the robbery."

"Except the victim recanted because Atwell was twice her size and she believed him when he said he'd come back and finish the job if she testified against him, but you and I both know he beat the shit out of her and he would have still done the jewelry store, so who are we kidding here?"

"Knowing and proving are two different things. I thought they taught you that in law school."

Alex had been a public defender for fifteen years, long enough to handle a young assistant prosecuting attorney. But Kalena

Greene wasn't a typical newbie. Alex met her during the Dwayne Reed trial a year ago when Kalena's boss, Tommy Bradshaw, wouldn't let her do more than escort witnesses to the stand. Since then, Bradshaw had given up trying to hold her back, her unflappable tenacity and innate trial instincts earning her the right to handle cases he usually reserved for more experienced lawyers.

Alex shared Kalena's love for the courtroom, but there were differences between them. Alex was white, tall, and athletic, deliciously rugged according to her partner, Bonnie Long. Kalena was African American, slender, slight, and attractive. If she spent time in the gym, it didn't show. But Alex had seen her in action enough not to mistake softness for weakness.

"Like I said, you should take the deal."

"If Judge West grants my motion, you've got no case. Knock it down to five years less time served."

"Wild Bill West cutting a defendant a break? That's what you're counting on?"

"The motion is solid. West might deny it, but Atwell will have great grounds for an appeal. You want to tell Tommy Bradshaw that you turned down my offer and blew this case just when he's given you your wings?"

Kalena ignored the bait and packed her briefcase. "You want to tell John Boy that he's going away forever?"

Alex wanted to say yes, she'd love to tell him that, because everything Kalena said about Atwell was true. He'd been in trouble since he was a teenager. One court-appointed psychologist, noting his disregard for himself and others, persistent anger, arrogance, lying, manipulation, penchant for violence, and lack of remorse or guilt, had diagnosed him with antisocial personality disorder.

Her motion to suppress had been an exercise in mediocrity that belied all her legal skills except for the one she was forcing herself to learn—the ability to do just enough to meet her obligation to her client while ensuring his conviction.

Ever since she'd won an acquittal for Dwayne Reed only to have him go on a killing spree, she'd promised herself that she would do exactly that rather than allow another monster back on the street. And that's what she'd done over the last year, leaving a credible paper trail of modest defense motions and driving soft bargains with the assistant prosecuting attorneys on the other side of the table. No one in her office had questioned her, and her clients had accepted her advice that their deals were the best they could get in light of the incriminating evidence.

Trials were trickier because there was an audience—judge, jury, and prosecutor—for everything she did. Every objection she made or ignored, every question she asked or avoided, every witness she chose to call, and every opening statement and closing argument she made had to be carefully calibrated to meet the constitutional standard of an adequate defense.

She'd tried half a dozen cases in the last twelve months, losing all of them. That wasn't an unusual track record for a PD, and none of the lawyers in the Public Defender's office appellate division had filed a motion for a new trial on the grounds that she'd failed to provide an adequate defense. The strength of the evidence against her clients had insulated her against critical scrutiny.

A few judges had raised their eyebrows when she'd let something slide, but she ignored them just as she ignored the occasional smirks from the assistant prosecutors, who were happy to reap the benefits. She glossed over any worry about her professional reputation or regret at her ethical lapses with memories of the innocent people Dwayne Reed had slaughtered and her determination to save others from the same fate. She accepted the irony that the images that woke her during the night also got her through the night, allowing her to forgive herself for what she'd done to her clients.

Atwell's case was different. There was no doubt that he was guilty, but there was substantial doubt about whether the search that resulted in the discovery of crucial incriminating evidence was legal. If she did her job, she had a great chance of winning—and losing again. She was straddling a line, a balancing act that threatened to rip her apart, leaving her wondering if she could turn her back on another client for the greater good.

She'd managed to write a subpar motion, gritting her teeth as she typed because it would have been so easy to write a great motion, but going on the record in open court proved more difficult than she had imagined, as she slammed the police and prosecutors for their callous disregard of John Atwell's constitutional rights against unlawful search and seizure. She didn't know whether it was because her client was watching or because of her ingrained courtroom combativeness or because she finally remembered that she'd become a public defender because there was honor in protecting the individual against the state when life and liberty were at stake. And it felt fantastic.

"My client understands the risks."

Kalena snapped her briefcase shut. "Good, because I'm not waiting for the judge's ruling. Today is Tuesday, September fourteenth. Mark it in your calendar, because when the sun goes down, the offer goes away forever, and so does John Boy."

Alex thought back to her conversation the week before when she told Atwell about the prosecutor's deal.

"What are my chances?" Atwell asked.

"Better than fifty-fifty," she said.

She didn't tell him that those were his chances in front of any judge but Wild Bill West, who applied his own brand of hang-the-bastard justice, making the odds in his court a hundred percent against Atwell. Alex knew that because the judge had persuaded Alex to join his private crusade after Dwayne Reed was acquitted, Alex agreeing to make it easy for the judge to throw the book at her most vicious clients, meeting with him after hours at his ranch to orchestrate the outcomes of her clients' cases.

"If I say no, can I change my mind later on?" Atwell asked.

"As long as the prosecutor doesn't change her mind."

"What happened in your case? Did they offer you a deal?"

Alex had killed Dwayne Reed while he was out on bail. She was charged with murder and acquitted, which gave her more street cred with her clients than she ever could have imagined.

"Doesn't matter. Every case is different."

Atwell thought for a moment. "Will the judge decide at the hearing?"

"No. He always takes these motions under advisement and rules later."

"Then there's no downside to going through with the hearing. I want to have a look at him. Get a feel for him."

They hadn't discussed the plea bargain again. When the hearing was over, Atwell whispered in her ear.

"The judge looked at me like I was roadkill he wanted to back up and drive over again. Tell the prosecutor I'll take the fifteen. That asshole is going to hang me."

If Alex ignored her client's instructions, he'd be convicted and never heard from again. If she didn't, she wouldn't have to worry about his future victims for fifteen years. And, she realized, she'd reclaim a part of herself she'd given away too easily.

"Hey, Alex," Kalena said, bringing her back to the moment. "What's it going to be, fifteen years or roll the dice with Wild Bill? I've got another hearing in twenty minutes."

Alex smiled. "Fair enough. We'll take the deal."

Kalena tilted her head up. "Really? Just like that?"

Alex shrugged. "You saw my client whispering to me. He thinks Judge West doesn't like him."

"Then why all the dancing around about fifty-percent discounts and five years less time served?"

"I was hoping there was some wiggle room, but you made it clear to me that there wasn't."

Kalena studied her for a moment. "Yeah. I guess I did, didn't I? I'll let the court know and get a hearing scheduled to enter the guilty plea. And, by the way, you really brought your A game today. I was impressed."

Alex smiled as Kalena left, then lingered alone in the courtroom, a place that had been her cathedral until she'd lost her faith in a system that too often got it wrong. It wasn't that countless guilty people went free, though some would in any system. It was the innocent victims of crimes she had hoped she would prevent by making certain that the worst of the worst didn't get the chance to commit them. If she could save one life, it would be worth the violation of her oath as a lawyer. Or so she'd kept telling herself until now. When faced with the choice in John Atwell's case of doing her job or abandoning her client, she'd stepped back across the line to the side where a criminal defense lawyer belonged.

Judge West opened the door from his office to the courtroom. "Alex."

She turned toward him. "Yes, Your Honor?"

"Tonight, eight o'clock, at the ranch."

Alex nodded as he closed his door. She'd been summoned.

SIX

Alex's clients had taught her a lot about the human capacity for shifting blame, dodging responsibility, and denying guilt. Some were robbers or rapists. Some beat their women and abused their children. Some killed for kicks or because of uncontrollable rage. Some blamed their victims, some said they were entitled, and some said they just didn't care. Regardless of their crime or their excuse, every explanation came down to the same refrain—mistakes were made, but not by me.

Alex was too harsh a critic of her own actions to take refuge in that sort of self-justification. She owned what she'd done. Dwayne Reed was dead. Nothing to be done about that except hope the nightmares would one day end. As for her deal with the judge, that was another matter altogether.

As she drove to his ranch, she realized that John Atwell's case had persuaded her that her partnership with the judge was over. She'd done her job for Atwell because of what she owed him as his lawyer, no matter the crimes he'd committed in the past or might commit in the future. There was more than honor in fulfilling her duty; there was power in doing the right thing, power that gave her the strength she needed to move on from Dwayne Reed and the deal she'd made with the judge. It was time to walk away.

She was nervous about telling him. She'd represented enough partners in crime to know what happened when one of them backed out of the deal. The other was rarely satisfied with his future former partner's vow to keep his mouth shut, often closing it for him—permanently. While she didn't think Judge West would kill her, she wouldn't underestimate his reaction. But knowing how good she would feel when she was free of him turned her dread to the joyful anticipation of something wonderful about to happen.

The judge's ranch was off Little Blue Road near the eastern edge of the city limits, the wooded, hilly acreage far removed from the county courthouse in downtown Kansas City. There was an old house and an older barn that housed half a dozen horses and a pony for his grandchildren to ride. It had the one thing that he valued more than anything else: privacy.

It was dark when Alex arrived, her headlights bouncing off the front porch of the house. Judge West's wife, Millie, was standing on the porch smoking a cigarette. She flicked it into the yard, turned, and went back in the house as Alex got out of her car, not even a wave to acknowledge her arrival.

It was always the same whenever Alex saw Millie at the ranch. They never exchanged a word, each of them pretending the other didn't exist. She'd learned Millie's name only when she found an article in the online archives of the *Kansas City Star* profiling the judge when he was appointed to the bench twenty-five years ago. The one time she'd asked him why they always met in the barn, never in the house, he said it was because his wife was bat-shit crazy and constantly accused him of having an affair anytime she saw him talking to another woman. He said it without elaboration and Alex never brought the subject up again.

It was a cool evening, and Alex gathered her light jacket around her as she made her way to the barn, the smell of manure hitting her in waves the closer she got. The barn door was open, a string of low-wattage lightbulbs casting weak light down the center of the barn. She stood at the door for a moment, watching the judge shoveling straw and manure from one of the stalls and dumping it into a wheelbarrow, his knee-high rubber boots caked in mud and muck.

"Come on in, or are you afraid of stepping in some shit?" he asked.

Alex glanced at her scuffed Danner boots and laughed. "It's nothing that won't wash off."

West smiled. "Then grab that pitchfork," he said, pointing to one hung on the wall to the right of the door, "and lend me a hand."

Alex didn't mind the work, though he'd never asked her to do it on any of her prior visits, welcoming it after a long day, glad for the chance to loosen her muscles and keep her mind off what she had to tell the judge. She quickly churned up a sweat, removing her jacket and getting into a rhythm as the judge cleaned out the stalls and she layered in fresh straw and bedding. An hour later they were finished and sitting on a wooden bench, each holding a cold bottle of beer.

"After a while," West said, "you don't even notice the smell."

"I'll take your word for it because I'm not there yet."

"Well, don't worry," he said, patting her knee. "Given enough time, you can get used to just about anything."

Alex flinched at his touch, pulling away as she set her bottle on the bench. "Why do I think you're not talking about horseshit?"

"Horseshit or bullshit, it all stinks, and somebody's got to clean it up. That's what you and I are doing. These stalls are no different than the people you defend, though my horses are a hell of a lot smarter. Your clients go through life crapping on everyone and everything, and, hell, half the time they get community service or probation. And the ones that go to prison don't stay there long enough because the fucking prosecutor gave them a sweetheart deal or because the prison is overcrowded. And you know what they do when they get out? They rape, rob, or murder someone else. Over half of them are back behind bars three years after they get out. You know what Missouri's recidivism rate is? It's fifty-four point goddamn four percent, third highest in the entire goddamn country."

Alex had heard the judge's speech enough times to know it by heart. For him, the statistics were personal insults.

"I know," Alex said as she stood and faced the judge.

He squinted at her, his head turned slightly to one side as if to get a better view of her.

"You look like someone who's got more to say, and I don't think I'm going to like it."

She took a deep breath and let it out. "I'm done. I can't do this anymore."

"All right. I'll clean the stalls on my own from now on."

"You know that's not what I'm talking about. Kalena Greene offered John Atwell a deal for fifteen years. He told me to take it and I did."

"You know that I was going to deny your motion."

"Yes, I know that."

"And what would have happened after that?"

Alex stiffened and stuck her hands in her jeans pockets, resenting that he was treating her like a schoolgirl. "Kalena would have withdrawn her offer and my client would have been convicted."

"That's right. And I would have sentenced him to life on the robbery and a hundred years on the armed criminal action and he would have been off the street forever. You do understand that."

Alex bristled. "Of course I do."

The judge rose, his face reddening. "That day you came in my chambers crying about what a bad man Dwayne Reed was, you told me that you'd do whatever it took to get rid of him and all the others like him. So what happened? Did you stay up late last night reading a John Grisham fairy tale and get all excited about the majesty of the law?"

Alex planted her hands on her hips, not backing down. They weren't in the courtroom, where she had to feign respect.

"Something like that. Anyway, I'm done. From now on, I'm playing all my cases straight. You and I can't meet like this anymore."

"For Christ's sake, Alex! You had the balls to shoot Dwayne Reed to death and now you're telling me that because you had a conscience fart you're gonna let John Atwell get off with fifteen years, which isn't even fifteen because he'll be eligible for parole in three fucking years!"

They stared at each other, Alex refusing to blink. "Kalena made the offer, I conveyed it, and my client accepted it. End of story. You and I are done."

"I don't think so. Wait here," Judge West said. He lumbered toward his house, went inside, and returned a few minutes later, handing Alex a large manila envelope. "Take a look."

She slipped her finger under the seal and pulled out a grainy eight-by-ten-inch photograph of her kneeling next to Dwayne Reed's body. In the photograph, she was holding his raised arm, the gun in his hand aimed at the ceiling, his finger on the trigger. Her hand was wrapped around his, her trigger finger on top of his.

Alex's skin burned, her gut twisting, as she glared at the judge.

"Where did you get this?"

"Doesn't matter. What does matter is that this photograph corroborates the prosecution's claim that you shot Dwayne Reed in cold blood and then fired his gun to make it look like self-defense. Now, the good news for you is that I acquitted you on the murder charge and double jeopardy prevents you being charged again, in state court, anyway. However, the U.S. attorney might take an interest in charging you with depriving your client of his civil rights. The Justice Department takes that sort of thing so seriously they're still trying to solve murders of black people in Mississippi back in the 1960s. What do you think they'll do with a murder of a black man by his white lawyer from last year?"

Alex's head was buzzing with questions. Where had the photo come from? How had the judge gotten his hands on it? Who could have taken it? There were no answers that made any sense. She swallowed hard, forcing the bile in her throat back into her stomach. If the photo was real, she was dead. If it wasn't, she was just as dead unless she could prove it was phony. Since she couldn't accept that it was real, she counterattacked.

"Nothing, because the photo is a fake," she said through clenched teeth. "I don't know who Photoshopped it or where you got it or how, but it's a fake."

"Are you saying that's not the way it happened?"

"I'm saying it's a fake and we both know it."

She slipped the photograph back into the envelope and threw it on the floor. Judge West bent down and picked it up, grunting with the effort.

"Well, now, that'll be for the jury to decide if it comes to that. And I don't know any lawyer whose career can survive two trials for killing the same man, even if she's acquitted both times."

Neither did Alex, though she wouldn't admit it. One of the lessons she'd learned in courtroom combat was to counterpunch when the prosecution thought they had the upper hand. It was the same lesson her mother had taught her when she was a little girl—never let them see you sweat, even if you're about to pee your pants.

"And I don't know of any judge who could explain how he tried to sucker the U.S. attorney into a bogus prosecution with a bullshit piece of evidence like this. I thought you were too smart for that, but if you're not, be my guest. I won't be bullied and I won't be blackmailed."

West grinned. "That's what I like about you, Alex. You're always ready for a fight, even if it's the wrong one, and that's enough to get most people to back off. But I'm not most people. If and when this photograph lands on the U.S. attorney's desk, my fingerprints won't be on it, but yours will be."

She shook her head, not believing she'd been so easily duped. Her fingerprints would give the photograph more credibility, especially since no one would believe her when she explained how they got there. She eyed the judge and the envelope, measuring the distance between them, arms at her sides, fists balled, and considered whether to try to wrestle the envelope away from him. He was bigger, maybe stronger, but she was younger, faster, and motivated.

West grunted, stepped back, and wrapped his free hand around the pitchfork.

"Tell me you aren't that stupid, Alex."

She let out a breath, releasing the tension in her coiled muscles.

"Not tonight. What do you want?"

"I want you to honor our agreement. Now, I'm willing to forget about the Atwell case."

"Why?"

"Because you didn't give me a choice. I'm bound by the plea agreement. And I'm more interested in how you handle your next case, not your last one."

"I've got a stack of cases on my desk. Which one are you talking about?"

"None of them. You're going to be assigned to a new case tomorrow. Your client has already confessed to a gruesome murder. All you have to do is go through the motions, get the discovery you're entitled to from the prosecutor, conduct a limited—and I mean limited—investigation so you can say you did, and when the prosecutor offers to let him plead guilty and be sentenced to life without possibility of parole instead of being executed, you will convince him to take that deal. Now, if you do that, why, then, this photograph will go back to where it came from and it will stay there."

First the judge hit her with the photograph and now he was telling her about her next case. She couldn't imagine how he knew what it would be. All she wanted was to get out of there.

"My new client, what's his name?"

"Jared Bell," Judge West said.

SEVEN

Alex jammed her car into reverse, turned around, and fishtailed back down the long drive, putting as much distance as she could, as fast as she could, between Judge West and her. She was so angry, her heart was slamming hard enough against her ribs that she was afraid it would explode or her ribs would shatter.

She'd been angry for much of the last year, though at first she tried to ignore the emotion, cramming her feelings into a dark closet, slamming the door and bracing her back against it. The euphoria that had consumed her after she was acquitted of murdering Dwayne didn't last. Like any drug, it wore off, and when it did, the door sprang open, leaving her raw inside and quick to lash out. Bonnie took the brunt of her outbursts, giving her time and space, until after a couple of months she'd had enough.

"You've got to see someone," Bonnie told her. "We can't keep doing this—you exploding and me picking up the pieces."

"I'm sorry. I'm trying. But," Alex said, shaking her head, "sometimes…I don't know…I just feel…Shit, I don't know what I feel except that I just want to scream, I'm so fucking pissed."

"About what?"

Alex ran her fingers through her short, dark hair. "About what? Are you kidding? I'm pissed that I got Dwayne Reed acquitted. I'm pissed that he killed all those people. I'm pissed that I killed him, and I'm pissed that I'm glad he's dead. I'm pissed that everything got so fucked-up and I can't stop fucking thinking and dreaming about it." Her eyes filled and she wiped away her tears. "And I'm pissed that I can't stop crying about it. It makes me feel so damn weak."

Bonnie wrapped her arms around Alex. "The last thing you are is weak, but that doesn't mean you're strong enough to deal with this on your own. Post-traumatic stress is a bitch. Nobody can go through what you did and come out on the other side the same person. So do us both a favor and get some help, or I'll end up more angry than you."

Bonnie recommended a psychologist, Dr. Jacob Daniels. Alex saw him for six months. He treated her with a combination of cognitive and exposure therapy, helping her to cope with her anger and guilt, though she couldn't tell him all the reasons she felt guilty. He taught her to use a type of meditation called mindfulness-based stress reduction, telling her that doing the focused breathing exercises was better than taking drugs.

The therapy had helped. She still had nightmares, but the boiling anger had cooled, except when something or someone like Judge West unleashed it. And while the tension between her and Bonnie had eased, she sensed that something else was bothering Bonnie, but when Alex pressed her, Bonnie just shook her head, reassuring her that everything was fine. They'd been together long enough that any other life seemed impossible. But she worried about Bonnie's unspoken concerns. Now when she woke during the night, it was as much to make certain Bonnie was still beside her as it was to shake off her nightmares.

Judge West had triggered her entire emotional package as if she'd stepped on a land mine when she walked into his barn. Her pulse was racing, her face was flushed, and she wanted to punch something, if she could just stop shaking. She pulled into the parking lot of a strip mall, the stores closed for the night, the lot empty. Cushioning her head on the headrest, she closed her eyes, breathing in and out until she was calm enough to think clearly.

Bonnie had taught her to triage when she found herself in the middle of a shit storm: focus on whatever was causing her the most pain, stop the bleeding, and then move on to the next crisis. Alex combined Bonnie's medical model with her own, working the facts, taking them as far as they would go, identifying the gaps and digging deeper to fill them in, while resisting the temptation to write a case off as a simple one, because she knew that's when a gap could swallow her whole.

The photograph was at the top of her critical list. She'd shot Dwayne Reed in the living room of his mother Odyessy Shelburne's house. Though she'd examined the photograph for only a moment, the setting looked like the crime scene. There was a body on the floor that could have been Reed, but the face was obscured. She was the woman kneeling next to him. That much was certain, and it might be enough to convince anyone else that the photograph was real, but Alex was certain it was a fake—not because it was inaccurate but because she couldn't imagine who could have taken it. There were only a few possibilities.

Odyessy Shelburne had wanted Alex convicted so badly that she perjured herself on the witness stand. She never would have withheld such damning evidence.

The only other witness to the shooting was Gloria Temple, who was dead. Gloria's cell phone was loaded with pictures, all of which Alex had seen, and the one Judge West was hammering her with now wasn't part of Gloria's collection. If it had been, Alex would be sitting on death row.

Detective Hank Rossi had investigated the shooting, and sending a criminal defense lawyer to prison would have been the high point of his career. If the photo had been out there before her trial, he would have found it, and Patrick Ortiz, the special prosecutor who'd handled the case against her, would have hung her with it.

If she was right about all of that, the alternative that the photo was a fake was still in play.

Judge West knew the prosecution's theory that Alex had staged the crime scene to make it look like self-defense, and he had access to the crime scene photos, which were part of the court file. If he was worried that Alex would back out of their deal, he could have manufactured the photo to keep her in line.

Or maybe, Alex thought, he hoped the photograph would force her to confess her guilt to him, her admission giving him a more powerful weapon to use against her. But if that was his plan, it hadn't worked. She hadn't confessed and never would. Not to him. Not to Bonnie. Not to anyone. Not ever.

If she was right that Judge West was behind the photograph and that he had been waiting for the right moment to use it, she had to prove that it was a fake. That was the only way she'd be able to make a clean break from him.

The judge wasn't the kind of person who would spend time hunched over a laptop manipulating images in Photoshop. Which meant he had to have had help, and the help was always the weakest link in any conspiracy. So all she had to do was figure out a way to prove the picture was phony, find whoever had created it, and then tell Judge West what he could do with it. Not easy, but it was enough to stop the bleeding.

Her new client, Jared Bell, was next up on her critical list. If the case against him was as strong as Judge West had said, Bell would be convicted or plead guilty regardless of which public defender represented him. So why would Judge West use his influence to get the case assigned to her and why would he go to such lengths to make certain she persuaded Jared to plead guilty? The inescapable answer rocked her. Jared Bell was innocent and Judge West wanted him to spend the rest of his life in prison for a crime he didn't commit.

A criminal defense lawyer's two worst nightmares were helping the guilty go free and failing to save the innocent. Alex had lived the first with Dwayne Reed, and now she was faced with the second.

EIGHT

Alex wasn't ready to go home. She needed more time to wind down and think and enough beer to help with the former without making the latter impossible. And that meant taking a trip to the Zoo.

The Zoo was a downtown dive bar at Twelfth and McGee, a narrow, shotgun joint with room for a couple of dozen people. There were stools along the bar, a few chairs against the back wall, and standing room only for everyone else. The bartenders did business in front of a floor-to-ceiling display of whiskey, and the surest way to get thrown out was to ask them for a drink made in a blender. The walls, ceiling, and anything that was nailed down were covered with graffiti, some patrons just signing their names, others bragging or begging, and a few making promises they couldn't keep.

Alex was a regular. She liked it when it was jumping with shoulder-to-shoulder people and she could get lost in the noise. But she was glad it was Tuesday night, because that wasn't a big night for the bar business and she needed a quiet place to drink in peace while she tried to find a way out of the wilderness.

Half a dozen people were scattered around the room when she took a seat at the bar, the stools on either side of her empty, and asked for a bottle of Bully! porter. It was ten o'clock. She turned her phone off, not wanting to be bothered. Taking an easy pull, she rubbed the back of her neck, feeling her knotted muscles give a little bit. Cranking her head from side to side, she saw Hank Rossi approaching her from the back of the bar.

"I'll have what she's having," Rossi said, taking the stool next to hers.

Alex shook her head. "Of all the gin joints..."

"In all the towns, in all the world, she walks into mine. *Casablanca*. Great flick, even if the cop was on the take."

She wasn't in the mood for company, especially his and especially if he liked *Casablanca* as much as she did. Rossi had arrested her for Dwayne Reed's murder. He'd also saved her life when he killed Gloria Temple. None of which made them pals, Rossi making it clear that he was just doing his job, neither of them trusting the other. It didn't matter that she'd been acquitted of murdering Dwayne and he'd been cleared in Gloria's shooting.

Rossi was long and muscled, with dark-eyed, craggy good looks that drew women close until the blood on his hands drove them away, blood that belonged to the bad guys who'd put up a fight, taken a shot at him, or just pissed him off too many times.

Alex was surprised that he would join her, certain he'd rather drink by himself in a toilet stall than have a beer with her.

"Here's lookin' at you, kid," Rossi said. He tilted his beer toward hers and they clinked bottles. "Didn't figure you for a Bogart fan."

"I was always more into Ingrid Bergman."

"Even if she was into Bogart?"

"Girl has to dream."

"I'll give you that, but I don't thing she would have gone for you tonight."

"Why's that?"

"'Cause you smell like horseshit. And I don't mean that metaphorically."

"Metaphorically? Don't tell me you're reading *Thirty Days to a More Powerful Vocabulary*."

"I am. Last night I got all the way up to *motherfucker*."

"Ah, but can you use it in a sentence?"

"Stone, you motherfucker, you smell like horseshit."

Alex cocked her head, fighting against a laugh and losing, not wanting to tell him where she'd been. "You're definitely getting your money's worth from that book."

"No doubt about that, even if I didn't think of you as the horseshit type."

"And I never think of you at all."

Rossi grinned. "We both know that's bullshit. Deep down I think you like me."

"There you go again, Rossi, doing all that thinking. Didn't your father warn you about working without tools? Besides, why do you care? It's not like I'm at the top of your Christmas list."

"I don't have a Christmas list. Hell, I don't even have a fucking stocking."

"Poor pitiful Rossi. Need a suggestion on where to put your lump of coal?"

"No, thanks. I'd rather keep it in the sunlight where I can admire its natural beauty. And, not that you're asking, but I'd say you could use a little sunlight."

"What's that supposed to mean?"

"It means you don't just smell like shit. The way you're hunched over and your face is all pinched, you look like you're trying to decide between going postal or fetal."

"You really know how to make a girl feel good about herself."

Rossi swiveled on his barstool, facing her. "Doesn't mean I'm wrong."

Alex straightened, flattening her palms on the bar and forcing a smile. "Is that better?"

"Now you just look like you've got gas."

"Fuck you, Rossi."

"No, thanks, but I get it."

"Get what?"

"All most people know about killing is what they see on television. Good guy kills the bad guy and goes home for dinner with the wife and kids like it was just another day at the office. But it's not, is it?"

Alex rubbed her hands around her bottle, setting it on the bar.

"No, it isn't."

"No, it isn't, is right. It changes you forever. I still get the nightmares, wake up sweating like it's all going down again, my heart trying to bust out of my chest."

Alex nodded and sighed. There'd been moments when Rossi had reached out to her like he cared. She hadn't known what to make of him in those moments, whether that was the real Rossi and the rest was just for show. But in this moment, she hoped it was the real Rossi, because he was the only person who truly knew what she'd been through. Bonnie's therapist had tried to understand but could never bridge the gulf between his compassion and her experience.

"I know the feeling, and I get so worked up, so angry, I can't get back to sleep. I just stay mad. Is it like that with you?"

He shrugged. "Nope. I thank God they're dead and I'm not and I go back to sleep, and you know why I can do that? It's because I don't feel guilty. I was doing my job each and every time, by the book on permissible use of deadly force. And when I had to go on the record, I told the truth. I've got a clear conscience, and that makes a world of difference."

Rossi's message was clear. Alex dropped her chin to her chest, biting her lip, anger swelling and rising from her belly. She sat up, squaring around at him.

"Is that what this is about, Rossi? You sit down next to me like this is a PTSD support group and pretend you give a shit about me? Why, because you think I've got a guilty conscience and if you give me some love, I'll come clean?"

"I guarantee you'll feel better. And why not come clean? You've got the double-jeopardy passport to freedom. Or you can spend the rest of your life hanging out in dive bars, drinking alone in the middle of the week, wondering if Bonnie's figured it out yet and what she'll do when she does and if you'll ever get another good night's sleep or if you'll ever stop being so pissed off at yourself for making such a fucking mess of your life."

Alex stood, trembling. Rossi had gutted her, and it was all she could do not to scream and take a swing at him or just puddle onto the floor and cry like a baby. She gripped the back of the barstool, steadying herself and gritting her teeth.

"Where the hell do you get off, Rossi? I was fucking acquitted, you miserable asshole! So take your bullshit psychology and stick it up your ass with your fucking lump of coal."

Rossi's face was a pool of calm. "You want my advice, Counselor, I'd get a grip on that anger. Makes you hard to live with."

Alex didn't answer. She dropped a dollar on the bar and left without looking back.

NINE

The public defender's offices were on the twentieth and twenty-first floors of Oak Tower at Eleventh and Oak, one of Kansas City's first skyscrapers. The original fourteen stories were doubled in 1929, and in 1974 the terra-cotta exterior was blanketed in stucco, a sad example of style buried by progress. Its days as class A office space long behind it, Oak Tower was perfect for public defenders, who didn't have to worry about impressing clients. Lawyers who dealt in life and death had bigger issues than the pale rose paint chipping off the walls and the threadbare carpet lining the halls.

On her drive downtown the next morning, Alex bounced back and forth between how Judge West had blackmailed her with the photograph and how Hank Rossi had dissected her psyche. Both had unnerved her in spite of the show she'd put on, leaving her feeling raw inside and out.

When Alex got off the elevator, no one was at the receptionist's desk, the secretaries' stations were abandoned, and the halls were empty. She'd started toward her office when Grace Canfield came out of the bathroom, wiping her swollen red eyes with a tissue.

Grace was one of the investigators in the PD's office. Middle-aged and stout, her black hair cut short and spiky and flecked with gray, she was a lifelong resident of Kansas City's east side, home to many of the African American clients Alex defended. She went to church with their families, worked their cases, and went to their funerals, giving her more street cred than any lawyer in the office; even the gangbangers called her Miz Grace.

"Grace, why are you crying? Where is everybody?"

"Oh, Alex," she said, fighting back tears, her voice catching. "It's Robin. She was killed last night in a car accident. They're all in the conference room."

Robin Norris had spent thirty years in the public defender's office, the last twenty running the operation. She hired Alex straight out of law school, raising her from a pup, as Robin put it after Alex won a case no one thought could have been won, and she took Alex back after the Dwayne Reed case when everyone bet she wouldn't. Her death left Alex numb, the reality not yet registering. Though she'd heard the words, part of her brain refused to accept the news, believing instead that someone must have made a mistake. She slumped against the wall, wide-eyed and gut punched.

"What happened?"

"She was out somewhere up north and lost control of her car and ran off the road. She was dead at the scene."

"Oh, my God!"

Grace sniffed and straightened, wiping her hands against her sides. "I know. I know, but if I don't get to work and get my mind on something else, I'm going to spend the whole day crying, and that's only gonna make me feel worse."

Alex went to the conference room, pushing the wooden doors open and stepping into a sea of sorrow. People were hugging as they sobbed or staring out the windows, dazed and mute. Others were milling around the room, lost. Alex moved from one to another, squeezing a hand, rubbing a back, and giving a hug, tears rolling off her cheeks, everyone muttering that it couldn't be real, that it didn't make sense, and that it wasn't fair, all of it true.

Looking out on the city, she saw the muddy Missouri River rolling past the north side of downtown on its way to St. Louis. A century and a half ago, bluffs a hundred feet high hid the view of the river until ancestral Kansas Citians carved through them, laying the streets that now ran two hundred feet beneath where she stood. Microscopic people glided by Oak Tower, as distant from her and her loss as those who had dug their way from the river. Robin's death had stopped time for her and everyone else in the room, the rest of the world swirling around them, sweeping past without a second glance.

"Can I have your attention, everyone."

Alex turned around to see the woman who had joined them. She was slender, her sandy hair cut in a bob. Half a head shorter than Alex, and in her forties, she was dressed in a dark-green pantsuit from the Hillary Clinton collection. On Alex's beauty scale, Bonnie was at the top and everyone else was ordinary, though this woman was ordinary-plus in spite of the pantsuit, the strength in her face and the glint in her hazel eyes setting her apart.

"My name is Meg Adler. I'm terribly sorry for your loss. I work in the St. Louis PD's office—at least I did until I got the call about Robin. I caught the seven a.m. flight on Southwest and got here as quickly as I could. I've been assigned to take Robin's place—not that anyone can really do that—until a permanent replacement is chosen. I know what a difficult time this is for everybody, but—and I don't mean to sound callous—we've got clients, cases, and trials. We'll let you know about funeral arrangements as soon as we can. I'll be stopping by each of your offices so we can get better acquainted. In the meantime, I know this may sound corny, but from what I've been told about Robin I think it's true—let's get back to work because that's what she'd want us to do."

Alex took the long way to her office so that she could walk by Robin's, lingering in the open doorway, imagining Robin sitting behind her desk, glasses halfway down her nose, engrossed in her latest bureaucratic tangle. She'd given up the courtroom to be an administrator, keeping the office afloat with the budgetary equivalent of bubblegum and Band-Aids.

The credenza behind her desk was crowded with framed photographs of her five children, a timeline of their lives. She wore last year's styles, buying them on sale to save money for her kids, did her own hair and nails, and told everyone else how great they looked. Fifty-five years old, she'd earned every wrinkle and every extra pound that she wished she could lose. She was a single mother, divorced when her oldest child was not yet ten, her ex-husband long removed from their lives. Alex had always marveled at Robin's grit, raising two families, the kids at home and the people at work. Thinking of both families made her heart hurt.

There were a few nonfamily photographs tucked in among the rest. One showed Robin shaking hands with the governor, one showed her in the bleachers at a Royals game after she caught a homerun ball, arms stretched to the sky in celebration, and another, taken six months ago, showed her receiving an award at the annual Missouri State Bar Association meeting at a hotel in St. Louis. Judge Anthony Steele, who'd recently been elevated from circuit court trial judge to judge for the Missouri Court of Appeals, presented an award to Robin for outstanding service. In the photograph, the two of them were shaking hands and smiling for the camera. Alex had been there. True to form, Robin gave all the credit for the award to the lawyers and staff in her office.

Alex smiled at the memory, not for the award but for what she saw later that night in the hotel bar. Robin and Judge Steele were huddled together in a dark corner, rubbing shoulders, their faces inches apart, oblivious to anyone else. She had kidded Robin about it the next morning, Robin telling Alex she was being ridiculous not only because Judge Steele was married but because both the judge and his wife, Sonia, were her close friends. But she was blushing nonetheless.

Though Robin never confided in Alex about her personal relationships, Alex knew that she didn't live a cloistered life. She and Bonnie had seen her around town with different men over the years, none of them Judge Steele and none of them wearing wedding rings.

Looking at the photograph now, Alex could understand if they had hooked up. Judge Steele was silver haired, with sparkling blue eyes and the kind of rugged good looks that improved with age, and Robin, in addition to being attractive, had the serenity, self-confidence, and zest for life that any man would have appreciated. And they were out of town, away from prying eyes, sharing the perfect cocktail for a one-night fling, the hell with marriage and friendship.

Knowing that Robin was dead made Alex wish that Robin did have that fling, even if she couldn't imagine Robin as a home-wrecking adulterer. She wanted to remember her alive and passionate, not lying dead in the wreckage of her car.

For Alex, Robin was the public defender, one not existing without the other. Robin didn't hesitate to criticize or praise, doing the former in private and the latter in public, telling complainers to suck it up. The only time Alex asked her when she planned to retire, Robin scoffed, saying she'd die on the job. And now she had. Hand at her throat, Alex shuddered and squelched a sob, hearing Robin's voice telling her to suck it up.

Meg Adler was waiting for Alex when she got to her office, sitting in a chair on the visitor's side of the desk, a file in her lap, and thumbing through messages on her iPhone.

"Oh," Alex said, her voice dropping an octave, her shoulders rounding, Meg's presence in her office a sharp reminder that Robin really was dead.

Meg looked up. "Oh, sorry. Didn't mean to camp out, but you're first on my list."

Alex nodded, hesitating in the doorway for a moment before walking past Meg and settling into her desk chair.

"Shitty way to start the day, huh?" Meg said.

"Not as shitty as it is for Robin's kids."

"Amen to that."

"Did you know Robin?"

Meg shrugged. "Not well. Saw her at meetings, that kind of thing. She was very well regarded. I do know that."

Alex knew it wasn't rational, but she couldn't help but resent Meg's presence. Not because Meg had said or done anything wrong but because Robin should have been sitting in the chair, not Meg. So she didn't respond, letting Meg carry their conversation.

Meg cleared her throat. "Look, I don't like this any better than you do. No, that's not right. I can't possibly hate this as much as you do, so I won't pretend that I do. I've been here for less than an hour and already I've gotten the wicked-stepmother look from half a dozen people. I get that, and believe it or not, I don't take it personally. I'm just doing my job, and it will be better for all of us if you mourn Robin without taking it out on me."

Alex took a breath and let it out, rubbing her face with her hands. "I'm sorry. You're right. It's just that this is all pretty fresh."

"And raw, both of which I realize are horrible understatements."

"Yeah. So what can I do for you?"

"You're the senior attorney in the office, been here longer than anyone else now that Robin is gone. I don't know how long it will take to find her replacement. All I know is that it won't be me. In the meantime, I could use your support."

"Sure. I'll spread the word that you're not the wicked stepmother."

Meg smiled as she rose. "Great. How about we have a drink after work one day this week. Maybe do that bonding thing all the management gurus get so mushy about."

The tightness in Alex's belly began to ease. "Yeah, sure."

Meg pointed to the picture of Bonnie on Alex's desk. "She your other?"

"Yep."

"Well, lucky you." She was halfway out the door when she turned around, tossing the file on Alex's desk. "I found this on Robin's desk with a Post-it with your name on it. Guess it's your case."

Ice shot through Alex's gut as she read the caption on the file, *State v. Jared Bell*. She laced her fingers together, afraid she'd shake if she picked it up.

"Yeah, I guess it is," she said.

TEN

Rossi didn't have to wait to be buzzed into the ER at Truman Medical Center. He'd been there often enough to interview witnesses, victims, and suspects that whoever was manning the desk hit the button as soon as they saw him, unlocking the door that led to the trauma unit.

He was on a first-name basis with many of the nurses and doctors, though Bonnie Long insisted on calling him Detective Rossi. He figured it was her way of keeping him at arm's length, which he knew she would do today once she realized why he was there.

Rossi was convinced that Alex Stone had gotten away with murder. It didn't matter that she'd been acquitted. That was a long way from being innocent. And it wasn't just that she'd gotten off. It was that she'd skated on one of his cases, and the combination stuck in his craw like a bone splinter even if the world was a better place without Dwayne Reed in it.

He knew plenty of homicide cops who had a case or two they couldn't let loose, cases they couldn't solve or that were solved wrong. His clearance rate was high enough that he'd avoided getting hooked. Dwayne Reed's case changed that, taking more of his time on and off the job than he'd like to admit.

He'd combed through Reed's case file half a dozen times over the last year, looking for something, anything that would prove he was right, coming up empty each time. He wasn't certain what he'd do if he found something, since Alex couldn't be retried for murder. He knew that the Justice Department had prosecuted people acquitted of murder in state court for civil rights violations. Maybe the U.S. attorney would be interested.

When he'd run into Alex last night at the Zoo, he couldn't resist picking at the scab again, peddling bullshit about not feeling guilty about the men he'd killed, hoping to make her feel worse. He didn't expect her to confess over a beer, but when he saw what bad shape she was in, he thought it was worth giving her a push. It wasn't going to happen then and there, but if he kept poking her, it might happen eventually. At least then he'd know for certain. And when he did, he'd figure out what to do about it.

He decided to take a run at Bonnie Long to gauge any fallout from the Zoo. If Alex was going to confess to anyone, it would be her, and he hoped she would be more likely to talk to him than Alex had been. He would reassure Bonnie that Alex couldn't be prosecuted and that all he was interested in was the truth. She might go for it and she might not, but he didn't have a better idea.

Watching Bonnie hustle in and out of treatment rooms, he understood why Alex had gone to such lengths to protect her, certain he would have done the same. Bonnie was simply beautiful, even with blood and vomit staining her white coat and her blond hair unraveling around her face. Rossi couldn't remember bluer eyes. And he'd seen her inner steel firsthand, which was as attractive as any physical feature.

That she loved Alex was a mystery to him but no greater a mystery than any love between two people. He'd chased after love long enough to know what he didn't know.

It had been a while since he'd seen Bonnie, and he wasn't certain she'd remember him. He waited until she was standing at the nurses' station filling out paperwork before approaching her.

"Hi, Doc. Remember me?"

Bonnie looked up from her clipboard. "Of course, Detective Rossi. What can I do for you?"

Rossi looked at the doctors and nurses walking past them. "Is there somewhere quieter we can talk?"

Bonnie's hand drifted to her throat. "Is Alex…"

Rossi raised his hand. "Don't worry. Nothing's happened. I just need to talk with you—in private."

Bonnie swallowed and nodded. "Very well."

She led him out of the ER, down a hallway to a small, windowless office furnished with a desk and two chairs.

"Your office?" Rossi asked.

"No. Just a spare. What's going on?"

"How's Alex doing?"

Bonnie folded her arms across her chest. "Detective Rossi, you wouldn't come here to ask me about Alex unless you had reason to think she wasn't doing fine, so get to the point. I've got patients waiting."

"Fair enough. I ran into her last night at the Zoo—that's a bar—"

"Downtown, I know. We go there sometimes."

"Right. Anyway, she looked like hell. This whole thing with Dwayne Reed is really tearing her up."

"Stop right there, Detective Rossi. When Alex came home last night, she told me how you treated her. I insisted she file a complaint against you for harassment, but that's not her way of doing things. However, it's very much my way, so if you bother either one of us again, you'll know what to expect."

Rossi had expected Bonnie to push back, but the threat of a complaint against him wasn't going to stop him. If she filed one, he'd just add it to his collection.

"Let me ask you something, Doc, just hypothetically. Suppose you got a patient in here, say, a little girl, nine or ten years old, and she's got a broken arm and burn marks on her leg. You ask the mom how she got hurt and the mom tells you the little girl fell down the stairs and stood too close to the heater. Now, you

49

know that's bullshit. You know that child's been abused. What would you do?"

"I'd report it to the authorities as I'm required to do under the law, and I've done that many times," Bonnie said with a self-assured shrug.

"But this time, the authorities investigate and decide that there's not enough evidence of abuse to prosecute. What would you do then? Would you throw up your hands and say too bad, so sad, the system sucks and there's nothing I can do about it? Or would you keep pushing because you're convinced you're right and no matter how little or low the victim is or how high or loved the perpetrator is, you know what's right?"

Bonnie blinked, looking past Rossi for a way around his question. Sensing her reluctance, he pressed.

"C'mon, Doc. We're talking a little girl here, and there's no one but you to protect her. Everyone else is saying it's over, move on. Next case. What are you gonna do?"

She raised her palm. "I'm a trauma doctor. I see people every day who are so badly injured there's nothing I can do to help them. That doesn't stop me from trying, but I've learned there are some things I can't fix."

"But you try anyway, and I'll bet you don't give up too easy."

Bonnie's mouth twitched and she shivered for an instant before regaining her footing. "The problem with your analogy is that there's nothing more I should do about Alex because she's innocent."

"The judge acquitted her because the prosecutor blew the case. That's not the same as being innocent."

"I don't care about any of that. I know Alex. She would never murder anyone."

Rossi shrugged. "You know what they say about love being blind."

"Why should I even consider the possibility that Alex is guilty? What do you know that the judge didn't know and that I don't know?"

"Did you ever see a movie called *The Man Who Shot Liberty Valance*?"

"No."

"Too bad. It's a great flick. Lee Marvin plays this psychopathic cowboy gunslinger who calls Jimmy Stewart out in the street so he can gun him down in a fair fight. But it's not a fair fight because Stewart is a tinhorn lawyer and he's no match for Lee Marvin, but he's got a gun and he goes out there anyway. John Wayne is watching from an alley where nobody can see him and he's got his rifle on Marvin. In the instant that Marvin and Stewart draw their guns and fire, John Wayne shoots Lee Marvin. Marvin is dead when he hits the ground. Everybody thinks Jimmy Stewart killed him and Stewart becomes a hero, the man who shot Liberty Valance."

Bonnie shook her head. "I don't like Westerns and I don't get your point."

"Dwayne Reed was a thug. He'd been carrying a gun since he got off his mother's breast. Alex was no match for him. If he'd had a gun, there's no way Alex could have beaten him. It wouldn't have been a fair fight."

Bonnie turned away from him, not responding.

Rossi didn't let up. "Tell me you haven't wondered about that. Tell me you haven't doubted Alex's story even a little. Tell me you aren't at least a little afraid that she's lied to you all along?"

Bonnie faced him, her face hot and trembling, biting off her words. "Tell me, Detective Rossi, that you haven't wondered what it's like to love someone, to trust her with your life and your future. Tell me you aren't at least a little afraid that you'll never know what that's like. And then tell me you don't have anything better to do than trying to ruin all of that for Alex and me."

"You said it yourself, Doc. Some patients are hurt so bad they can't be fixed. Same thing for relationships. If that turns out to be the case for you and Alex, it'll be on her, not me." He took a business card from his wallet, tucking it in a side pocket of her white coat. "You ever want to talk to me, give me a call. My cell number is on the card."

"You go to hell!"

She stormed out of the room. Rossi gave her a moment before following, satisfied he'd shaken Alex and Bonnie's tree. Now all he had to do was wait and see what fell out of it.

ELEVEN

Alex stared at Jared Bell's file, her neck and back stiffening, afraid that if she picked it up, she would be shaking hands with the devil. She could have her secretary return it to Meg Adler with a note that she was too busy to handle the case. She could try swapping it with a colleague for another case. Or she could do what she knew she had to do not only because of Judge West but because it was her job—suck it up and pick it up.

At this early stage, there would be only two documents in the file, the probable cause statement, written by the investigating police detective, and the complaint, filed by an assistant prosecuting attorney. The two documents went together, the probable cause statement forming the basis for the complaint.

She'd never gotten these documents before her client's initial appearance in court, which was also where she usually met her client for the first time. In a high-profile case, she might meet her client at the jail before the initial appearance, but even then, she wouldn't have the probable cause statement and the complaint. So how did she end up with the file now?

Meg Adler had told her that she found the file on Robin Norris's desk bearing a Post-it note with Alex's name on it. It was possible that Robin had learned about the case yesterday, requested the file in advance of Jared's initial appearance, decided to assign the case to Alex, and told Judge West of her decision, but three things bothered her about that sequence of events. She'd never known Robin to do something like that before. The

Post-it note wasn't on the file when Meg gave it to her. And Robin was dead.

Alex shook her head, warding off paranoid conspiracy theories. Meg had no reason to make up the story about the Post-it note. And Robin worked hard to maintain good relations with the prosecutor's office, the police, and the court. Someone in the prosecutor's office could have given her a courtesy call, telling her about Jared's case, trading an early copy of the file for a favor in another case. Robin could have reviewed the file and decided that Alex should handle it and told Judge West in order to expedite matters at the initial appearance.

Alex couldn't say for certain that something like that had never happened before because Robin didn't tell her how she handled each and every case. Nor would Alex have expected her to do so, but there was one way to find out if that was what had happened this time.

She called Robin's secretary, Patty, who maintained a master calendar for all the cases in the office. Patty protected her turf so well that people in the office compared her to the Hand of the King in *Game of Thrones*.

"Patty, it's Alex."

"Oh, my God, Alex. This can't be real, it just can't."

Alex waited for Patty to compose herself. "I know. It's awful, but I need you to do something for me."

Patty sniffled and cleared her throat. "Sure. What is it?"

"I've got a new file for a client named Jared Bell. I need to know when his first appearance is scheduled."

"Hang on. Let me check.... Well, that's weird. It's not on the calendar. You know that I enter all relevant dates before I give a new file to Robin."

"Did you give this file to her?"

"You said the defendant's name is Jared Bell, right?"

"Right."

"I don't remember seeing that file at all. What are you doing with it?"

"Meg Adler gave it to me. She said she found it on Robin's desk this morning with a Post-it that had my name on it and assumed that Robin had assigned the case to me."

"Well, I don't have any record of it, but I had a doctor's appointment yesterday, so maybe it came in after I left. This is how stuff falls through the cracks. Whoever took that file off my desk should have known better, Robin included. Meg should have given the file to me first."

"I guess you'll have to train her."

"Don't think I won't. Let me check on the initial appearance and get back to you," Patty said and hung up.

Alex didn't think her problems with Jared's case could get any worse, but they did when she opened the file and began reading the probable cause statement. The first line read, *I, Detective Hank Rossi, #4278, knowing that false statements on this form are punishable by law, state that the facts contained herein are true.*

"Shit!" Alex said, slamming the file onto her desk.

Another dance with Rossi was the last thing she needed, especially after what happened at the Zoo and what happened with Bonnie when she got home. Bonnie took one sniff and ordered both of them into the shower. Afterward, wrapped in their robes, they sat on the bedroom floor drinking wine and ruffling their dog Quincy's fur. Bonnie waited until Alex had finished her glass of wine.

"Okay, give. What terrible thing happened today?"

"Do I look that bad?"

"Yes, but you smelled worse. Where did that come from?"

Alex knew that she had to give Bonnie enough of the truth to make sense of her appearance, and that meant telling her she'd been to the judge's ranch. She'd never told Bonnie about her visits to the ranch, claiming she was meeting a witness in one of her cases.

"I was in Judge West's court today. He was going on and on about his damn horses and how wonderful they are and I was trying to be polite so I said that I'd love to see them sometime. And he said what about tonight, and what was I going to do? Of course, if I'd known he was going to ask me to help him muck out the stables, I would have come up with an excuse. But I wasn't quick enough."

"You're kidding! He made you shovel horseshit?"

"Well, he didn't make me. I just couldn't figure out how to say no. Except for the smell, it wasn't that bad. I needed the exercise, and who wouldn't want to help a horse?"

"That explains the smell, but it doesn't explain why you looked so beat-up when you walked through the door."

Alex dropped her chin to her chest and sighed. "No, it doesn't."

Bonnie draped her arm over Alex's shoulder and pulled her close. "Come on. Out with it."

Alex left out that Judge West was blackmailing her, limiting her confession to her encounter with Rossi at the bar. They argued over what to do about it, Bonnie wanting her to file a complaint against Rossi with the police department, Alex refusing, saying she could handle him. Their fight killed the cuddling vibe, the argument ending with them sleeping back to back, the middle expanse of their king-sized bed separating them. Bonnie was gone when Alex woke up in the morning. But Rossi was there, stuck in her head like a bad song playing over and over.

Alex's computer pinged, announcing that she'd received an e-mail. It was from Patty. Jared Bell's initial appearance was Friday morning, September 17, at nine o'clock.

"Shit!" she said again, plucking the probable cause statement from the file.

Rossi stated that he'd gotten a call about a dead body in Liberty Park at 1:15 a.m. on Tuesday, September 14. He identified Jared as a twenty-eight-year-old white male, approximately 150 pounds, with black hair, summarizing how Jared had led them to the victim. He described the ligature marks and the bruised impression on her chest in the shape of a cross. He included Jared's statements denying he had touched the body while acknowledging that he was familiar with the victim but didn't know her name. Rossi described going with Jared to his tent and finding a cross that appeared to match the wound on the victim's neck.

The probable cause statement recited that Rossi then took Jared into custody and advised him of his Miranda rights and that Jared consented to continuing to answer questions. Jared stated that he had consensual sex with the victim in his tent several hours before he reported finding her body. Not owning a watch, he was uncertain about the time.

Rossi continued questioning Jared at police headquarters. At nine twenty a.m. on Tuesday, September 14, Jared stated that after having sex, they quarreled and he strangled her, dumped her body in the creek, and stole her cross.

The report identified six people who were camped out in the same area, noting that none of them acknowledged hearing or seeing anything suspicious or related to the crime. None of them had permanent addresses.

The last paragraph of the probable cause statement recited that the coroner, Dr. Bruce Solomon, had examined the body at the county morgue and informed Rossi that he had observed evidence of genital trauma at the external vaginal opening consistent with forcible rape. Rossi ended the statement by saying that the victim was unidentified.

The complaint charged Jared with forcible rape and first-degree murder of one Jane Doe. Kalena Greene had signed the complaint.

Alex leaned back in her chair, the file in her lap, reconsidering her speculation that Judge West wanted Jared convicted not because he was guilty but because he was innocent. Taken at face value, the probable cause statement was compelling. So why force her to handle the case and make sure Jared took a deal for a life sentence? Why not let Kalena go for the death penalty, which would satisfy the judge's appetite for maximum justice?

The answer came to her. No defendant would ever agree to a plea bargain that included the death penalty. And a death-penalty case would be more closely scrutinized. Once Jared was convicted, the Midwest Innocence Project might jump all over Jared's case and Judge West would have no way to control that. If the judge was using Jared to protect the real killer, a plea bargain was his only option.

Which brought her to the bottom-line question. Who was Judge West protecting? The easy answer was that he was the killer, but that was too big a leap for her. He'd never given her any indication he was capable of such a crime. Still, she knew firsthand the human capacity to kill when pushed too far. And she also understood a killer's unabashed determination to get away with murder.

TWELVE

Alex wanted a look at Jared Bell before his initial appearance. She had to get a feel for him, get some sense of how he got caught up in whatever Judge West was orchestrating and whether she'd be able to pry both of them out of that trap.

Jared had confessed to murder, but that didn't mean he wasn't being set up to take the fall for crimes he didn't commit. He wouldn't be the first person to confess to something he didn't do after being questioned throughout the night by an aggressive cop like Rossi.

And his confession didn't match all the charges. For starters, Jared hadn't confessed to the rape. If he was willing to admit murdering the victim, why deny raping her? That there was evidence of forcible rape didn't mean Jared was the rapist. It was possible that the victim had been raped, or engaged in rough sex, before she had sex with Jared, neither of which Alex could rule out, given what little she knew about the victim.

But that wasn't all. According to Rossi, Jared said that he and the victim argued after they had sex and that's when he strangled her. If Jared had raped her, that sounded more like second-degree murder, knowingly causing the death of another during the commission of a crime, than first-degree murder, knowingly causing the death of a person after deliberation on the matter. If convicted of second-degree murder, he'd have a shot at parole one day.

And if the sex was consensual, Alex might even be able to convince the jury that it was involuntary manslaughter—recklessly causing the death of another. That was a Class D felony, which carried a maximum sentence of four years.

It was a short walk from her office to the county jail. The building was officially known as the Jackson County Regional Detention Center, a name that politicians liked better. Everyone else called it what it was—the jail, all seven floors of it.

The jail population was segregated by floor. Those with serious mental health problems and openly gay and transsexual inmates were housed on the second floor, an arrangement that made Alex want to scream whenever she set foot on the floor. Instead, she continually lobbied the county to stop equating the two.

The third floor was for inmates who had no prior incarcerations, resulting in a population of mostly young inmates. Jared fit that profile. The crimes he was charged with didn't. Rape and murder qualified him for the seventh floor, home to sex offenders and high-profile inmates.

Alex rode the elevator past the fourth and fifth floors, which were reserved for inmates who had served real time in state or federal prisons, and past the sixth floor, which housed women. She stepped off on seven, looking through a windowed wall into another room, where the corrections officers, or COs, worked. On the far wall of that room, there was another bank of windows, through which she could see the inmates. Having little else to do, they gathered at those windows to see who had come to visit.

At any one time, she might have half a dozen clients in the jail. Once they saw her, they would point at themselves, miming their question. *"Are you here to see me?"* She'd smile and mouth her apology, pointing at the chosen one. She'd called ahead, letting the COs know whom she wanted to see.

She scanned the faces lined up against the windows, shaking her head at the familiar ones, wondering which of the others was Jared Bell, her answer coming when a skinny white man with vacant eyes and mangy hair peeled away from the windows and shuffled toward a waiting CO.

Another CO escorted her to an interior meeting room big enough to accommodate a scarred metal table bolted to the floor and a pair of chairs. Jared entered through another door, chin down and hands jammed in the pockets of his jumpsuit, eyes darting around the room like a mouse looking for a morsel or a way out.

"Hi, Jared. I'm your lawyer, Alex Stone. Please take a seat."

He slid down in his chair until his legs were stretched beneath the table almost to Alex's side.

"Okay," he said, after a moment.

"Are they treating you all right?"

He shrugged. "Yeah, I guess so. Nobody's given me any trouble."

He was pleasant, soft-spoken and polite, without a hint of pent-up rage or inclination to violence, the kind of person a jury might warm to and the kind of person who could be manipulated into taking a fall. His sunken eyes, sallow complexion, and yellowed teeth spoke to his time living on the street.

"Where are you from?"

"Goodland, Kansas."

"Boy, that's all the way west to the Colorado line, isn't it?"

He gave her a shy smile. "Yes, ma'am."

Alex returned the smile, holding his gaze for a moment, trying to make a connection.

"When was the last time you were home?"

He shrugged. "Three or four years, right after I got out of the army."

"What was your rank when you got out?"

"E-4."

"Like a corporal except you weren't a junior noncommissioned officer."

His eyes got wide. "You know your ranks."

Alex smiled. "I've represented my share of vets. How long were you in the service?"

Jared swirled his hands on the table's Formica surface as if he was making patterns in the sand. "Two tours, four years."

"Did you see a lot of action?"

He ducked his chin, looking away. "Everybody did. That's how it was in the sandbox."

Alex shook her head. "Boy, I can't imagine what that was like."

"No, ma'am, you can't. I can promise you that," he said, tugging at the sleeves of his jumpsuit, the fabric hanging on him, the outfit at least a size too big.

She nodded. "I believe you. Thank you for your service."

His voice rose as he hunched his shoulders to his ears. "Everyone's always thanking us for our service, 'cept that doesn't mean much, 'cause they don't know what it's like over there so they don't really know what they're thanking us for, you know what I mean, ma'am?"

It was Jared's first show of anything approaching anger, making Alex wonder what might be boiling beneath his soft-spoken façade.

"I guess I do, Jared. I suppose it's hard for anyone who hasn't been through it to understand what it was like, so I won't pretend that I do."

His face softened again. "Thank you, ma'am."

"But when I get to know you, I'll have a better idea what it was like and I'll thank you for your service then. In the meantime, I want you to know I'm glad to represent you."

He furrowed his brow. "Why's that? I'm a homeless nobody."

"Because I know what it's like when your life is on the line and you feel outnumbered."

"How you know what that's like?"

"I'll tell you when we've got more time. When you were in Afghanistan, you looked out for your buddies and they looked out for you, right?"

His eyes fell, his voice dropping to a whisper. "Tried to."

"Well, this is a different kind of war and I'm going to look after you," she said, wincing inside, hoping to make good on the promise, knowing she might have to break it.

Jared thought about what she said and smiled. "Then I guess I should be the one thanking you for your service."

"You're welcome," Alex said, pleased that she was building rapport. That was the key to building trust, and trust was the key to finding out what she needed to know. "Have you ever been charged with a crime before?"

"No."

"Okay, so here's how your case is going to play out. Your initial appearance is Friday morning at nine. I'll meet you in the courtroom. That's when the judge will set bail. It will probably be too high for you to get out, so I'm afraid you'll be here for a while."

"That's okay. Been on the street a long time. Like they say, three hots and a cot."

Alex grinned. "Not many of my clients see it that way. You've been charged with forcible rape and first-degree murder. In a month or so, the prosecutor will ask the grand jury to formally indict you on those charges. If you're convicted, you could get life in prison without parole, or the death penalty."

She paused, gauging his reaction. Jared's face slackened, and what little color he had melted away, his eyes fluttering. She expected that, but not the small smile that leaked from the corners of his mouth, as if he was telling himself, *I told you so*. He was revealing pieces of himself, but she didn't know what they meant.

"And a few months after that, we'll have a preliminary hearing. That's when the prosecutor will put on enough evidence to convince the judge that you should stand trial. And six months to a year from then you'll go to trial unless we make a deal."

Jared perked up. "What kind of deal?"

"Too early to say, but it would probably mean pleading guilty to a lesser offense to avoid the death penalty or life without parole. Something that would give you a shot at eventually getting out."

He shook his head. "They ain't ever lettin' me out."

Alex cocked her head. "Why do you say that?"

"'Cause that's the way it is."

"Innocent people confess to crimes they didn't commit more often than you could guess. It happens for all kinds of reasons. And someone who's been to war and who ends up living on the street may be even more likely to do that just because of all the stress you've gone through. I'll come back after court and we'll go over everything that happened. And I'll dig into everything the police did to get you to confess. If there's a way to keep your confession from the jury, I'll find it."

"I hear you," he said, his chin down. "But…"

Alex leaned toward him, holding her breath, waiting to see if he would recant his confession. Jared looked away, saying nothing. Alex pressed him. "But what?"

He leaned back in his chair, took a deep breath, and let it out. "It don't really matter anymore."

"What doesn't matter?"

His eyes were red and wet. "All of it. Everything. I been headed here a long time, and now that I am here, it don't matter anymore."

Her clients rarely told her the truth, especially the first time she met them, even when they were confronted with persuasive physical evidence, like DNA and fingerprints. The street-smart ones who'd spent their lives perfecting the arts of deception and denial would tell her without flinching that they knew it looked bad but it wasn't them, that the eyewitnesses were liars and the lab tests were wrong, that they'd been at their mother's house watching television when the crime occurred. When she'd tell them to get real, they'd ask what kind of deal they could get, not admitting their guilt but offering to testify against somebody. *Who?* she'd ask. *Anybody,* they would say. Whatever it took.

Jared Bell told her something she didn't hear very often from her clients. He was where he belonged. Maybe because he was guilty and nothing he could do would change that or maybe because he was innocent and nothing he could do would prove that.

"Well, it matters to me," she told him.

On her way out, Alex stopped to talk to Calvin Lockett, one of the corrections officers. Alex had cultivated a friendship with him, making it a point to ask about his family, sharing news of hers. It had paid off more than once when Calvin let her know about an inmate too eager to testify against one of her clients.

He had worked the jail for twenty years, using the time to become an unofficial jailhouse psychologist, adept at diagnosing what he called an inmate's roots, the tangle of bad breaks, bad judgment, and plain meanness that put them in his charge. He grew up poor and black like many of them, puzzling about how he ended up on the other side of the steel bars. Rail thin and graying, he watched over the inmates, shaking his head and clucking his tongue.

"Hey, Calvin," Alex said. "How's it going?"

"Same old, same old."

"I've got a new client, Jared Bell. What's your take on him?"

"Boy's a midnight screamer. Wakes everybody up with all his racket."

"Nightmares, huh? Any idea what they're about?"

Calvin shrugged. "Some people say dreams don't mean a thing. I don't buy that. Man dreams of making love to a beautiful woman, that's what he needs. Man dreams he can fly, he's trying to escape his troubles. Man that's a midnight screamer, well, that's his demons trying to get out."

"You talk to him about his nightmares?"

"Don't need to talk to him. I heard enough."

"What did you hear besides his screaming?"

Calvin paused, looking around to make certain they wouldn't be overheard. "Whoever that girl, Ali, is—or was—you ask me, he killed her. That's what's waking him up. He's calling her name, saying he's sorry."

Alex's heart picked up a beat. According to Rossi's report, Jared said he didn't know the victim's name and Rossi hadn't identified her. Knowing her name would jump-start Alex's investigation.

"What, exactly, did Jared say?"

"He kept calling her name, saying 'I'm sorry, Ali, I'm sorry.'"

"I don't suppose he mentioned her last name."

Calvin smirked. "You ever hear of a demon with a last name?"

Alex thought about her recurring nightmares, the ones in which Dwayne Reed appeared out of the darkness, reaching for her with one hand, the other clamped around Bonnie's throat.

"I can think of at least one," she said.

THIRTEEN

Rossi got back to his desk in the homicide unit, playing out in his head his next visit with Alex Stone, wanting that encounter to appear as accidental as the one at the Zoo actually had been. He was trying to figure out how to make that happen when his boss, Mitch Fowler, hollered at him from the door to his office.

"Rossi! My office! Now!"

Fowler was the commander of the homicide unit. He yelled at Rossi because he could and because it was his idea of strong leadership. Fowler lived in and by the book, while Rossi used the book as a doorstop. Fowler spent his days crunching numbers on overtime and closed cases, his hair thinning as his waistline swelled, frustrated that Rossi's name was always at the top of both lists. Rossi's overtime cost their unit too much money, but his closure rate made it impossible for Fowler to dial him back.

Rossi grabbed his cell phone, holding it to his ear, pretending to be talking to someone on the other end, one finger in the air signaling to Fowler that he'd be there in a minute. No one was on the other end, but he couldn't resist pimping Fowler. He watched Fowler from the corner of his eye, waiting until Fowler's face blossomed red before he pocketed his phone, slow walking to Fowler's office. By the time he got there, Fowler was behind his desk, thumping a pencil against his belly. There were two chairs on the visitor's side of the desk, one of them occupied.

"Hey, Rossi," Charlie Wheeler said. "How's it hangin'?"

Wheeler was Rossi's first partner when he joined the homicide unit. His parents were wealthy physicians who sent him to Pembroke Hill, Kansas City's private prep school, and to Princeton, where he got an engineering degree. He'd disappointed them when he enrolled in the academy the day after he graduated, telling Rossi he never grew out of playing cops and robbers. Rossi nicknamed him Mr. Mayor since he shared the name of a popular former holder of the office.

He was black, which would have given him a leg up with the brothers on the east side if they trusted the cops and if they couldn't sense his upper-class, Ivy League background a mile away. Despite the badge, he was an engineer at heart, more pen-and-paper problem solver than throw-down motherfucker.

One day they chased a suspect into an abandoned house, Wheeler taking the front, Rossi going in the back. The suspect put a bullet in Wheeler's left leg before Rossi took him out. His wife, Lorraine, reminding him that their two kids needed their father, convinced him that it was time he stopped chasing bad guys and used his engineering degree. Wheeler didn't want to quit the force, so they compromised and he transferred to the traffic investigation unit and started reconstructing accidents.

Rossi occasionally used him as a sounding board, appreciating how Wheeler could deconstruct a case, finding the flaws and pointing him in the right direction. Rossi bought him a beer after Alex Stone was acquitted, running the case past him. Wheeler told Rossi he agreed with him but since Alex had been acquitted, he had no choice but to let it go. Rossi said he couldn't, and Wheeler said that was the difference between an engineer and a homicide cop.

Rossi shook his hand. "Free and easy, Mr. Mayor. How's the leg?"

Wheeler patted his thigh. "Still got a limp, but Lorraine says it's not enough to get me out of mowing the lawn."

Rossi laughed. "I hear that. What brings you over here?"

Wheeler pointed at a file on Fowler's desk. "Like I told the commander, I've got a case I'd like you to take a look at. My boss said your boss would have to okay you doing that."

Rossi turned to Fowler, whose perpetual scowl notched another downturn. "He said take a look, not take it over. Are we clear?"

"Clear as ever, boss," Rossi said. "Follow me," he said to Wheeler.

Rossi pulled a chair next to his desk, motioning to Wheeler to take a seat, Wheeler sighing as he did, rubbing and stretching out his left leg.

"Just a limp? Looks like it feels worse than that," Rossi said.

"Depends on the day. Sometimes I get pins and needles that won't quit. Sometimes it gives out on me and sometimes I can mow the lawn." He patted his stomach. "But it's a good excuse for packing on the weight."

Rossi grinned. "And what's your excuse for the bald head and glasses? You didn't have those the last time I saw you."

Wheeler smiled and nodded. "That, my friend, is just me getting where we're both going, only I'm getting there first. But it makes me glad you killed the prick that shot me so he could get there ahead of both of us."

"Makes me glad too. What's with your case?"

Wheeler spread his file on Rossi's desk, separating the photographs from the accident report and a diagram of the scene. "One-car accident last night north of the river, way west on Barry Road. Westbound car goes around a curve where the road turns to the south, driver loses control, goes down an embankment, and smacks into a tree. The driver is dead at the scene due to massive head trauma."

"So? Happens all the time. What do you need me for? Maybe she fell asleep at the wheel or maybe it was suicide."

"Maybe, but she didn't leave a note and the family says no way. She was happy, wasn't in debt, wasn't on drugs, and as far as anyone knows, wasn't in any kind of trouble. And, there's one more detail."

"What's that?"

"The accident location. According to her oldest son, who's a senior in college at UMKC, his mother never went north of the river unless she was going to the airport, and this location is a long way from KCI. He had no explanation for why she was where she was."

Rossi took sip of cold coffee. "Which leaves you where?"

"Suspicious. I won't know more until we get an autopsy report to rule out drugs and alcohol and until I get a chance to flyspeck the vehicle and do a complete reconstruction of the accident."

Rossi nodded. "Okay, you've got a case with a lot of questions. I still don't get why you want me to look at it."

"The victim was Robin Norris. Ring a bell?"

Rossi's eyes popped. "The Robin Norris who runs the public defender's office?"

"Yeah. That Robin Norris. We found her cell phone on the floor in the front of her car. We pulled her phone records. She made a call just before the accident."

"Who'd she call?"

"Alex Stone."

Rossi sat up. "How 'bout that."

"Yeah, how about that. I was going to pay her a visit and ask what they were talking about, but I thought you might like to come along."

"Wouldn't miss it."

FOURTEEN

Grace Canfield knocked on the open door to Alex's office. "You wanted to see me?"

"We've got a new case for a guy named Jared Bell. He's charged with forcible rape and first-degree murder and his initial appearance is Friday morning at nine," she said, holding up Jared's file.

"And you've already got the file? How many times has that happened?"

"Zero, but we can't say that anymore. Make a copy for yourself and bring it back to me. Then start digging. I want to know everything there is to know about him—family, friends, priors—whatever you can find. He was in the service, so we'll need those records too. And I'd like to have as much as you can pull together before court."

"Why the rush? Nothing ever happens at the initial hearing except for the judge setting bail our clients can never post."

"You're right, but there's something about this guy that's off and I need to figure out what it is."

"All of our clients are off one way or the other or they wouldn't be our clients," Grace said.

Alex raised a hand, telling Grace to stop. "Yeah, yeah, yeah. I get that. But when I was talking to Jared..."

"Wait a minute. You've already talked to him? At the jail?"

"Yes. Already. At the jail."

"He's that high profile?"

"No. Near as I can tell, he doesn't even have a profile. He's a homeless vet who confessed to murder but not rape who says he's never getting out because he's been heading to jail for a long time. Calvin, my buddy at the jail, says he wakes up in the middle of the night screaming to someone named Ali that he's sorry. We don't have an ID on the victim yet, so look for anyone by that name because we're gonna need that if we're gonna have a shot at putting this on someone else."

Grace cocked her head, a glint of worry in her narrowed eyes. "Girl, you got that look I haven't seen in a while."

"What look is that?"

"It's your I-Am-Sasha-Fierce-and-I'm-gonna-save-the-world-one-poor-soul-at-a-time look."

Alex smiled. "Something wrong with that?"

"Just one thing. That look works for Beyoncé when she's onstage shaking her booty, but, girl, you lost that look for a reason," Grace said, leaving with the file.

Grace was right. She'd lost that look because she'd lost hope that she could make a difference. Even on the rare occasions when she won, all she did was send her clients back to the same lousy world that had raised them to be criminals and where that was the only job skill they had. She'd learned to live with that, convincing herself that she was defending the Constitution as much as any client, making certain that their rights were protected regardless of their guilt or innocence.

But her ideals had been no match for Dwayne Reed. They hadn't been strong enough to protect the people he killed or to stop her from killing him. If Grace had seen that look in her today, maybe she could feel that hope again and turn Jared Bell from someone's fall guy into her salvation, if she could find a way around Judge West.

Five minutes later, Meg Adler rapped on her door.

"I ran into a couple of people in the lobby that need to talk to you."

Alex looked up from her desk. "I didn't get a call from the receptionist."

"I told her that wouldn't be necessary."

Alex furrowed her brow, staring at Meg. "Why?"

Charlie Wheeler stepped from behind Meg and into Alex's office. "Because I asked her not to. I'm Detective Wheeler," he said, showing her his badge.

"And," Meg said, "I believe you know Detective Rossi. I'll leave you to your business."

Rossi followed Wheeler, the two detectives fronting Alex's desk, looking down at her. Alex tensed, angry that Meg had let them ambush her, depriving her of a chance to figure out why they wanted to talk with her and how she would handle them. That Meg was new and they didn't know each other was no excuse. *Protect your people* was the first rule for any boss, and Meg had served her up, letting them catch her wide-eyed and openmouthed. If it had just been Wheeler, she might have given Meg a pass. But nobody got a pass when it came to Rossi.

Rossi led off. "Sorry for barging in."

"No, you're not," Alex said. "It's what you do. The question is why?"

"We need to talk to you."

"I gathered that. What happened? Did you lose your phones? Forget how to make an appointment? Or were you just in the neighborhood and decided to drop by?"

Wheeler started to sit in one of the two chairs in front of Alex's desk but she cut him off.

"Don't bother. Whatever you want, you won't be here long enough to sit."

"Why the hostility?" Rossi asked.

"I'm busy. Next time I show up at your work uninvited you'll understand."

Rossi shrugged. "I spend my day getting interrupted. No reason to come out swinging."

Alex leaned back in her chair, arms crossed. "Fine. What do you want?"

Rossi looked at Wheeler. "It's your case, Mr. Mayor."

"I'm in the traffic investigation unit," Wheeler said. "I'm investigating Robin Norris's accident."

Alex clenched her jaw, Wheeler's statement breathing life into the unformed dread she'd felt since learning that Robin was dead. There could be only one reason Wheeler and Rossi were in her office. Robin's accident wasn't an accident. If they had information, she wanted to hear it.

"I'm sorry," she said, motioning them to sit. "It's been a shitty day."

"I'm sorry for your loss," Wheeler said.

"Thanks. What makes you think Robin's case is a homicide?"

"What makes you ask that?"

"Because if it was an accident, he wouldn't be here," Alex said, pointing to Rossi. "So what's going on?"

Wheeler deflected her question. "When was the last time you saw Ms. Norris?"

Alex turned her head to the side, thinking for a moment. "I'm not sure. I probably saw her in the office yesterday or the day before."

"When was the last time you spoke with her?"

"Like I said, yesterday or the day before."

"What did you talk about?"

"Just hi and how are you, in the hall, that sort of thing."

"Nothing more substantive, maybe something about one of your cases or something going on outside the office?"

"No. Robin was always under the gun. She didn't have a lot of time for chitchat and there was nothing going on in any of my cases that we needed to discuss."

"What's your cell phone number?"

Alex frowned. "My cell phone number? Why do you ask?"

"Please, Ms. Stone, your number?"

"Don't worry," Rossi said, "he's not going to call and ask you out."

"Maybe you should give him yours. He might ask you, and the change would do you good," Alex said.

Wheeler coughed into his fist, unable to hide his smirk. "Your number, Ms. Stone."

"Fine, if it will get this over with faster. It's 816-555-1331. Now it's your turn. Why do you need my number?"

"We recovered Ms. Norris's cell phone at the scene. Her last call was to you."

Alex grimaced. "Really? If you knew that, why did you ask for my number?"

"Just confirming that we had the right one."

"Well, I didn't get a call or a message from Robin."

"Do you have your phone?" Rossi said.

Alex didn't like that she was the only one answering questions, though she knew that was a standard cop interrogation technique. Although she had nothing to hide, she couldn't stop her pulse from racing as she retrieved her phone from her pants pocket.

"Right here," she said, holding it up.

"Can I have a look at it?" Rossi said.

"After I do." Alex unlocked the phone, her mouth dropping open when she saw that she had a message. "That's weird. I've got a message, but I don't remember getting a call." She clicked through to the voice message screen. "The caller ID says it was from Robin."

"Put the phone on speaker and play the message," Rossi said.

Alex hesitated, hating that she had to share the message with anyone, especially Rossi. Robin had intended the message for her, not them. What could be more intimate, more private, than a friend's last words?

"Play it, Counselor," Rossi said.

She nodded, realizing she didn't have a choice, tapping the touch screen, taking a quick breath when she heard Robin's voice.

"Alex! I've got to talk to you! Oh, my God!"

The message ended with a garbled mix of Robin's scream and the crunch of collapsing steel.

The three of them sat in silence, staring at Alex's phone, each of them hard-bitten enough to think they'd heard it all only to find out in that moment how wrong they were.

"We're going to need your phone," Rossi said, his voice surprisingly soft and gentle. Alex nodded and turned away, clutching her middle. "You can get a new phone with the same number."

"What about saving Robin's message? Won't I lose it when I change phones?"

"I've been down this road before," Rossi said. "Your voice mail is saved on your carrier's server. Do you have any idea what she needed to talk to you about?"

Alex shook her head. Robin rarely called her after hours, respecting her employees' needs for a private life. So the call had to have been some kind of emergency, and the only one she could think of was Jared Bell's case. And that wasn't something she wanted to discuss with Rossi. "None."

"The accident happened north of the river, way west on Barry Road. Can you think of any reason she was in that area?" Rossi asked.

Alex was glad for a question she could answer with a clear conscience. "No idea."

"What time was the call?" Wheeler asked.

Alex examined her phone. "Last night. Ten fifteen."

"Where were you when the call came in?"

Alex straightened, feeling a little less vulnerable for the moment. "At a bar. I'd turned my phone off. That's why I didn't hear it ring."

Wheeler took Alex's cell phone and dropped it into an evidence bag.

"Were you with anyone? Can anyone vouch for you?"

Alex nodded. "Yeah. Him," she said, pointing at Rossi. "Your partner and I were having a beer."

FIFTEEN

Wheeler and Rossi waited until they were out on the street before discussing their meeting with Alex.

"So what's your take?" Wheeler said.

"Other than that Alex is lying about not knowing what Robin Norris wanted to talk with her about?"

"What makes you think she was lying?"

"The way her face fell when you asked her the question. She couldn't even look at you. I've seen that face a thousand times. It's the what-who-me-couldn't-be special. Never fails and never works."

"You sure you're not reading too much into that given your history with her? She's got a solid explanation for why she didn't get the phone call, since the two of you were kicking back a few brews. And by the way, what were you doing going drinking with her?"

Rossi crunched his brow, staring at Wheeler. "I didn't go drinking with her. I was at the Zoo drinking by myself. She came in. I sat down next to her. End of story."

"No, it's the same old story. You didn't have to sit down next to her. You're never going to leave it alone, are you? What did you think was going to happen? You'd get her drunk and she'd confess? And even if she did, so what? She was acquitted. And that is the end of the story."

"Not for me. And don't forget, you invited me to this party after her name popped up, so quit telling me to let it go."

"Look, I get it. We've all got at least one case that will eat our ass until the day we die."

"Even in traffic?"

Wheeler stepped back. "Fuck you, Rossi!"

Rossi put up his hands. "Sorry, Mayor. That was out of line."

"Damn straight it was. I know why you can't let this one go."

"And now you're gonna tell me even though I'm not going to ask."

"You know I am. You don't give a rat's ass about Dwayne Reed. Nobody misses that prick. But you can't get over the fact that Alex Stone beat you."

"It's more than that."

"What?"

"She used me."

"How?"

"To put a bullet in Gloria Temple. That's how she beat me. I killed the one witness who would have put Stone away."

"You've told me that story a dozen times. No way Alex could have set that up. Shit, you saved her life."

"Like you said, she beat me."

Wheeler studied him. "Man, you are fucked-up." He pulled the evidence bag containing Alex's phone from his jacket pocket. "I may regret this, but are you in?"

"Yeah. I'm all in."

"Okay. My boss will square it with yours. Just be sure you're all in on Robin Norris, not Alex Stone."

Rossi put his hand on Wheeler's shoulder. "Don't worry. I know how to multitask."

"Oh, yeah?" Wheeler grinned. "What's next on your to-do list?"

Rossi pointed across the street to Ilus Davis Park. "I'm going to have a seat on a bench, let the sun shine down on me, and watch all the girls go by."

"And hope that Alex Stone is one of them?"

"You're a wise man for a mayor."

Ilus Davis Park was an outdoor mall flanked on the north by the federal courthouse and on the south by city hall and named after another former Kansas City mayor. The five-acre park had a statue of Davis, a reflecting pool, a memorial to the more than two hundred city employees who'd lost their lives in the line of duty, and a monument to the Bill of Rights.

It also had enough trees and shrubs to make it a perfect place for Rossi to sit and watch the entrance to Alex's building without her knowing it. He was betting that she was so shaken by the message on her phone that she'd have to get out if only to clear her head and, if Rossi was lucky, talk to someone, probably Bonnie. If she did that, he'd take another pass at Bonnie. He settled onto a bench with a good line of sight and waited.

Twenty minutes passed before Alex emerged, heading south on Oak. Rossi gave her a head start before following, puzzled when she didn't turn into the garage where he knew she parked her car. He was even more curious when she crossed Twelfth Street, angling toward the Jackson County Courthouse. She wasn't carrying a file or a briefcase, so he doubted she had a hearing. He couldn't imagine a less likely place for Alex to go to lay down her burden.

He stopped on Oak, just north of Twelfth, standing in the shadow of a bail bonds office, and watched her enter the courthouse because he couldn't follow her immediately without her seeing him.

Once she was inside, he trotted across the street, past the bronze statue of a mounted President Andrew Jackson, the county's namesake, and up the stairs to the courthouse doors. Peering through the glass, he saw her standing in front of the lobby elevators.

When she disappeared into one of the elevators, he went inside, the deputies waving him through security, and watched as her elevator door slid shut. The number of each floor was displayed above the elevator, lighting up as the elevator reached that floor. The car in which Alex was riding made its first stop on the fifth floor. Rossi watched the numbers. When the car began its descent, he took the stairs to the fifth floor, coming out in the center of a wide, oval-shaped rotunda ringed by four courtrooms. Doors at each end opened into interior corridors leading to offices for each judge's staff and chambers.

It was near the end of the lunch hour, and the expansive hallway was filled with lawyers, litigants, jurors, and courthouse personnel getting ready for their afternoon sessions. Alex wasn't among them and she wasn't in any of the courtrooms.

She could have gone into one of the interior corridors to see a secretary, law clerk, or judge, but that didn't make sense if he was right about her reason for being there. And he couldn't go prowling through those offices without having to answer more questions than he could ask.

There was another possibility. She could have realized he was following her, led him to the fifth floor, and jumped on another elevator, giving him the slip. Either he was wrong about her knowing something about Robin Norris's death or she'd beaten him again.

SIXTEEN

Alex stood outside Judge West's courtroom, looking through the glass set in the upper half of the swinging double doors at the lawyers huddled in front of the bench. The court reporter had moved alongside them with her steno machine to capture what they were saying in hushed voices the jury couldn't hear, while the jurors studied ceiling tiles and the handful of spectators checked their e-mail. It was twelve forty, well past the usual time for a lunch break, but Judge West was notorious for long sessions and short recesses.

Knowing that he had to break sooner rather than later, Alex decided to wait for him in his chambers, hoping his secretary and law clerk had gone to lunch so she wouldn't have to make up an excuse for a private, unscheduled meeting with the judge. She let out a quick sigh of relief when she found their offices empty, sucking in a sharp breath as she stood in front of the closed door to Judge West's chambers. She hesitated for a moment, debating whether to let herself in, deciding that Wheeler and Rossi hadn't left her a choice.

She'd always felt uneasy in his chambers even before they became coconspirators. It wasn't just his prickly gruffness or the perpetual dusk he maintained with drawn shades and muted lighting. And it wasn't the dark woodwork and black leather chairs or the absence of any trace of kith or kin. It was how well the shadows suited him.

In her nightmares, he strode toward her on legs welded from steel prison bars, swinging arms made of long-handled gavels in punishing arcs at her head, his corpulent body bursting at the seams as a putrid discharge boiled over his collar. He kept coming at her, his eyes shrunk to red slits, his mouth torn in an executioner's snarl, until she turned and ran, only to be caught by Dwayne Reed, who pinned her against the wall, one hand clamped around her throat, the other ripping at her clothes until she broke free, pulling a gun, both of them laughing at her until she pulled the trigger again and again and woke up screaming.

Alex never told her therapist that Judge West haunted her dreams along with Dwayne Reed. Physician-patient privilege was not a safe enough sanctuary for that confession. Nor did she tell Bonnie, too afraid that once Bonnie tugged on that thread, she wouldn't stop until she'd unraveled her.

She understood why she couldn't escape him in her dreams, but that wouldn't stop her from confronting him about Robin Norris's death. Had he told Robin how to handle Jared Bell's case? Had she refused and unwittingly signed her death warrant? What would drive him to such extremes? She would demand answers, and if she wasn't satisfied, she'd go to Rossi and tell him everything because there wasn't room on her conscience or in her dreams for Robin.

The door from the hallway swung open, making her jump, clutching her hand to her chest, wondering how she would explain her presence in his chambers to Judge West's secretary, until she realized it wasn't his secretary. It was a wan-faced, slim-shouldered man dressed in a charcoal-gray suit, his silver hair buzzed close to his scalp, patchy in places. A round gold pin the size of a quarter was stuck to his lapel, an eagle perched at the top, its wings wrapped around the sides.

"Oh," the man said, staring at her through his black-framed glasses, his eyes more curious than startled.

Before Alex could answer, Judge West came through the door from the courtroom, his black robe billowing around him like a storm cloud. He glanced at Alex and the man, then, hanging his robe on a coat stand, lumbered to his desk and dropped into his chair.

"Her I know," he said, pointing at Alex, "but who the hell are you?" he asked the man.

The man chuckled and tugged at his collar, then shook his head. "I'm sorry. I get so turned around in these big buildings I'm not sure where I'm supposed to go or how to get there. I'm looking for the probate court and I'm guessing this isn't it."

"Next floor down," the judge said.

"Thank you, and I'm sorry for intruding," the man said and left.

"Who was that guy?" Judge West said.

"Beats me," Alex said. "I've never seen him before."

"Jesus fucking Christ! I've told the county a dozen times we need more money for courthouse security and they keep telling me I'm crying wolf. Well, mark my words, one of these days, some nutcase is going to waltz right past our five-and-dime security team of overweight and out-of-shape deputies and spray a few hundred rounds into a jury pool, and then we'll see who's crying wolf, by God!"

"He didn't look too dangerous to me. He was probably an out-of-town lawyer who doesn't know his way around the courthouse."

"That's not the goddamn point, Alex. The goddamn point is that a stranger walked right into my chambers and nobody asked him who he was, why was he here, and did he have an appointment."

Alex nodded.

"For that matter, I could say the same thing about you, except for the part about you being a stranger. So what are you doing here?"

He was a bully and bluster was his natural state. At times, she let herself believe that he'd bullied her into joining forces to railroad her most heinous clients into a life behind bars, but in her honest moments she knew that wasn't true. She'd been a willing partner. He'd exploited her guilt-driven weakness, but that didn't make him responsible for what she'd done. She owned that, which made it easier to stand up to him in spite of his threat to ruin her life.

"Robin Norris is dead."

He rocked back in his chair, arms folded across his belly.

"So I heard. Damn shame."

Alex balled her fists, arms at her sides. "Is that all you can say?"

He spread his hands. "What would you have me say? I didn't know her well, but from what I knew, she did a good job and I assume she had a family. But accidents happen and some days life is a shit sandwich. Seems to me that *damn shame* covers that and a lot more."

"The police think it wasn't an accident."

West leaned forward, shuffling papers on his desk, not looking at her. "What makes you say that?"

Alex watched him for a moment, his nonchalance not what she expected, wondering if it was too practiced, his way of keeping his emotions in check.

"Because two detectives came to my office to talk to me about it."

"Why would they do that?" he asked, leaning back in his chair again.

"You think they'd tell me? One of the detectives, a guy named Wheeler, is in the accident investigation unit, but the other detective was Hank Rossi, and he's strictly homicide. If he didn't think Robin might have been murdered, he wouldn't be involved in the investigation."

Judge West laced his fingers together across his belly. "Why are you telling me this?"

She looked at him, hesitating for a moment, then plunged in. "A woman from the St. Louis PD's office, Meg Adler, is filling in for Robin. She brought me Jared Bell's file first thing this morning. She said she found it on Robin's desk with a Post-it note with my name on it, but the file was never logged in. It just showed up out of nowhere."

West narrowed his eyes. "Get to the point, Counselor."

Alex took another deep breath. "You told me I was going to be assigned to Jared Bell's case. The next thing I know is that Robin is dead, Bell's file is on her desk with my name on it, and no one knows how it got there."

The judge pulled his chair tight against his desk, color flooding his cheeks. "If I were you, I'd be very careful with the next thing that comes out of your mouth because I don't like your tone or your implication."

Alex planted her palms on his desk, boring in on him. "Did you talk to Robin about Jared Bell's case? Did you tell her how I was supposed to do my job?"

Judge West eased back, a thin-lipped smile cutting across his face. "No. Anything further, Counsel?"

Alex didn't blink. "Yes. Where were you last night at ten fifteen?"

He gave her a weary grin like a parent whose patience has been strained to the limit. "In bed listening to my wife snore."

"Did you have anything to do with Robin Norris's death?"

The judge remained impassive. "No."

Alex hung her head for a moment, then straightened and turned away.

"Anything further, Counsel?"

She shook her head, her back to him.

"Then let me give you some advice. The next time you accuse me of murder, try digging up some evidence first, like a photograph maybe. In my experience, that's much more persuasive to a jury."

Alex stiffened at his mention of the photograph, unwilling to let him turn the tables on her. She faced him, her jaw set.

"Photograph or no photograph, if I find out you're responsible for Robin's death in any way, so help me God, I will burn you down!"

"Really?" West said, his face as calm as that of a card player holding a winning hand. "When did you take up arson? I thought you favored shooting the unarmed and defenseless."

She cocked her head to the side, showing him a steely smile. "I'll make an exception for you."

SEVENTEEN

Alex pounded down five flights of stairs to the street, taking her anger and frustration out on each step. She couldn't decide what was worse: that she'd let Judge West goad her into threatening to kill him or that she'd accused him of murder.

By the time she reached the first floor, she'd burned enough energy to think clearly. What mattered was whether she believed his denial and his alibi. She couldn't picture him rear-ending Robin's car, forcing her off the road. It was easier to imagine him whispering in someone's ear about a problem that had to be solved in a hurry, never mind the details.

If the judge was responsible for Robin's death, she was culpable as well, even if the law wouldn't draw that link. She'd given in to her weakest self by joining hands with West, making it easy to draw a straight line from that moment to this. She had to find out the truth about Robin's death, no matter the consequences. She couldn't leave it up to Rossi, because he wouldn't hesitate to use the investigation as another way to bring her down. And she couldn't ask anyone for help without putting them at risk by dragging them into the deal she'd made with the devil.

When she left the courthouse, she saw the man who'd walked into Judge West's chambers staring up at Andrew Jackson and his horse. She was about to pass him when he turned, head still raised, and ran into her.

"Oh," he said.

"That's two *oh*s in one day," Alex said.

"Yes, it is," he said with a smile. "That's my limit, I'm afraid."

He was an inch shorter than her, his gray complexion waxy in the sunlight. She was close enough to make out the detail on his gold pin. There was a navy blue inner circle inscribed with *Service—Valor—Sacrifice*. A map occupied the center of the pin with *50th* superimposed over it. The words *Vietnam War* appeared beneath that. A small rectangular ribbon in green, gold, and red was attached to the bottom of the pin.

Alex pointed to the pin. "You served in Vietnam?"

"Eighty-Second Airborne, 1968 to 1970."

"Long time ago."

"But not forgotten."

"Nor should it be," Alex said, hesitating for a moment. "Did you find the probate department?

"I did, but everyone was at lunch. I'll have to try again, but next time I'll know where I'm going."

"Since you didn't know your way around the courthouse, I take it you're not a lawyer."

He laughed. "Oh, no. I was looking into a matter for a friend, another vet, that's all. I'm retired, so I don't have much else to do."

The man was so courteous and disarming that Alex warmed to him immediately, their pleasant conversation a welcome antidote to her confrontation with Judge West.

"What did you do before you retired?"

"Pretty much the same thing, helping vets, so I guess you could say I didn't work very hard or I never retired."

"I know a few lawyers who do probate work. I'd be happy to give you their names."

"Then you must be a lawyer."

"Guilty," Alex said.

"And a good one, if I'm any judge of people." He stuck out his hand. "Mathew Woodrell."

"Alex Stone," she said, shaking his hand.

"A pleasure," he said. "Nice to know a lawyer if I ever need one."

"Well, you won't want it to be me."

"Why's that?"

"Because I only represent poor people accused of crimes."

"Then I hope you're right."

She watched him walk away, then look back at her and give her a little wave. A westbound bus was stopped on the other side of Twelfth Street. When it left, she saw Rossi standing on the sidewalk. They stared at each other, neither of them moving, waving, or nodding, until Rossi turned his back and walked away.

EIGHTEEN

Alex stopped at a phone store on her way home and bought a new phone, keeping her old number. The salesperson confirmed Rossi's explanation that her voice mail was stored on the carrier's server and not on the phone. She'd sync the new phone with her laptop to restore everything else that was on her old phone.

Bonnie was on her hands and knees, wrist deep in dirt, working along the edge of a flower bed that bordered their patio when Alex got home. Alex watched her from the den window that looked out on the backyard. Soil littered the patio's redbrick pavers behind her. Alex couldn't tell whether she was digging a trench or digging to China.

Bonnie was the gardener in the family. She delighted in choosing the plantings, putting them in, and nurturing them from one season to the next, taking Alex by the hand for a tour and explaining about annuals and perennials, irises, day lilies, impatiens, and hydrangeas, and junipers and ferns and all the rest. Alex never got past the colors, telling Bonnie she liked the purple and yellow flowers and the green bushes until Bonnie poked her in the arm and called her a moron.

Alex could judge Bonnie's mood by how she gardened. The more time she took, the more at peace she was. The faster she moved, the harder she dug, the more riled up she was, and at the moment, she was hitting the soil like a jackhammer.

She needed Bonnie's help dealing with Robin's death, but she was struggling with how much to tell her, especially since it looked like Bonnie was fighting her own battle. It was the same tightrope she'd been walking for a year, and she felt like one of the Flying Wallendas teetering on a wire suspended over the Grand Canyon, the wind swirling around her.

Grabbing two beers from the refrigerator, Alex went outside. Their dog, Quincy, had been napping in the late-afternoon sun beneath a black wrought-iron table surrounded by matching chairs. He bolted toward Alex, jumping up and planting his paws on her chest, his tail wagging at warp speed, as if he hadn't seen her in years. Alex stroked his back from head to tail.

"Hi, baby dog! Did you miss me today?"

"Don't get excited," Bonnie said over her shoulder. "He did the same thing to the meter reader a while ago."

"I know. What can I say? We raised a dog that loves everyone. Where did we go wrong?"

She rested a beer bottle against Bonnie's neck, condensation running off the bottle and mixing with Bonnie's sweat. Bonnie sighed, stopped digging, and reached for the bottle. She stood, took a drink, and wiped her mouth.

"You always know what this girl needs," Bonnie said.

"That's why you're my girl. How long have you been out here?"

"I got off at three, so I've been out here since about three thirty, a couple of hours."

"That's a whole lot of digging. You must have had a lousy day."

They sat in wrought-iron chairs beneath an oak tree that shaded the patio. Bonnie rubbed her bottle against her cheek, closing her eyes for a moment.

"You could say that. From the hangdog look you're wearing, I'd say yours wasn't any better."

"That's for sure. I don't know anything about your day, but mine was awful. When I walked in the office this morning,

I found out that Robin Norris was killed in a car accident last night."

Bonnie covered her mouth with her hand. "Oh, dear God! What happened?"

Alex let out a sigh and shook her head. "She lost control of her car and it went off the road, hit a tree, and she was killed."

Bonnie reached for Alex, hugging her tight, Alex resting her head on Bonnie's shoulder. "How awful."

"And it gets worse," Alex said, sitting up. "She was leaving me a voice message when it happened but I didn't hear the call come in because my phone was off."

"Where were you?"

"At the Zoo."

"With that asshole Rossi?"

Alex nodded. "And guess who's investigating the case?"

"Rossi?"

"Yeah. He and another detective came to my office today because they found Robin's phone at the scene and the call log showed that her last call was to me. They wanted to know what we talked about. I hadn't even noticed I had a message until they asked me about the call. We listened to the message together." She paused and gulped, choking on her memory of the recording. "She said she needed to talk to me and then she screamed and I heard the car hit the tree and then…nothing."

Bonnie rubbed Alex's back. "Oh, my. I can't imagine how awful that was. Do you have any idea why she was calling you?"

"I don't know. She kept saying she had to talk to me, but I have no idea what about. That's what I told Rossi, and I could tell by the look he gave me that he didn't believe me. It's bad enough that Robin is dead, but now I've got to put up with his bullshit again."

"That's not the only bullshit he's shoveling at us."

Alex's stomach clenched. "I don't think I like the sound of that."

"Me neither, but it is what it is."

"What's what it is? What's going on?"

"Rossi paid me a visit this morning."

Alex's jaw dropped and her heart skipped a beat. "What was that about?"

"What do you think? He won't let the whole Dwayne Reed thing go."

"What's that got to do with you?"

"He pretended that he was concerned about how you looked when he saw you at the Zoo. He thinks you feel so guilty about killing that prick that it's eating you up, but he didn't fool me. He doesn't give a shit about you—or me, for that matter."

"That's not exactly news."

"No, but here's the headline. He doesn't think you feel bad about killing that douche bag Dwayne. He thinks you feel guilty because it wasn't self-defense and he's hoping that you confessed to me and that I'll rat you out. The guy is un-fucking-believable!"

Alex twisted in her chair, eyes wide, torn between outrage at Rossi and fear that Bonnie might believe him.

"What did you tell him?"

"What do you think I told him? I told him to go fuck himself."

Alex took a deep breath. "Thanks. I'm sorry he put you through that. I don't know why he won't leave us alone."

Bonnie leaned forward and put her hand on Alex's knee. "Because, babe, he thinks you're a badass, stone-cold killer."

Alex set her beer on the table, forcing her voice to sound matter-of-fact. "And what do you think?"

"I think you killed that son of a bitch because he threatened you and me. I think if you hadn't killed him, he would have raped and killed me and then gone after you. I think he was a crazy psychopath who wasn't going to stop unless somebody stopped him, and I give thanks every day that you did. That's what I think."

"So you don't think I'm a badass, stone-cold killer?"

Bonnie cupped Alex's face with her hands and kissed her deeply. "I've known you were a badass since the day we met. And I've seen what you've gone through since that day, and if you were a stone-cold killer, you wouldn't have had one nightmare. You'd have just added a notch to your belt. You did what you had to do and you've paid the price."

They cried, hugged, and kissed, coming up for air when Quincy nosed between them, making them laugh.

"What a dog!" Alex said. "He doesn't want to be left out." She wrapped her hand in Quincy's fur. "Is it because you're an only child?" she asked the dog.

"We can always fix that," Bonnie said.

"You want another dog?"

"No. I want a child."

Alex was speechless. Of all the things she expected Bonnie to say, that wasn't one of them. When they decided to move in together, they talked about having kids one day, Bonnie saying she wanted to carry the baby, but it had never been more than casual conversation.

"You sound serious."

"Honey, I am serious. I've been thinking about it for a long time. I was going to bring it up a year ago, but then everything happened, and our lives have been so crazy, there was never a good time. Remember asking me if there was something bothering me? Well, that was it. I didn't know if it was the right time to bring it up."

"And after everything that happened today, you think this is a good time?"

"I know. At first I didn't think it made sense, but the more I thought about it, the more sense it made. We love each other. We're going to be together forever, right?"

Alex grinned. "You know it."

"Well, I'm thirty-six and the clock is ticking. And I'm sick and tired of assholes like Dwayne Reed and Hank Rossi screwing with our lives. If we wait until the rest of the world leaves us alone, we'll die barren old ladies with drool cups strapped under our chins. It's our lives and it's time we started living them. And, besides, I'll look fabulous pregnant."

It was the kind of crazy logic that did make sense. More than that, it was a commitment to their future and a powerful statement by Bonnie that she'd stand by Alex no matter what. Alex had never loved her more than at that moment.

"Well, I guess we better buy a turkey baster."

That night as they lay in bed, Alex propped herself up on one elbow and studied Bonnie as she slept, grateful for the gift of her love and scared to death that she would squander it. She fell back on her pillow, closed her eyes, and prayed for sleep.

NINETEEN

Friday morning, Grace Canfield met Alex outside the courtroom of Associate Circuit Court Judge Noah Upton, who would preside over Jared Bell's initial appearance. Grace gave her an up-and-down appraisal, nodding her head and pursing her lips.

"Uh-huh," she said.

"Uh-huh, what?" Alex asked.

"Since when do you wear your fancy black pantsuit and white ruffled blouse to an initial appearance? That's what. And am I wrong or are you wearing blush?"

"What on earth are you talking about? I wear black pantsuits all the time," Alex answered, ignoring the question about her makeup.

"Not the one with the fancy stitched pattern on the jacket lapels that Bonnie gave you for your last birthday, and you were the one who told me that makeup violated your official lesbian dress code."

Alex folded her arms across her chest, not wanting to admit that Grace was right. When she woke up this morning, she felt something she hadn't felt in a long time—happy. Bonnie loved her and wanted to start a family. Last night's anxiety about whether she would ruin all of that had given way to a morning filled with images of the two of them pushing a baby stroller down the sidewalk on a warm summer day. She didn't know how long the feeling would last before harsh reality set in again, but she would ride the wave as long as she could. Getting ready for work had felt more like getting ready for a date, so she dressed up and put on a little blush for Bonnie, who giggled and groped her, nearly making both of them late.

"Do we really have to talk about this now?"

"No, but you start coming to work like this all the time and we're gonna talk about it, because I'm gonna want some of whatever's put a skip in your step."

Alex laughed. "Fair enough. What did you find out about our client?"

Grace shook her head. "Nothing that'll do you any good this morning. I talked to his mother, Diane. She still lives in Goodland, Kansas. She was so glad to hear he was alive that she couldn't stop crying. When she finally did, she told me they hadn't heard from him in a couple of years. Said he came home from the war a mess and they woke up one day and he was gone."

"Did she know anything about someone named Ali?"

"Only that she heard him calling out her name in his sleep, but when she asked him who that was he said he didn't know what she was talking about."

"Anything else?"

"We can find out if Jared's been treated at the VA hospital if he signs this release." Grace opened a thin manila folder and handed the form to Alex, who slid it into her case file. "I can request his service records, but that takes a while."

"Not if we can cut through the red tape."

"Girl, if you got a pair of them scissors, let me have 'em."

"I don't, but I met someone yesterday who might. His name is Mathew Woodrell. He's a Vietnam vet who helps other vets with their problems."

"Where do I find him?"

"I don't know. Check with Veterans Affairs. He was in the Eighty-Second Airborne."

"You don't have a phone number or e-mail address?"

"Sorry. I only talked to him for a minute. He said he'd just come from the probate clerk's office. He was trying to help another vet with something. Maybe they've got contact information."

"Description?"

"He's a little guy, not more than five-seven, short gray hair, has to be in his early seventies at least, and he was wearing a military pin for having served in Vietnam."

"And he's white," Grace said.

"Yeah. How did you know?"

"Because white is the default race for white people. If he'd been black, you would have said so."

Alex raised her eyebrows, blushing. "I...I..."

"Never thought about it. I know. Most white folks don't. Well, that's a start." Grace glanced at her watch. "It's go time."

"Then let's go," Alex said, leading the way into the courtroom and taking her place at the defendant's counsel table.

Kalena Greene was already seated at the prosecution's counsel table. She and Alex exchanged good mornings as two deputies escorted Jared into the courtroom, shuffling, his wrists and ankles shackled. He gave her a shy smile. Alex smiled in return, pleased that she'd made a connection, putting her arm around his shoulder for a moment.

"Hi, Jared. Say hello to Grace Canfield. She's an investigator in my office."

"Hey," he said to Grace.

"Hey, yourself," Grace said. "Alex is the best. She's gonna take real good care of you."

"Hope so," he said.

Alex was struck again by how soft and quiet Jared was, as if he was afraid to raise his voice. She had difficulty imagining him as a killer. Even though he may have killed while serving in combat, he didn't strike her as the kind of civilian who had slid down that slope all the way to murder.

"How are they treating you, Jared?" Alex asked.

He shrugged. "Okay. Everyone's pretty much leaving me alone."

"I hear that. Like I told you yesterday, we won't be here long. This hearing is mostly a formality."

"Like the army, huh. Rules for everything."

"Yeah. Like the army. A couple of quick things before the judge comes in. Have you been treated at the VA hospital here?"

"A few times, mostly when the PTSD got crazy. They gave me some meds and told me to go to group therapy."

"How'd that work out?"

He looked at the floor. "I sold the meds and skipped the group."

Alex saw no reason to chide him. He'd have plenty of time for treatment in prison if she didn't get him out, and if she did win his freedom, that would be the time to talk about getting well.

"I need you to sign this release," she said, sliding the form toward him and handing him a pen, "so we can get your medical records. We may need the doctor who saw you to testify about your PTSD."

"Are you sayin' I could get off because of that?" he asked after signing the release, his signature more of a scrawl because of the handcuffs he was wearing.

"One second," Alex said, handing the form to Grace. "Hand deliver it and tell them we need the records right away."

"Sure thing. You know how excited bureaucrats get when someone tells them that."

Alex raised her eyebrows at Grace.

"I'm on my way," she said. "I'm on my way."

Alex turned back to Jared. "Sorry. We may be able to use your PTSD as a defense, but if we're going to do that, I have to find out everything about you, including whatever happened in Afghanistan that caused your condition."

He hung his head, closing his eyes as a tremor rippled through his torso, then opening them and shaking his head. He didn't say anything and Alex didn't push.

TWENTY

Everyone stood for the judge, sitting when he did. He was in his early forties, with blond hair, great cheekbones, and blazing white teeth, making him well suited for the televised courtroom he'd never see as an associate circuit court judge.

"The court calls case number F458-2013. Counsel, state your appearances."

"Kalena Greene for the people."

"Alex Stone for the defendant, Jared Bell, who is also present. We'll waive reading of the charges."

"Very well. Bail?"

"My client is indigent, Your Honor. Short of releasing him on his own recognizance, he can't make any bail you're likely to set. But, for the record, the defendant requests bail be set at ten thousand dollars."

Kalena sprang to her feet. "For a vicious rape and murder by a homeless man with no ties to the community? I don't think so, and I don't care if he can't make a ten-dollar bail. The court should send a message that people who commit violent crimes won't be allowed back on the street before trial. Bail should be denied."

"He's also a decorated war veteran who's been charged, not convicted," Alex said.

"I agree with both of you," Judge Upton said. "Mr. Bell is innocent until proven guilty, but given his current circumstances, notwithstanding his military service, for which we are all grateful, and the nature of the charges, bail is set at one million dollars. Anything else?" Both lawyers shook their heads. "Hearing nothing, we are adjourned."

"Here," Kalena said, handing a file to Alex after the judge and Jared left. "It's the investigating officer's report and the complaint."

Alex had been waiting for this moment to find out whether someone in the prosecutor's office had given an advance copy of the file to Robin Norris.

"Thanks, but I've already got a copy."

Kalena squinted at her. "What do you mean you've already got a copy? From who?"

"You heard about Robin Norris, right?"

Kalena's face fell as she let out a breath. "Yes, and I'm so sorry. I didn't know her well, but I never heard a bad thing about her. What a blow."

Alex was struck by her sincerity, reminded again of one of the things she cherished about the practice of law. She and many of the lawyers in the Prosecutor's Office were friends, and no matter how hard they fought over a case, they could still kick back over a beer. She and Kalena hadn't gotten to that point yet, but this felt like a first step.

"Robin had five kids, and I can't stop thinking about them."

"How are they doing?"

"I don't know. I've been so busy with this case, I haven't had a chance to get over there, but I'm going to stop by tonight."

Kalena put her hand on Alex's wrist. "Please give them my sympathies."

"I'll do that. Anyway, about the file. Robin's interim replacement is a woman from the St. Louis PD's office named Meg Adler. She found the file on Robin's desk yesterday. My name was on a Post-it note stuck to the file, so Meg assumed Robin wanted me to handle the case. That's all I know."

"Hmm. That's so odd."

"Why? Is it that big of a deal?"

"Depends on how you look at it. Whether you got the file yesterday or today doesn't impact the case. But how you got the file might be."

"Why?"

"Because my boss' policy is to wait until the initial appearance to produce this file, and because this is my case, I'm the one who would produce it. You know Tommy Bradshaw and what a stickler he is for stuff like this."

"Yeah. He was like that when we were in law school together. Which means someone in your office didn't follow your policy or someone outside your office sent the file to Robin Norris."

"If it came from my office, whoever did it could lose their job. My boss has fired people for less. I have to tell him what happened, and when I do he'll turn the office inside and out to find whoever leaked it."

"Really? Why? You said my getting the file early won't impact the case."

"That's not why he'll turn it into an inquisition. The guy is paranoid about leaks, worse than the White House. And the only thing that will drive him crazier is if someone outside the office did it, because whoever did that is sticking his nose where it doesn't belong. So, yeah, it's a very big deal."

"But as long as it doesn't impact the case, how about sending me the standard discovery before the grand jury indicts my client?"

Kalena smiled and shook her head. "Then I'd be the one looking for a job. Besides, I won't have all that stuff before the grand jury convenes. We're still working the case up, and I'll save you the trouble of asking me to reduce the charges to a misdemeanor. You're not that stupid and I'm not that easy, especially when the death penalty is in play."

That was the response Alex expected unless Kalena was getting pressure to put the case on a fast track to a plea bargain, her response making it clear that she wasn't.

"Never hurts to ask. Can you at least tell me if the victim has been identified?" Kalena hesitated. "C'mon. Don't make me wait for the grand jury for that information. You're going to release her identity to the press anyway."

"We're not quite there yet, but I'll give you a call as soon as I can."

"Fair enough," Alex said. She had gathered her things and begun to walk away when she stopped and turned back toward Kalena. "By the way, who else in your office had access to the file?"

"Everyone," Kalena said.

TWENTY-ONE

Alex went home and changed into faded jeans, a long-sleeved navy polo, and boots. She played fetch with Quincy in the backyard using one of the many tennis balls he'd stashed around the house and yard, waiting for him to tire while she thought about Jared's case.

When she met him at the jail, she didn't ask him to tell her his version of what happened. She was more interested in getting a sense of him and beginning the process of building a rapport. The more he liked, trusted, and believed in her, the more likely he'd be to tell her the truth. She was under no illusion that he'd ever tell her the entire truth. Few, if any, of her clients did that. The most she hoped for was that he'd tell her enough of the truth that she could build a defense. And the more she knew about the case when she had that conversation with Jared, the more she could tell when he was lying.

Rossi's investigative report and the prosecutor's complaint gave her the outlines of the state's case. It would be a while before she got any discovery from Kalena Greene and before Grace Canfield tracked down Jared's army buddies or anyone else who might know something useful. That left the crime scene.

The courtroom was Alex's favorite place, but the crime scene, alive with smells, colors, and textures and speaking a sign language peculiar to the horror it had witnessed, was a close second. The challenge was figuring out what the scene was trying to say.

She didn't have the police photographs, the forensic report, or the physical evidence taken from the scene or Jared's confession.

And that was fine with her. She wanted to see the scene through her eyes first. There would be other versions told by people with an agenda, but the crime scene didn't have an agenda. Though bloodstained, it was pure.

She'd driven by the scene countless times, the grassy, overgrown stretch of ground flitting past in her peripheral vision. It was flanked by I-435 on the west, Truman Road on the north, and Twenty-Third on the south. Jackson County had two courthouses, one downtown and another in Independence, Missouri, which bordered Kansas City's easternmost edge. She regularly used both Truman Road and Twenty-Third to get to that courthouse, never thinking to detour onto the winding side streets that led to where the murder had occurred.

She exited from I-435 onto Truman Road, passing a porn shop called Erotic City. Its sign towered above the store's roofline, enticing customers with the promise of literature, films, books, playthings, and videos. Once when she and Bonnie were about to pass the store, Bonnie made her stop, claiming she couldn't live another day without knowing the difference between pornographic literature and pornographic books. She discovered that the difference was in the price and walked out with a few delightful playthings.

According to Rossi's report, the police had entered the area from the north. Alex did the same, thinking to retrace Rossi's steps. The north end was narrow and studded with stunted trees, their limbs bent and bare, and clusters of runaway weeds that tugged at her jeans as she strode past. The ground was riddled with hidden rocks and cracks in the earth that could snag a careless ankle and twist an unguarded knee.

The area opened up as she approached the center, which was flat and grassy, with few of the hazards of the north end, making it an inviting place to pitch a tent. The southern end was tapered like the north, with woods so thick she couldn't see Twenty-Third Street.

A creek running north and south cut through the area at an angle. She was on the east side. There was another hundred yards of grass and scrub on the west side of the creek, with the interstate just beyond.

Rossi's report described a campsite with a number of tents. Now there was only one, set deep in the shadow of a rock wall carved out of what was once a bluff marking the eastern border of the unofficial campground. Murder was bad for property values, even in a homeless encampment, Alex thought. Or maybe it wasn't the murder. Maybe it was the scrutiny that came with the murder. Either way, the campgrounds had been abandoned save the one tent. Grace would have a hard time running down anyone who had been there that night.

Rossi's diagram of the scene put Jared's tent near the midpoint between Truman Road and Twenty-Third Street. She had no trouble finding his campsite. The grass was still beaten down and faded from where the tent had been. And it was the only vacant site with crime scene tape ground into the turf by an anonymous boot.

She made her way to the lone remaining tent, stopping when she was within twenty feet. The tent flap was half-open and she could hear someone stirring inside.

"Hello in the tent," she called out.

There was no reply.

"Anybody home?"

Silence, then a raspy, smoke-addled voice answered. "Who gives a shit?"

Alex bit her lip, trying not to laugh. "I do. My name is Alex Stone."

"Good for you. Go away."

"I'd rather talk to you first."

"And I'd rather be the queen of England, so it looks like we're both gonna be disappointed."

"No reason for both of us to be disappointed. All I want is to talk to you. That's a hell of a lot easier than you giving up all of this to marry Prince Charles. And I've got twenty dollars for you if that will help."

A burst of lung-busting coughing exploded inside the tent, after which a short, skinny woman wearing sweatpants cinched around her bony hips and a grease-stained yellow T-shirt stepped into the sun. Her gray hair was stringy and tangled and her eyes were bloodshot. She opened her mouth, sucking in air like it was hard labor, running her tongue where her teeth had been and sticking out a scrawny hand.

"Like the man says, show me the money."

Alex approached, catching a whiff of the woman's stench, a sour, curdled odor like garbage left to rot in the sun.

"C'mon, now," the woman said, snapping her fingers, "I ain't got all day."

Alex held out a twenty-dollar bill and the woman grabbed it in a flash.

"Were you here the other night when they found that woman's body in the creek?"

"You a cop?"

"No. I'm a lawyer. I represent Jared Bell. The police arrested him for murdering that woman."

"Poor Joanie," the woman said, fishing a cigarette from her T-shirt pocket. "Got a light?"

Alex caught her breath at the mention of the victim's name. "Sorry, I don't. You said her name was Joanie."

The woman looked at her, squinting. "You deaf?"

Alex had represented enough homeless people to know how unpredictable they could be, whether because of mental illness or substance abuse or both. She didn't want to antagonize the woman, so she kept her tone even and neutral.

"No."

"So why you askin' me was her name Joanie when I just got done sayin' 'poor Joanie'?"

"I'm sorry."

The woman dug into her sweatpants, pulling out a lighter. She put the flame to her cigarette and drew long and deep, hacking and sputtering as she spoke.

"You're so sorry about everything and none of it's got anythin' to do with you."

Alex nodded. "You're right. Let's start over. I'm Alex Stone. Who are you?"

"Gladys Knight. The Pips are around her somewhere."

"Nice to meet you, Gladys. Tell me about Joanie. What was her last name?" Alex asked, happy to play along.

"How the hell should I know? Last names are the last thing anybody around here cares about."

"Was Joanie staying in one of the tents that were here the night she was killed?"

The woman's cigarette had burned down to her fingers. She flicked it onto the ground. "You think I keep track of who comes and goes?"

"I think you haven't survived this long without paying attention to what's going on around you."

The woman squinted at her. "True that, and so's stayin' out of what don't concern me. And that goes double for you and Joanie and that no good, cocksucking, murderin' Jared whatever the hell his last name is."

Alex narrowed her eyes, studying the woman, anxious to find out whether her accusation was based on Jared having been arrested or whether she knew something more. She pulled out another twenty-dollar bill.

"Even if it doesn't concern you, I'd sure like to know why you think my client is a murderer."

The woman snatched the twenty, wadding it up in the palm of her hand with the first one.

"Wouldn't you, now?" she said, grinning.

Alex forced a half smile. "Yes, I would."

"Well, I'll tell you what I told the cops. Go to hell and don't call me when you get there."

She turned and disappeared into her tent, zipping the flap closed.

Alex waited a few minutes to see if the woman would return, calling to her but giving up when there was no response, uncertain whether the woman knew anything or had just played her for forty bucks. Rossi's report made no mention of witnesses who had seen or heard anything, giving credence to the woman's claim that she had told him nothing. Convinced that she wouldn't get any further, she walked to the creek to see where Joanie's body had been found, glad to at least have a first name for the victim, hoping the woman hadn't scammed her about that as well.

She reached the creek bank, looked down, and nearly fell in when she saw a young girl, no more than ten, with alabaster skin and long, corn-silk hair lying faceup, eyes closed, her head resting in the soft mud, her legs stretched out in the water, her arms spread like wings.

"Oh, my God!" Alex cried, her hand on her chest, terrified she'd found another murder victim.

The girl's eyes popped open. Seeing Alex staring down at her, she scrambled to her feet and dashed through the water and up the other bank before Alex could say another word. Without uttering a sound or looking back, the girl ran alongside the creek, vanishing into the trees at the south end. All Alex could do was watch her go.

Alex bent over, hands on her knees, and took a series of deep breaths until her heart stopped pounding. Who was the little girl? Was she playing a harmless game or was she reenacting the murder scene, and if she was, how could she have known the details and what could have possessed her to do such a thing? Alex had no answers to any of her questions.

She turned back toward where Jared's tent had been. The woman had come out of her tent again but went back inside as soon as Alex saw her. Hands on her hips, Alex did a slow turn, taking in the grounds and seeing a sign that had been planted in the ground, christening the area as Liberty Park. Alex thought about that name, imagining what it was like to live and die in this place, and decided that Janis Joplin had been right when she sang *Me and Bobby McGee.* Freedom was just another word for nothing left to lose.

TWENTY-TWO

Alex would have preferred to spend more time at the scene, walking through the crime scene the way Rossi had laid it out, looking for anything that might contradict his report, but the little girl changed all that. She was getting away and the scene wasn't going anywhere.

Unless the girl was a runaway, she had to live close by. Alex couldn't see any houses from where she stood, but she knew there weren't any on Truman Road or Twenty-Third Street. And Alex doubted the child had crossed eight lanes of interstate highway to get to the creek. That meant the child most likely lived to the east, somewhere on the other side of the cliff.

Alex ran for her car, gambling that the child would head for home rather than remain in the woods at the south end of Liberty Park. If she was right, she had a chance of finding the girl before she could hide behind a locked door and parents who would shield her from the lawyer for an accused murderer.

Back in her car, Alex followed the street where she'd parked up a hill and into an unfamiliar neighborhood. The streets were narrow, winding bands of asphalt, crumbling along the edges, bordered by drainage ditches thick with overgrown grass and weeds. She had to be quick without hurrying or risk losing control of her car on the serpentine roads.

Houses and trailers were scattered haphazardly along the streets, some bunched together, others standing alone, many of them so old and run-down that a stiff wind would blow them away. Pit bulls and Dobermans patrolled their turf, snarling and barking when she passed by. Signs saying *Keep Out* and *Beware of Dog* were plentiful enough to convince any door-to-door salesman—or lawyer—to try her luck elsewhere.

No one was working in their yard or sitting at a window or on their front porch. No children were playing on swing sets or in the street. There was no one at all, which wasn't unusual on a weekday afternoon, when adults were likely at work and children in school, but there was something about the neighborhood that felt alone or abandoned. Maybe it was the dilapidated, neglected conditions, or maybe it was something missing in the lives of the people who lived there. Whatever the cause, it gave her a prickly uneasiness, making her anxious to find the little girl, talk to her, and get out of there.

Several times she thought she caught a glimpse of the girl darting among the trees, her long blond hair matted against her neck. But when she slowed for a closer look, no one was there, making Alex wonder if what she'd seen was just the sun reflecting off the leaves rustling in the breeze, the elusive images tantalizing enough for her to keep searching.

She wound her way through the neighborhood again and again before catching a woman parking a white Chevy Impala in a driveway she'd passed twice before. The car was missing its hubcaps and a rear brake light. A sheet of plastic was duct-taped over the missing passenger window on the driver's side, and the left quarter panel was rusted out above the wheel well. The driveway belonged to a saltbox house with a roof that sagged in the middle and siding that was peeling in places and fading in others. A storage shed sat at the back of the driveway, its door padlocked with a heavy chain.

Alex stopped in front of the house, rolling her window down and calling to the woman when she got out of her car.

"Excuse me, ma'am."

The woman had copper-red hair courtesy of a bad dye job and enough makeup for a drag queen, her glittering green eye shadow visible at a distance. She wore jeans that were too tight for the heft she carried and an even tighter shirt stretched over mountainous breasts subdivided by the strap of the purse slung between them.

"Yeah," the woman said.

Alex got out of her car and crossed the yard to the driveway, glad that there was no dog in sight.

"I'm looking for a little girl, probably about ten. She's wearing shorts and a T-shirt and has long blond hair."

The woman blinked, glancing over her shoulder at the thicket of trees behind her. It was enough to make Alex think the woman not only knew the child but was also looking for her.

"She your kid?" the woman asked, the corners of her mouth twitching.

"No."

"Relative of yours?"

"No."

"You even know her name?"

"I don't," Alex said, not liking the way the conversation was going.

"What makes you think she lives around here?"

"I saw her playing in that creek that runs through the area...I don't know what to call it...There's a sign that says Liberty Park."

The woman cocked her head at Alex, one eyebrow raised. "Uh-huh. What do you want with her?"

Alex smiled, trying to keep their conversation casual and friendly, knowing the more questions she was asked, the fewer answers she would get to her own questions.

"I just want to talk to her."

"About what?"

"The other day, a woman's body was found in the creek right where she was playing, and I thought maybe," Alex said, holding up her palm, "and I know it's probably a long shot—but maybe if that's someplace she liked to play, if she was down there a lot, she

115

might have seen somebody or something that would help me find out what happened."

The woman squinted at her. "You a cop?"

Alex took a breath, shaking her head, knowing that this was the moment when things could go south. Most people didn't like getting involved in anything outside their own lives, especially cops, courts, and crimes. It was a toss-up between whom they disliked more—the police who might one day arrest them or the lawyers who they suspected would get the guilty off on a technicality unless they happened to be the one who was guilty.

"No, I'm a lawyer and I'm representing a man whose been charged with murdering that woman."

The woman crossed her arms over her chest, tightening her jaw. "Well, I don't know nothing about no little girl or dead woman."

Alex studied her for a moment, the woman returning the stare. Alex broke eye contact first, digging her wallet out of her jeans and removing a business card.

"If you happen to hear anything or run across that little girl, I'd appreciate it if you would give me a call," she said, handing the card to the woman. "My client's life could depend on it."

The woman reluctantly took the card without looking at it, her downturned mouth sour proof that she was unmoved by Alex's appeal.

"Sure," the woman said.

Alex drove away, watching the woman in her rearview mirror, the woman crumpling her business card and dropping it on the ground. Just as Alex rounded a curve, she saw the little girl dash out from behind the storage shed, running to the woman's side, ducking behind the woman and out of Alex's sight.

She stopped in the middle of the street, debating whether to turn around. The woman was probably the child's mother and had done what any mother would have done when a stranger tried to draw her daughter into a murder investigation. Confronting her now would only make the woman more protective, but Alex had to take that chance, because the longer she waited to talk to the girl, the more likely the mother was to make sure the girl told her nothing.

Alex spun the wheel and drove back to the house, slamming her hand on the steering wheel when she saw the empty driveway. The woman, the girl, and the Impala were gone.

TWENTY-THREE

Hank Rossi slowed his car as he approached the scene of Robin Norris's fatal accident on Northwest Barry Road, pulling off onto the westbound shoulder and parking behind Charlie Wheeler's car. Getting out, he surveyed the scene.

It was a rural area, with only a few homes in the vicinity, none of them close to the accident scene or one another. Barry Road ran generally east and west, though from where he stood, it curved to the south before straightening back to the west. The ground dropped off from his side of the road at a severe angle, sloping down to a grove of trees, one of which was scarred from the impact of Robin's car. Wheeler was standing in front of the tree, running his hand across the damaged trunk.

"Careful you don't get a splinter, Mayor," Rossi said.

Wheeler hobbled up the slope, slowed by his bad leg, rubbing his thigh when he reached the road. "About time you got here."

Rossi pointed to the tree. "Is that the smoking gun that's going to make our case?"

"More like the last dot in a long string of dots that we're going to connect."

Rossi rubbed the back of his neck, craning his head to loosen his muscles. "Okay. So where's dot number one?"

"Follow me. Not much traffic for a Friday afternoon, but pay attention anyway. I don't want to spend my weekend filling out reports explaining how you got run over." They waited for a break in traffic before walking to the painted yellow line dividing the two lanes. "You see that curved tire mark that starts in the westbound lane in the middle of the curve?"

"Yeah."

Wheeler turned toward the south edge of the road. "That tire mark goes all the way across the eastbound lane to the point at which the victim's car left the road."

"That's a big skid mark. What's it mean other than she was going too fast?"

"I'll get to her speed in a minute. And don't call it a skid mark. It's either a yaw mark or a spin mark. A yaw mark is caused when a driver makes an abrupt steering maneuver to avoid an object in the roadway or to stay on the road when entering a curve too fast. But a spin mark is caused when one vehicle impacts another."

"So how do you know whether it was a yaw mark or a spin mark?"

"The easiest way to tell is if there's also a dark scuff mark at the point of impact."

Rossi studied the westbound lane. "I don't see anything like that."

"Me either."

"So we're missing a dot. What does that leave us with besides her speed? How fast was she going, anyway?"

"I can't calculate her speed without knowing whether that's a yaw mark or a spin mark. The equations are different."

"Are you telling me you don't know how fast she was going?"

Wheeler looked at him, pursing his lips and shaking his head like a disappointed parent. "Did I say that?"

"Then you do know."

"Damn right I know."

"But you aren't going to tell me yet, are you? You're going to make me sit through your introductory class in accident reconstruction, aren't you?"

Wheeler smiled and clapped him on the shoulder. "Yes, I am. And there will be a test. Now, let's get back to my classroom," he said, leading Rossi to his car.

He pulled an envelope filled with photographs from the front seat, thumbing through them until he found the ones he wanted, then spreading them out one at a time on the hood of his car.

"The victim was driving a Honda Accord. The driver's side collided with the tree. You can see how badly damaged the car was in these photographs. The Accord does really well in crash tests, including side impacts, but the force of this impact was just too much. It shoved the driver's side of the car all the way to the midpoint of the cabin. Robin Norris took a direct hit. The blow to her head was enough to kill her, and if it hadn't, the internal injuries would have done the job."

Rossi winced. "Christ Almighty."

Wheeler laid out three more photographs. "These show damage to the rear bumper," he said, pointing with a pen. "The right rear corner of the bumper has several scrapes and scruffs with a horizontal orientation. We found dark blue paint in those scuff marks that matches the paint color used on Missouri license plates. And there's a hole in the bumper about twelve inches from the ground with rough edges that are consistent with tearing."

Rossi picked up one of the photographs. "It looks like there's a scrape extending from the hole to the right side of the car."

"Go to the head of the class. All of that is consistent with a rear-end collision."

"Except for one thing. The photographs don't tell you when the rear-end collision happened. Somebody could have hit her in a parking lot six months ago."

"As a matter of fact, someone did hit her in a parking lot, but it wasn't six months ago. It was three weeks ago."

"How do you know that?"

"I checked with her kids. They told me and I've got a copy of the invoice from the body shop that put on a brand-new bumper. She got the car back last week."

"Damn, Mayor. Someone did knock her off the road."

Wheeler grinned. "Which makes that tire mark a spin mark and explains why the collision was to the side of the car. Someone hit her and she spun out, pinwheeled down the embankment, and smacked into the tree."

"What was she doing out here anyway? Didn't one of her kids tell you that she never went north of the river unless she was going to the airport?"

"It was her oldest," Wheeler said, consulting his note. "Name is Donny."

"So is this where you tell me how fast she was going?"

Wheeler put the photographs back in the envelope and turned toward the road. "She came around that curve doing seventy-five in a forty-five. Whoever hit her couldn't have timed it better. He got her at the exact point in the road when the impact would make her spin out of control."

"That's way too fast for anybody to take that curve. I'll give you that," Rossi said, "but it still could have been an accident. Could have been some kid hot-rodding and he came up on her and couldn't slow down in time."

"Maybe, but she would have seen him coming and probably would have pulled over to let him go by instead of trying to outrun in him on an unfamiliar dark stretch of road. But she was already doing seventy-five in a forty-five, and for my money, there's only one reason she would have been doing that. Someone was chasing her."

Rossi nodded. "Yeah. And she was running for her life."

They leaned against Wheeler's car, staring at the road, catching the draft from the few passing cars, each breaking the case down from his own perspective. Wheeler was imagining the accident, seeing the vehicles and the road: speed, force of impact, and the coefficient of friction adding up to murder.

Rossi saw the drivers. The killer was faceless for now, height, weight, and gender to be determined. Robin Norris was easier to see, her eyes wide, pupils dilated with fear, her mouth open as she gasped, not believing what was happening. He saw her knuckles whiten as she gripped the wheel, jamming her foot on the gas pedal, her head snapping back at the first impact, screaming and clenching her eyes at the end. But before that final moment, in the midst of her panic, he saw Robin grab her cell phone and punch in Alex Stone's number.

"I don't get it," Rossi said, breaking their silence.

"Get what? The initial impact? Because that's not a problem once we find the other vehicle. The damage to the front bumper will match up to the rear bumper on the victim's car like a jigsaw puzzle."

"Not that. Why did Robin call Alex Stone? If she was going to call anyone, she should have called 911 for help. How was Stone supposed to help her?"

"You're right. That doesn't make sense," Wheeler said.

Rossi tugged at his chin. "Unless she wasn't calling Stone to ask for her help."

"Then why the hell else would she have called her? To tell her who was about to kill her?"

"Maybe, but she could have told that to the 911 dispatcher."

"Then why the call?"

Rossi looked at him. "To warn her. Warn her that whoever was after her was going to come after Stone next."

Wheeler thought for a moment, nodding. "I'll buy that, especially if the victim figured there was no time for 911 to send help."

"Don't call her the victim. Her name was Robin Norris. She had kids, a job, and a life."

Wheeler laughed. "What happened to my asshole ex-partner who never called a victim anything but a vic? Did he grow a heart?"

"Yeah, but let's make it our secret."

"So now what?"

Rossi shrugged. "We go by the numbers. If I'm right, Robin knew her killer and knew there was a connection with Alex Stone. So we start by asking Alex who that might be and, just in case she doesn't know or doesn't want to share with us, we build a list of people who tie them together."

"And then we ask them who would have wanted to kill Robin and wants to kill Alex."

"Exactly."

"And if that doesn't work?" Wheeler asked.

"You find the car that hit Robin's car and I keep my eye on Alex until someone tries to kill her."

"Just like that?"

"Just like that. And you thought accident reconstruction was easy," Rossi said.

TWENTY-FOUR

But Rossi knew there was no such thing as an easy murder case. Some cases, like Jared Bell's, came together faster than others, but calling them easy didn't do justice to the victims or their families, whose pain and loss lasted forever. He called those cases quick closers, but he'd never call them easy.

And there was nothing easy about Alex Stone. He could convince her that Robin Norris had been murdered, but she wouldn't believe that the murderer might be after her as well, not if she heard it from him. And she definitely wouldn't believe that he was trying to protect her. She wouldn't trust him to tell her the right time without checking her watch. He couldn't blame her, because he felt the same way about her. Protecting someone he wanted more than anything else to bring down was just the latest contradiction in a job filled with them.

The day was starting to turn when Wheeler drove away, leaving the photographs with Rossi. A thin layer of gray cloud cover moving in from the north was chasing away the sun, the distant sky darkening behind it. The breeze kicked up, an advance party for the coming storm.

Rossi studied the incoming front, betting he had time before it arrived to do what he had in mind. He called Alex. She answered on the third ring.

"It's Rossi," he said.

"I know. Ever hear of caller ID?"

"Just making sure. Where are you?"

"In my car on my way home. What do you want?"

"I want you to meet me at the scene of Robin Norris's accident."

Alex didn't respond immediately, Rossi letting the silence take care of itself.

"Why?" Alex said after a few moments.

"I need you to see how it happened."

"Why?"

Rossi hated answering, hated her having something on him, but there was no alternative. "Because I need your help."

"My help? You need my help."

He sighed. "Yes, Counselor. It pains me to say so, but yes, I need your help."

"Why don't I believe you?"

"We both know the answer to that question. Give me ten minutes with you at the scene and then you can decide whether I'm just bullshitting you."

Another pause.

"Okay. I can do that. When?"

"Now. I'm out here on Barry Road where it happened," he said, giving her directions.

"Can we do it next week? It's Friday and I've had a long week and a longer day that isn't over yet. I'm on my way home to clean up and go visit Robin's family."

"You've got all weekend to make your condolence call. I need you out here now."

More silence.

"You do, don't you. I like that," she said, picking up on the urgency in his voice. "Okay. I'm on my way."

Half an hour later, Alex pulled up behind Rossi's car, joining him on the shoulder, not saying anything. He watched her study the scene, arms crossed against her chest, looking first at the road, following the tire marks, and then focusing on the damaged tree trunk. He watched Alex's eyes well up, saw her clench her jaw as her face reddened and she wiped the tears away, taking a deep breath.

"Is that the tree?"

"Yeah. You can take a closer look if you want."

Alex sidestepped down the embankment, standing in front of the tree, first pressing her palms against the scarred bark, then leaning in, her forehead resting on the trunk, arms wrapped around it. After a moment, she stepped back, brushing her clothing and wiping her eyes again. She walked up the slope toward the road, ignoring Rossi's offered hand as she reached the shoulder.

"So how did it happen?"

Rossi walked her through it just as Wheeler had done for him, answering her questions, letting her sift through the photographs, waiting until she stacked them together and returned them to the envelope.

"The tire mark, the damage to the rear bumper, and Robin's speed all make a strong case that someone intentionally forced her off the road," he said.

"Maybe, but what you've got won't hold up under a decent cross-examination, not without more. All you've got is evidence of an accident, not a crime. You've got nothing on the other car or the other driver or any motive."

"We'll find the car and the driver and we'll figure out the motive."

"Try to get it right this time," Alex said.

Rossi beat back his temptation to take the bait. "I'll do that."

"So why did you drag me out here? I can't help you fill in any of those blanks."

Passing cars flew by, trailing small plumes of road grit, drivers in a hurry to beat the storm and start their weekend. Rossi leaned against his car as a big-wheeled pickup thundered past, waiting until it had rounded the curve.

"Let me ask you a question. Let's suppose my theory is right but it's you in the car. You're driving like a bat out of hell because someone is chasing you out in the middle of nowhere. You're scared shitless that you're going to die. What would you do?"

She cocked her head, furrowing her brow. "Really?"

"Yeah, really. Put yourself in Robin Norris's shoes. What would you have done?"

Alex sighed, thinking. "I'd lead the asshole to the nearest police station."

"Okay, but you've never been on this stretch of road in your life. You've got no idea where you are, let alone where you can find a police station. What then?"

"I'd call 911, tell them what was happening, and ask them to send help in a hurry."

"That's what I'd do too. That's what anyone would do."

Alex's eyes widened, her mouth dropping half-open. "But Robin didn't do that."

"No," Rossi said. "She didn't."

Alex covered her mouth with her hand. "She called me. Why would she do that?"

"Think about it. What possible reason could she have had?"

Alex turned her back to him, hands on her hips, making a slow circle as she thought, stopping when she was facing Rossi again.

"She knew or thought she knew who was chasing her and wanted to tell me."

"If it had been you and you knew who it was, who would you have called?"

She nodded her head. "I'd have called 911. It doesn't make sense. If she knew who was after her, why call me?"

Rossi didn't answer, wanting her to work it out on her own so she would believe it.

And then it hit her. She slumped against the side of Rossi's car, bracing herself with her hands, staring down the embankment at the tree.

"She was trying to warn me." She slapped the car with one hand, bolting upright, facing Rossi. "If she had just wanted someone to know who was after her, she would have called 911. She knew she wasn't going to outrun this guy. She knew no one could get to her in time to save her. She was trying to warn me. That had to be the reason."

Rossi kept his voice even and quiet. "Warn you about what?"

She wrapped her arms around her middle, squeezing hard, looking back and forth from the road to the tree. "That this guy was after me too. Holy shit! How is that possible?"

"And that's why I need your help. What was going on between you and Robin that would make both of you targets?"

Alex dropped her arms to her sides, shaking her head and arching her eyebrows.

"Nothing. I mean nothing except work, but she didn't work on my cases. She was the perfect boss. All she did was assign them to me and tell me not to fuck them up."

"Did you socialize with her outside of work?"

"No."

"Was she having any personal problems that she talked with you about, maybe something about someone threatening her?"

Alex waved off his question. "No, nothing at all. She was my boss. We were colleagues. I didn't know much about her personal life. And if she was having some kind of problem, she didn't tell me about it."

"Then it has to be something connected to work. What's the most recent case Robin assigned to you?"

TWENTY-FIVE

Alex knew all about the autonomic nervous system, knew that it was the part of the peripheral nervous system that accounted for involuntary functions like heart rate, perspiration, and pupil dilation, and knew that it was better than any lie detector. She'd seen it in action whenever she caught a witness lying on cross-examination. They'd twitch or tic or their eyes would bug out or they'd look away or down or they'd burn bright red or they'd erupt in flop sweat. One way or another, their bodies would give them away and there was nothing they could do to stop it.

Only the best liars and poker players could suppress the involuntary reactions and facial movements that gave away the truth. She'd learned to do that when it came to Dwayne Reed, but Rossi had caught her off guard, her evolutionary flight-or-fight impulses overwhelming her, sending her heart rate soaring, dampening her armpits, and stretching her eyes as wide as silver dollars. She couldn't have felt more exposed if she were naked.

"Jared Bell," she said.

"That's my case."

"I know that," Alex said, willing her voice to remain in its normal octave and not stammer. "You act like you didn't know I was handling it."

"I didn't."

Alex was relieved as her heart rate began to slow and her facial muscles to relax, hoping without faith that Rossi hadn't noticed her mini-meltdown. If he was telling the truth, something she never assumed, he couldn't have been involved in getting Jared's file to Robin, but she wanted to be certain.

"How could you not know?"

"I never know who's defending one of my cases until the prosecutor needs me. And why would I care about Bell? The guy admitted to having sex with the victim and we found the crucifix she was wearing at the time she was killed in the back pocket of the shorts he had on when he says he found her body. And he confessed. The case couldn't be any tighter. Whether you or somebody else pleads him out makes no difference to me. But I'll tell you what I do care about."

"What's that?"

"Why did you practically shit your pants when I asked you what was the last case Robin Norris assigned to you? And what does Jared Bell have to do with all of this?"

Alex deflected his question, using what she'd learned from the homeless woman in Liberty Park to put Rossi on the defensive.

"Do you know the victim's name?"

"What's that got to do with this?"

"Just answer my question. Do you even know that her first name is Joanie?"

Rossi narrowed his eyes at her. "Who have you been talking to? Her name hasn't been released."

"Then you do know her name. Joanie."

"Yeah. Joanie Sutherland. Who leaked that information to you? Was it that assistant prosecutor, Kalena...whatever her last name is?"

"It's Kalena Greene, and no, she keeps everything in her vault. I got it the old-fashioned way, by investigating my client's case. And your case isn't as tight as you think."

Rossi thought for a moment. "So you found a witness who knew the victim's name?"

"Just her first name. You gave me her last name," Alex said.

Rossi ducked his chin, pursing his lips. "Okay, score one for the defense. Now answer my question. Why did you pinch a loaf when I asked you about the last case Robin assigned to you?"

Alex had had time to regroup. She couldn't tell him about her deal with Judge West, but she had to give him something that was plausible.

"I'm trying to save the life of a client accused of a capital offense while also trying to deal with my boss's death when you drag me out here to tell me that not only was Robin murdered but that her death might have something to do with my client's case. So, yeah, that knocked the pins out from under me for a minute, but my panties are clean. Score one for you if that's what you call rounding the bases."

Rossi stared at her, waiting for any hint of a tell that would give her away, but she was steady, her face flat and cool, her arms at her sides, her hands soft and open.

"Here's the way it is," he said. "Someone murdered Robin Norris, and my bet is that the last thing she ever did on this earth was try to tell you the identity of her killer because she was scared he would come after you next. Now, if you want to blow that off, pretend that I'm playing games with you, there's nothing I can do about it. But be sure you tell your girlfriend so when she goes to the morgue to identify your body, she'll blame you and not me."

Alex felt the heat rise in her neck and cheeks again, not because Rossi had caught her flat-footed, but because he'd played the Bonnie card.

"Leave Bonnie out of this. You've been sticking your nose in our relationship too much as it is."

Rossi shrugged. "I'm just saying."

"And I'm just saying maybe Robin wasn't trying to warn me but maybe she was trying to tell me who was chasing her so that I would make sure the bastard was caught and put away. Maybe she called me instead of 911 because she trusted me more than she trusted the cops."

"Either way, it doesn't matter."

"How's that?"

"Either the killer is coming after you anyway or once he thinks Robin told you who he is, he'll definitely come after you and you'll be just as dead."

The first drops of rain splattered on the road, hissing. Alex turned her face skyward, wishing the rain would wash all of this away, knowing that it couldn't possibly rain that hard. She let the water run off her face, running her fingers through her hair and shaking her head, then taking a deep breath.

"So what do we do?"

"Help each other. Do you think we can do that?"

Before Alex could respond, Rossi's phone rang. He answered and listened.

"Okay. I'm about fifteen minutes out," he said and clicked off. "You know someone named Mathew Woodrell?"

"Sort of. I met him yesterday at the courthouse. Why?"

"He just tried to kill Jared Bell."

TWENTY-SIX

Alex followed Rossi, both of them shooting past slower-moving vehicles. The sky had opened, hammering them with sheets of rain that reduced visibility until Alex could barely see Rossi's taillights. She stayed with him, not wanting him to question Mathew Woodrell or Jared alone.

She opened her phone, put it on speaker, and called Grace Canfield.

"It's me, Alex. What have you found on Mathew Woodrell?"

"Not a damn thing."

"Not good. No luck in the probate clerk's office?"

"That was my first stop. No one fitting his description was there yesterday or the day before or as long as anyone could remember. I called the Kansas City Veterans Affairs office and they'd never heard of him. My husband has an uncle who was in the Eighty-Second Airborne. They've got their own veterans association. He checked their membership directory. There were a couple of guys named Mathew Woodrell, but they've been dead for years."

"Shit!"

"What's the problem?" Grace asked.

"He just tried to kill Jared Bell."

"Get out! How could he do that? Jared's in jail."

"Tell me about it," Alex said and clicked off the call.

Ten minutes later, Alex parked behind Rossi in metered spaces in front of the jail. Rossi ignored the meters but Alex couldn't bring herself to do that, searching her glove box for change and jamming quarters into the coin slot, getting soaked in the process. She raced into the building, cursing that she'd let Rossi get the jump on her, only to find him standing in the first-floor lobby talking to Kalena Greene.

Kalena was wearing the kind of black sheath dress designers promised would take you through the day and the night. Her makeup was perfect and her nails were freshly done. Reliably fashion-unconscious, Alex cringed, knowing her bedraggled, wet-rat look was even worse than usual compared to Kalena. That normally wouldn't have bothered her, but Kalena was sporting more than fashion; she was radiating authority, something Alex had to undermine or risk being shoved aside. She joined them, interrupting their conversation.

"How's my client? Is he okay? I want to see him immediately and I want to know how there could have been such a breakdown in security."

Kalena took the interruption in stride. "Short story, your client is fine. He was stabbed in the neck, but he's going to be okay. They stitched him up and he's in isolation until we figure this thing out."

"What about Mathew Woodrell?" Alex asked. "I met him yesterday at the courthouse. How'd he end up in jail today and why did he attack my client?"

"I can answer the first part of your question," Kalena said. "Late yesterday afternoon, he walked into a liquor store, aimed a gun at the cashier, and walked out with a fistful of money and kept walking until the police arrested him a couple of blocks from the store."

Alex shook her head. "Unbelievable. He seemed like a harmless old guy."

"Not so harmless," Kalena said. "Half an hour after he got on the men's floor, he came up behind your client and stabbed him in the neck."

"With what?"

"His glasses, if you can believe that."

"Like in the third *Godfather* movie," Rossi said, "when Michael Corleone's kid is getting baptized and his henchmen are busy knocking off Corleone's enemies. I think it was the Vatican's banker that got killed that way, only the killer used the banker's glasses. Woodrell used his own. Must have been pretty sharp glasses."

"Wait until you see them," Kalena said. "He filed down the ends of the frame on each side until they were like a shiv. Then he covered the ends with rubber caps, the kind you'd use to keep your glasses from sliding off."

"Smart," Rossi said. "The kind of thing that no one is going to check."

"They will from now on," Kalena said. "Jared was lucky. When Woodrell jumped him, Jared threw an elbow that knocked Woodrell to the floor. Otherwise, it would have been worse than the proverbial flesh wound."

"But why?" Alex said. "Why try to kill Jared?"

Kalena sighed. "That's the next crazy part of this. The corrections officers subdued Woodrell, put him in a single cell, and called the police and my office. Standard procedure when something like this happens."

"Dispatch called me because Jared Bell is my case," Rossi said.

"And I got here first. He's waived his right to counsel but he won't answer my questions."

"Why not?" Alex asked.

"Because he says he'll only talk to you."

"Why me?"

"That's what we're going to find out."

Kalena led them to a room on the second floor. A corrections officer was stationed outside the room and another was inside. Woodrell was seated at a table, legs and wrists shackled, his wrists cuffed to a steel hoop bolted to the table. He'd transformed from the dapper gentleman she'd met at the courthouse to an unshaven, disheveled, jumpsuit-clad inmate, though he was just as calm.

There were two chairs on the opposite side of the table. Kalena and Alex each took a seat. Rossi stood in the corner.

Alex thought for a moment, deciding where to start. An effective interrogation depended on either fear or trust. Woodrell had no reason to fear her, and his insistence on talking to her suggested he trusted her. Though they'd spoken only briefly the day before, she must have made a favorable impression, so that was where she'd begin.

"So, Mathew. Yesterday you told me that you wouldn't need a criminal defense lawyer, but it looks like you do."

"No," he said, his voice quiet and sure, "I don't."

"How can you say that? You committed an armed robbery yesterday and today you assaulted someone with a deadly weapon."

"I'm guilty of both, which makes a lawyer unnecessary, don't you think?"

Alex shook her head. "It makes it even more important that you have a lawyer. Since the person you assaulted is my client, I can't represent you. If you can't afford a lawyer, the court will appoint one for you."

"Yes, yes, Ms. Stone. I know all about my rights. Ms. Greene read them to me and we had a nice discussion about them, after which I signed a waiver."

"Fair enough, then. Ms. Greene said you wouldn't answer her questions but that you would answer mine. Why is that?"

"Because there are things you need to know."

"Such as?"

"Your client is a murderer."

"My client has been charged with murder. He hasn't been convicted."

"I'm not talking about that woman in the creek."

Alex cocked her head at him. "Then what murder are you talking about?"

"My daughter. Jared Bell raped and murdered my daughter."

TWENTY-SEVEN

Alex fell back in her chair, eyes wide and blinking, stunned like she'd been sucker punched. She looked at Kalena and Rossi, both of them slack-jawed, both of them taken by surprise as well.

She took a deep breath, studying Woodrell for some sign of artifice. His shoulders were soft and rounded, not bunched up around his ears, his face was slack, and his breathing was smooth. His hands were still, cupped around the hook in the table. His body was at ease except for his watery, pinched eyes. She thought about Jared and the name he shouted in his sleep, her stomach clenching at the realization that Woodrell might be telling the truth.

"Was her name Ali?"

Woodrell leaned his head to one side, nodding, the corners of his mouth quivering. "So he told you."

"He didn't tell me anything. One of the corrections officers told me that he wakes up during the night calling that name."

Woodrell sniffed, his eyes reddening. "Ali was her nickname. Her full name was McAllister Woodrell." He ducked his chin, chuckling. "I know. What a name, but McAllister was my wife's maiden name. She insisted on naming our daughter McAllister because it reminded her of one of her favorite authors, Flannery O'Connor. Flannery is an old Irish clan and McAllister is Scottish, so my wife said if using the family name was good enough for Flannery, it was good enough for our daughter. Except it was a mouthful and everyone ended up calling her Ali."

It was impossible for Alex not to smile at the story, told with a father's sweetness. In spite of what he'd done, she sensed that Woodrell was a good man driven to extremes by a terrible loss, something she understood. He had a story to tell and he'd begun with the ending, though Alex sensed he had more to say.

"Tell me about your daughter."

Woodrell sighed, smiling softly. "She was a good girl. Full of spunk. Like her mother. A tomboy, but a looker, hair black as a raven and a grin filled with more mischief than a sailor on leave. And she was strong and graceful, you know, like a gymnast or a dancer. And headstrong," he said, chuckling again. "Like when she decided to join the army. Her mother raised hell about that, but you couldn't tell Ali anything once she got something in her head."

"Is that where Ali and Jared met, in the army?"

He nodded. "Yes. I don't know exactly when or how. All I know is that they were on the same base in Afghanistan. She e-mailed us that a soldier was harassing her, 'coming on to her' was the way she put it. She wasn't interested, but he was real pushy. She didn't go into a lot of details, but we got the picture."

"Did you ever find out who that was?"

Woodrell clenched his jaw. "Not till after. The army told me it was Jared Bell."

"The army told you that it was Jared?"

"They didn't have to. I could read between the lines."

"Was Jared prosecuted?"

He tightened his grip on the hoop in the table, his knuckles whitening. "How could they when he was the only witness and they believed the story he told?"

"What story was that?"

Woodrell's face twisted, his voice rising, his cheeks shuddering. "He said they were off the base and were kidnapped by the Taliban, that they made him watch while they raped Ali and then blew her brains out. And would have killed him too if they hadn't been scared off by incoming fire from an Apache helicopter. By the time more troops got there, it was just Jared and my dead baby girl."

"Was there an autopsy?"

He shook his head, puckering as if to spit, thinking better of it. "They put her in a box and sent her home. All we knew then was that she was killed in combat. I had to fight the army to get the rest of the story. By then it was too late to prove Jared raped her because we had her cremated."

"What makes you think Jared lied about what happened?"

"His story never made any sense to me. What were they doing off base when they were supposedly kidnapped? When the helicopter showed up, why didn't the Taliban put a bullet in Jared? And what about Ali's e-mails? And why did the army stonewall me every time I asked questions? I'll tell you why! They're covering up for one of their own. That's why!"

Woodrell banged his cuffed fists on the table, hanging his head and crying. Alex reached across the table, covering his hands with hers. They stayed like that for a moment, until he gently shook her hands away, straightening and sniffling as tears rolled down his cheeks.

Alex looked at Kalena. "Do you have a tissue?"

Kalena was riveted on Woodrell, Alex's question bringing her back. "Oh, yeah. Sorry," she said, digging a tissue from her purse and handing it to Alex.

Alex stood and leaned toward Woodrell, who sat stone still as she patted his face, muttering when she finished.

"I'm sorry."

"You had a terrible loss and that's nothing to apologize for. Where do you live, Mathew?" she asked, moving their conversation back to the present.

He cleared his throat and rolled his shoulders. "Columbus, Ohio."

"When did you get to Kansas City?"

"A few days ago."

"Why did you come here?"

"The army wouldn't do anything about Ali. I talked to the police at home and they said there was nothing they could do. No one would do anything and Jared was going to get away with murder, which meant it was up to me to do something. I owed that much to my daughter. I've been looking for Jared for the last two years. Even hired a private detective until I ran out of money. After he took my last dollar, he told me to set up a Google Alert for Jared's name, so I did that, and when I saw the newspaper article saying that he'd been arrested, I got in my car."

"To do what?"

He shrugged. "At first all I wanted to do was talk to him, to somehow make him tell me the truth and admit what he did to Ali. But when I got here, I realized that wouldn't be enough. I had to make sure he paid. That's why I went to see the judge handling his case. I wanted to tell him about Ali so he'd be sure Jared didn't get off on some technicality. But the way Judge West yelled at you and me when he found us waiting for him in his office, I knew he wouldn't listen. The man was as bad as the army."

Alex flinched when he mentioned finding her in Judge West's chambers, stealing a glance at Kalena to see if she picked up on it, uncertain what to make of her blank expression. She sat back in her chair, wrapping it up with as much nonchalance as she could muster, one beat shy of saying *"yada, yada, yada."*

"So you robbed the liquor store in order to get arrested so you could deal with Jared on your own?"

Woodrell nodded, his chin down, his gaze fixed on the table.

Alex paused, her palms on the table. There was nothing more to be learned. His only proof that Jared had raped and murdered his daughter was a father's pain. All she wanted was to get out of there without drawing more attention to herself and Judge West.

"Mathew, I'm very sorry for your loss. I hope you'll reconsider your decision not to seek counsel. A lawyer may be able to make a good argument about extenuating circumstances that the court could consider at sentencing."

He looked up at her, his face once again gray and waxy. "I've already been sentenced."

"I'm sure you feel that way. I can't imagine what it would be like to lose—"

"No. You don't understand. I have end-stage cancer. The doctors give me no more than a few months. I don't think any lawyer could get me a better deal than that."

TWENTY-EIGHT

Alex, Rossi, and Kalena stood on the sidewalk outside the entrance to the jail. The storm had passed, leaving the air damp and chilled, the sky shot through with orange licks painted by the setting sun.

"Well, that was a first for me," Kalena said.

"Which part?" Rossi asked. "All he wanted was justice for his daughter's killer. He's not the first father to want that."

"You know that's not what I mean. The army investigated and said there was no case. Woodrell may not like it, but that's the end of it. A lot of victims' families get angry when they think the system blew it, but he's the first I've seen that committed a crime so he could get put in jail and take his revenge."

"What's he supposed to do?" Rossi asked.

"Live with it," Kalena said. "The system isn't perfect, but it's all we've got."

"What about you, Counselor?" he said to Alex. "Bad guy gets off. What would you do?"

Alex saw the glint of a smile in the corners of Rossi's mouth and was determined not to let him provoke her the way he had when she ran into him at the Zoo. She pretended she was in court, where the first rule was to never let them see you sweat.

"Like Kalena said, every lawyer knows the system isn't perfect."

"Forget you're a lawyer. Suppose the bad guy kills someone and gets off, and suppose you're afraid now he's gonna come after you or someone you love. Would you take a page out of Woodrell's book?"

Alex turned the question around. "Let's try it this way. Remember that you're a cop and the person you thought was guilty was acquitted. Would you respect the verdict or would you keep going after that person?"

They stared at each other, neither giving ground.

"Am I missing something here?" Kalena said. "I was talking about Woodrell. What are you guys talking about?"

Alex looked at Rossi, letting him answer, daring him to tell an assistant prosecuting attorney that he was harassing her.

Rossi shook his head. "Nothing."

"Yeah," Alex said. "Just kicking around hypotheticals."

"Then try this one," Kalena said. "Jared Bell is convicted—and that's not the hypothetical part—and I put Woodrell on the stand at sentencing to tell his story. Even if your client wasn't charged or convicted, Judge West can consider evidence that he raped and murdered Woodrell's daughter when he imposes sentence."

"Hypothetically, he could, but it's not likely. Not when the only evidence is the unsupported allegations of a father so distraught that he robbed a liquor store so he could try to kill my client."

"Maybe, but you and your client should consider the possibility. And, by the way, what did Judge West say to Woodrell that made him go off?"

Kalena made her question sound more chatty than inquisitive, and Alex matched her tone, not mistaking her purpose, knowing that they hadn't suddenly become gossiping girlfriends.

"What can I say? Wild Bill was being Wild Bill."

"In his chambers?"

"Yeah."

"I hope you weren't woodshedding the judge on one of my cases," she said, an eyebrow raised in mock concern.

"Are you kidding? Trying to have an ex parte chat with Wild Bill about a pending case is like asking to get my ass kicked. I just wanted to tell him that my office may have to ask for some extensions because of Robin Norris's death. Things are pretty crazy at the moment."

Kalena nodded. "And Woodrell just barged into West's chambers? That must have been something to see."

"You saw him. He was a man on a mission. Besides, he had no way of knowing what a jerk Wild Bill can be."

"Was that before or after you ran into him on the courthouse steps?"

Kalena wasn't fooling Alex with her soft cross-examination, the kind of questioning that seems innocuous until the other shoe drops, and Alex wasn't going to stick around for that. She glanced at her watch, shrugging like the answer was an insignificant detail.

"Before. Hey, it's almost seven o'clock and I've got to get home."

"Don't you want to make sure your client is okay? I'll take you back upstairs to make sure you won't have a problem getting in to see him."

Alex gave her a tight-lipped smile. "Thanks, but you said he was all right, so that can wait until Monday, and if I don't get home soon, Bonnie is going to kill me. We're supposed to go see Robin's kids tonight," she said, hustling to her car before Kalena could take another shot at her.

Rossi waited until Alex drove off.

"What was that all about? She came in demanding to see her client and leaves without checking on him because you said he was okay?"

"I could ask you the same thing about your little two-step with her."

Rossi gave her his flat cop street stare. "Don't."

Kalena leaned her head back a fraction. "Okay," she said, drawing it out. "What's your first reaction, Detective, when someone forgets to mention an important part of a story?"

"That they didn't forget."

"Alex said she met Woodrell at the courthouse on Wednesday, but she didn't say anything about meeting him in Judge West's chambers. Why do you suppose she left that out?"

"Because she didn't want us to know she was having an ex parte conversation with the judge? So what? I thought you lawyers did that all the time."

"I don't."

"Then what's your point?"

"Something strange happened in a case I've got with Alex. She showed up today at the initial appearance and she already had a copy of the investigative report and the complaint."

Rossi shrugged. "Why's that so strange? Isn't she entitled to that?"

"Sure, but our office never provides it until the initial appearance, not before. It's just weird. I asked her how she got the file and she said Meg Adler gave it to her."

"Who's Meg Adler?"

"She's filling in for Robin Norris."

"Huh. Then why wasn't Meg Adler talking to Judge West about getting more time instead of Alex?"

"Fair question. According to Alex, Meg Adler found the file on Robin's desk. There was a Post-it note with Alex's name on it so she assumed Robin wanted to assign the case to Alex."

"Let me guess," Rossi said. "It was the Jared Bell file?"

Kalena stared at him, openmouthed. "How'd you know?"

"It's my case."

"I know that, but how did you know it was also Alex's case?"

Rossi filled her in on Robin's last-second call to Alex, Wheeler's reconstruction of the accident, and his visit at the scene with Alex.

"If Robin was going to call anyone," Rossi said, "she would have called 911, but she called Alex instead. My working theory is that Robin knew the identity of her killer and called to warn Alex that the killer would come after her."

"Did you tell Alex that?"

"No. I walked her through the accident scene and let her put it together. She came to the same conclusion I did."

"What was her reaction?"

Rossi stroked his chin. "Shock, disbelief—at first."

"Then what?"

"I asked her what was going on between her and Robin that would make someone want to kill both of them. She says there was nothing going on, says their relationship was strictly professional and that Robin left her alone unless she fucked something up."

"So either she's lying about their relationship or it's one of their cases. Which do you think it is?"

"Maybe both, but when I asked her what the last case was that Robin assigned to her, she almost messed herself."

Kalena nodded. "Jared Bell."

"Jared Bell. And now you tell me that someone sent the file to Robin ahead of schedule. Not a big thing by itself."

"But a lot of cases are about a bunch of little things that spin out of control."

"So how did Jared's file end up on Robin Norris's desk?"

"I don't know. My boss hung everyone in our office by the fingernails to find the leak, but no one knows how it happened."

Rossi thought for a moment. "Would Judge West have had access to the file?"

"Of course. But why would he send it to Robin Norris?"

"Who knows? But that could be another one of those little things, and since there are no rules against me having an ex parte conversation with the judge, I think I'll ask him."

Kalena grinned. "He's starting a trial on Monday. He'll love it when you show up in his chambers."

"Why not? Who wouldn't be glad to see me?"

Alex had no doubt that Kalena and Rossi would talk to Judge West about Mathew Woodrell and use that pretext to get the judge's version of his conversation with her. She picked up her cell phone as soon as she rounded the corner heading away from the jail, intending to call him so they could get their stories straight, dropping her phone in her lap when she realized making that call would leave an electronic trail leading back to her.

Heading south on Main Street, she pulled into the parking lot of a convenience store and bought a prepaid cell phone, worrying that she was becoming like one of her drug-dealer clients, glad to have learned a few of their lessons. Keeping her face down to avoid security cameras, she handed money to the cashier, pocketing the change and the phone.

Back in her car, she drove further south. Months ago, Judge West had given her his unlisted phone number, telling her that it rang only in his home office and instructing her to use it only in emergencies. She clicked on the burner phone and tapped in the number. A woman answered on the fourth ring.

"Who is this?"

Caught off guard because no one other than the judge had ever answered her calls, Alex hit the brakes and was almost rear-ended by the driver behind her, who hit her instead with a blast of his horn and a raised middle finger. Waving her apologies, she drove on. The woman was agitated, her voice sharp and demanding. Though Alex had never spoken with the judge's wife, she had no trouble imagining that this was how Millie West would sound.

"Mrs. West?"

"Yes. This is a private number. Now, who is this? If you're selling something I'm hanging up."

"It's Alex Stone. I'm calling for Judge West."

Millie didn't respond, her silence making Alex wonder whether the call had been dropped.

"Mrs. West? Are you still there?"

"Yes, but my husband isn't."

"Can you give me his cell phone number?"

"If he wanted you to have it, you already would," she said and hung up.

Alex smacked her palm against the steering wheel, her attempt at clandestine communication an utter failure. She'd squandered the anonymity of her burner phone. Its number was now included in the call records of the judge's phone, and his wife could identify her as its owner. She was reminded again how easy it was to make the stupid mistakes that landed her clients in prison.

TWENTY-NINE

Bonnie was waiting for Alex when she got home, dressed, pressed, and ready to go in a pair of dark-wash skinny jeans, a coral open-front blazer over a white silk blouse buttoned at the neck, the tail hanging over her jeans, and three-inch heels showing off her legs, as if they needed any help. Hands on her hips, she took one look at Alex and shook her head.

"I'm not going anywhere with you looking like that. Where have you been? Never mind," Bonnie said, raising a palm. "I don't want to know. Take a shower and put on something clean. We'll pay our respects to Robin's family and then we'll get something to eat. I'm famished, so get moving. Chop, chop," she added, clapping her hands.

Alex grinned, enjoying Bonnie's dismay at her appearance. It was one of their rituals, Bonnie pretending to be annoyed, Alex pretending to be sorry, both of them keeping their tongues firmly in their cheeks.

"On my way. I'll be ready sooner if you lotion my back when I get out of the shower."

"Oh, no. If I do, the only thing we'll be having for dinner is each other. Now, get moving, sister."

Standing in the shower, hot water pulsating on the back of her neck, she thought about the little game they'd played when she walked in the house. Their relationship was made of such moments. They were familiar and easy, like muscle memory, only for lovers. But this one was so out of sync with the day she'd had that she didn't know what to make of it or Bonnie or them.

She was absent the day they taught how to integrate murder and death threats into a quiet home life.

She and Bonnie had always shared whatever was going on at work, dancing around client and patient confidentiality like most couples who swore their mates to secrecy, picking one up when things went wrong, patting the other on the back for a job well done. Intimacy wasn't just about sex or just about their private life. It was about intertwining everything, blurring the line between where one of them ended and the other began.

Alex worried that her life was becoming compartmentalized, Bonnie in one box, Dwayne Reed and Judge West in another, their box getting crowded with the additions of Hank Rossi, Jared Bell, Mathew Woodrell, Robin Norris, and her killer. She had tried convincing herself that Judge West was building this wall between her and Bonnie, but she knew that she was the one laying the bricks, each made of the secrets she was keeping from the woman she loved.

And now Bonnie wanted to bring a baby into their lives at the very moment that Robin's killer might have set his sights on her. Overcome at the image of Bonnie standing at her grave, holding their baby in her arms, she began to cry, pounding the shower walls with both fists, turning her back to the wall and sliding to the floor, letting the water beat down on her.

"Are you drowning in there?" Bonnie said, knocking on the bathroom door a few minutes later.

Alex pulled herself up. "Not yet. Be out in a second."

She put on faded denims, a untucked pale blue checked shirt beneath a gray and blue wide-striped sweater, and a pair of black Kick Hi boots, ran her fingers through her damp hair, applied ChapStick to her lips, and pronounced herself ready.

Minutes later they were in Bonnie's Audi, the satellite radio playing Billy Joel's "Just The Way You Are," a song they claimed as theirs, repeating the promise not to change they'd made to each other when they fell in love. Settling back in her plush leather seat, inhaling Bonnie's perfume and surrounded by tons of high-performance German engineering, Alex felt cocooned and safe. For the first time all day, she thought they would survive all of this, though she had no rational reason to think so, only that she would find a way. When they stopped for a traffic light, she leaned over and pulled Bonnie toward her for a long, deep kiss.

"Boy!" Bonnie said when Alex let go. "I guess I'm buying dinner."

Robin had lived in Overland Park, which was on the Kansas side of the Kansas City metropolitan area. The state line was a convenient geographic demarcation that allowed Kansas residents to claim the attractions on the Missouri side—professional sports teams, high-end stores and restaurants, art galleries and museums—as their own while disavowing Kansas City's failing public schools, persistent crime rate, and gangs as someone else's problem. Except for Robin, who'd taken the good with the bad, dedicating herself to representing the dropouts, drug addicts, and gangbangers who'd found their way to her public defender's office.

She'd lived on a quiet, tree-lined street in a modest stone and stucco house with a two-car garage, a semiparched lawn, and a basketball net mounted on a steel post on the side of the driveway. Four cars were parked in front of the house, two others in the driveway.

Bonnie slowed as they approached the house. Two men got out of one of the cars in the driveway, one of them limping.

"Don't stop. Keep going," Alex said.

"Why? What's the matter?"

"That's Rossi," she said, pointing at the men, "and the one with the limp is a detective named Wheeler."

"So? I'm no fan of Rossi, but why should we let him keep us from offering our condolences to the family? If they can, we can too."

"Just keep going. I've had enough Rossi for one day, and they aren't there to offer their condolences."

Bonnie drove past the house, glancing at Alex. "How could you know that?"

Alex took a deep breath, her stomach churning. "Because Robin was murdered. It's Rossi and Wheeler's case. They're probably there to tell the family, which makes it the wrong time for visiting."

Bonnie stopped the car at the end of the block, turning to Alex, her eyes narrowed, her mouth tight.

"And you were going to tell me this when?"

"Soon," Alex said, her face reddening. "Tonight, okay? I just found out this afternoon, and when I got home, you were ready to go and you told me to jump in the shower and then next thing I know, here we are."

"No. There's no 'next thing I know here we are.' Not after we've been in the car for twenty minutes. You couldn't have mentioned it?"

"I know. I know and I'm sorry. It's just that…" She stopped, blinking, shaking her head and then staring out the window. "This has been…" She hesitated again, turning back to Bonnie, swallowing hard, and letting out a deep breath. "Some kind of day."

Bonnie eased up, putting her hand on Alex's shoulder. "There's more, isn't there?"

Alex nodded.

"About Robin or something else?"

"Both."

"Are you in trouble?"

"Maybe."

"Are you going to tell me, or do I have to worry without knowing what I'm worrying about?"

Alex looked at her, torn between adding another brick and knocking down the wall. Her eyes filled; a tremor rattled outward from her belly. She'd been holding so much back, and all she wanted was to let it go.

"Yeah," she said, her voice thick. "I'll tell you everything. Let's go home."

THIRTY

"Who's going to tell them, you or me?" Wheeler asked Rossi as they walked toward Robin's house.

"I'll take the lead," Rossi said, "then you can fill in the details. What do we know about the family?"

Wheeler shrugged. "Five kids, bunched together, ages sixteen to twenty-one, I think."

"Father?"

"Out of the picture. They've been divorced for years."

Rossi rang the bell. A young man wearing jeans and a Kansas Jayhawks T-shirt answered the door. He was average height with an average build and light brown, almost blond, hair, a round face, and soft features, his connection to his mother apparent.

"Yes?"

Rossi and Wheeler showed their badges. "I'm Detective Rossi. This is my partner, Detective Wheeler. Are you one of Robin Norris's children?"

"I'm Donny, the oldest. What's this about?"

"We want to talk with you about your mother's accident. May we come in?"

He furrowed his brow, hesitating. "What's going on?"

"We'd rather talk about it inside, if that's okay with you."

He nodded. "Sure. Sorry. Come on in."

Donny led them into the den. It had a high ceiling and was furnished with comfortable, overstuffed chairs and an L-shaped sofa. There was a fireplace on the back wall flanked by windows and surrounded by inlaid stone rising to the ceiling. The lighting was soft, the fabrics warm, the ivory carpeting accented with a maroon oriental rug beneath a mahogany coffee table, the top of which was covered with two large pizza boxes and a half-empty carton of Coke.

A couple Rossi guessed to be in their late fifties or early sixties was sitting on the long side of the sofa. He had silver hair, blue eyes, and a ruddy complexion and was wearing a navy blazer, gray slacks, and a blue oxford-cloth shirt. Her blond hair was cut in a shiny bob. Her short-sleeved lavender dress showed off her toned arms and well-defined calves. They were a handsome, prosperous-looking couple.

An unshaven man around their age wearing Dockers and an untucked polo shirt leaned against the wall by the fireplace studying his smartphone. A boy and two girls who looked to be in their late teens stood in the middle of the room talking while juggling slices of pizza and sodas. A fourth child, a girl closer to sixteen, was leaning against a wall near the unshaven man, pecking away on her smartphone.

"Everybody," Donny said, "this is Detective Rossi and Detective Wheeler. They want to talk to us about Mom's accident."

"Well, actually," Rossi said, "we'd like to talk to Ms. Norris's children."

Donnie and the older kids formed a line, shoulder to shoulder, as if they were used to being introduced as a group or answering roll call. They all shared the same features gifted to them by their mother. The youngest girl had dark hair and angular features similar to the man at the fireplace. Donny made the introductions.

"These are my sisters Carrie and Rachel and my brother Josh. And that's Kim over by the fireplace."

Carrie, Rachel, and Josh shook their hands. Kim stayed where she was, silent, grim faced, and sullen.

"I'm sorry for your loss," Rossi said, all the kids nodding except for Kim, who shook her head and disappeared into the kitchen.

"And I'm their dad," the man at the back of the room said as he walked toward them, chest puffed out. "Ted Norris," he added, shaking both Rossi's and Wheeler's hands.

He was half a head shorter than Rossi, his nose crooked like it had been broken at least twice. His hair had once been dark like his daughter's but now was a slicked-back muddy gray. He had the red-speckled cheeks and rheumy eyes of a man who'd spent a lifetime getting the last drop out of the bottle. Rossi could smell the whiskey evaporating through his skin along with the stench of cigarettes in his clothes.

"Helluva thing," Norris said. "Robin was a great gal and these are great kids. Gotta give her credit for that. Everybody knows I didn't have anything to do with it, not that I didn't want to or didn't try. We had five kids in six years before she gave me the boot. My little Kimmy was only five years old, but she turned out okay in spite of her no-account old man."

He flashed yellow teeth in an expectant grin, waiting for his kids to contradict him and tell him he wasn't so bad after all and that he deserved some of the credit, but none did. Instead, they shifted their weight from one foot to the other, heads down or turned away, avoiding eye contact with their father.

The couple on the sofa rose, the man clearing his throat. "Ted, why don't you get going and let the detectives do their job."

Norris shot a hot look at him, eyes flashing, teeth bared. "Why don't you hit the road, Tony? You're not family."

"I'd like Uncle Tony and Aunt Sonia to stay," Donny said, turning to Rossi. "Uncle Tony is a judge and Aunt Sonia was our mom's lawyer."

Norris glared at his son, squeezing his arm. "You always took your mother's side."

Donny yanked his arm free, his jaw clenched. "That's because there never was another side."

"You little punk! I oughta…" Norris raised his hand, palm flat, his face crimson.

Rossi grabbed Norris's wrist before he could hit Donny.

"I'd take the judge's advice if I were you, Mr. Norris."

Norris raised his other hand, this time in surrender. "Okay, okay. Let's not everybody get excited." Rossi released him. Norris brushed his hands down his sleeves and straightened his collar. "So I'm getting thrown out of my own house again. I guess some things never change."

Rossi walked outside with him.

"I don't need a damn escort," Norris said.

"Just want to make sure you get to your car okay."

"So I don't come back inside and kick your ass?"

"So I don't cuff you, throw you in the back of my car, and let you spend the night cooling off in jail."

"Big man when you got a gun and all I've got is a…"

"Hangover and a bad attitude," Rossi said. "So shut the fuck up and get your ass out of here while you still can."

Norris climbed into a white Ford Escort parked on the curb and drove off. Rossi waited until he was gone, memorizing the license plate.

Everyone, including Kim, was gathered around the dining room table when Rossi returned. The judge rose to meet him.

"I'm Anthony Steele, and this is my wife, Sonia," he said, putting his hand on her shoulder.

She looked up at Rossi. "You handled that very well, Detective. Ted Norris is a nasty drunk."

"I'm convinced," Rossi said. "What's your relationship to the family, Your Honor?"

"No need to be so formal, Detective. We're not in court. Robin was one of our closest friends. Sonia and I were young marrieds when we started law school. Robin was in our study group and we've been friends ever since."

"We've known them all our lives," Donny said. "They've always been Uncle Tony and Aunt Sonia to us."

"I'm a trusts and estates lawyer," Sonia said. "I wrote Robin's estate plan and I'm helping the kids sort through the process. Fortunately, Robin took out a substantial term life policy when she was young enough to afford it. There will be enough for all the children's education and a little something to get them started after they graduate."

"Did their father know about the policy?" Rossi asked.

"At the time, yes. They both had policies making each other the beneficiary. Robin made the kids the beneficiary after the divorce. I don't know whether she ever told Ted."

"So," Judge Steele said, "what brings two detectives out on a Friday night to talk about a traffic accident?"

Rossi had delivered enough bad news to know that people responded to it in many different ways. Some were so shocked they couldn't speak. Some fell apart, crying or fainting. And some buried their reaction under a masquerade of calm that others mistook for grace under fire but that Rossi knew, more often than not, was the calm before the storm.

He took a seat at the table and looked around, making eye contact with each of the children. Donny and Rachel returned the look, their hands folded on the table and steady, oblivious to what was to come. Carrie blinked away tears, hands in her lap. Josh shifted in his chair, unable to get comfortable. Kim stared at him, dry-eyed and expectant, as if she knew what he was going to say and that it was bad. He didn't disappoint her.

"Your mother was murdered."

THIRTY-ONE

Alex sat at their kitchen table watching the dawn break. She'd been there all night after confessing to Bonnie, sleeping in fits and starts, her head on her arms, jolting upright at her latest nightmare. She'd left nothing out, telling Bonnie everything beginning with her confession that she hadn't killed Dwayne Reed in self-defense and ending with buying the burner phone. Bonnie had listened, drawing out the details like she was taking a thorough history from a reluctant patient, not editorializing, just making certain she got the information she needed for a diagnosis.

Alex didn't cry and Bonnie didn't yell. They were more than civil. They were professional, Bonnie going over everything again and again, Alex reminding her they'd covered all of that, Bonnie saying yes but she was just trying to understand. They'd opened a bottle of wine when they began but neither took a sip. Bonnie turned to coffee as the enormity of what Alex had done became apparent.

"Is that it? Is that everything?" Bonnie asked after three hours.

The knots in Alex's back and neck had unraveled the more she talked, draining her tension and anxiety, leaving her limp and depleted. But now that it was Bonnie's turn to react, whether to console, condemn, or forgive, her muscles began to tighten and twist again.

"Yes," she said, stiffening. "That's all of it."

Bonnie sat back in her chair, cradling her coffee cup, eyebrows raised, mouth pursed in contemplation.

"I don't know what to say."

"I know," Alex said.

Bonnie set the cup on the table, running both hands through her hair, then around her neck, crossing her arms over her chest and shaking her head, letting out a long breath.

"I mean, I don't even know where to begin."

"You don't have to begin. This is all on me."

"What's that even supposed to mean?" Bonnie asked, her flat-faced clinical detachment giving way to anger and anguish. "How could this all possibly be on you? You could lose your job, your law license, and probably go to jail, and, oh, by the way, someone may try to kill you, and you don't think this doesn't affect me? Or us?"

Alex wrapped her arms around her middle, rocking back and forth. "Of course it does. But I'm taking the responsibility."

"How?" Bonnie asked, throwing up her arms, her voice rising. "Are you going to start packing a gun and wearing body armor until Rossi catches Robin's killer? Are you going to turn yourself in for murdering Dwayne Reed? What would be the point of that? It's not like I haven't heard of double jeopardy. Are you going to turn in your law license and rat out Judge West? Are you going to quit your job and check into rehab like politicians and celebrities who totally fuck up their lives? Maybe you'll find a twelve-step program for people who make the biggest fucking mistakes! Hi, my name is Alex and I'm a moron! Just exactly how are you going to take responsibility, because I'd really like to know?"

Alex stopped rocking, dropping her hands in her lap and hanging her head. She was too worn-out to cry. All she could do was take Bonnie's body blows like a punching bag.

"I don't know."

"And what about us? Are you planning some grand noble gesture like breaking up with me so when this shit storm hits—and it is going to hit sooner or later—none of it blows back on me?"

Alex raised her head. She'd thought of nothing else during her confession because it was the only thing she could think of to protect Bonnie.

"I'll be out today."

Bonnie stood, planting one hand on the table, cupping Alex's chin with the other and squeezing.

"Like hell you will. No way am I letting you off that easy."

Bonnie's cell rang before Alex could respond. Bonnie answered, listening and shaking her head.

"Christ! I'll be there in ten minutes." She clicked off the call. "School bus carrying a bunch of kids back from a high school football game got T-boned by a fire truck. I don't know when I'll get back, but you better be here when I do."

She picked up her purse and ran for the door, racing back to kiss Alex on the forehead.

"We'll figure this out. Don't ask me how, but we will."

In the morning light, Alex knew Bonnie was wrong. Bleary-eyed from lack of sleep, she could see clearly enough to know that much. She wouldn't expose Bonnie to a killer, but that wasn't the only harsh reality they faced. No one's well of forgiveness was that deep. No one could live with someone who'd done what she'd done. And even if Bonnie never uttered a word of reproof, never brought up any of her sins again, Alex knew she'd forfeited Bonnie's trust. That would corrode their relationship as surely as anything else, and Alex wouldn't put Bonnie through that. She wrote her a note, packed a bag, and walked out.

THIRTY-TWO

Alex spent Monday morning staring out her office window trying to not to think about anything. Not after the weekend she'd had.

She didn't want to think about the conversation she had with Judge West when he called her early Saturday. On her cell phone. Not on her burner phone, his indifference to leaving an electronic trail that tied them together another reminder that, as far as he was concerned, she was the one at risk in their relationship, not him. He listened as she told him what to say if Rossi and Wheeler showed up in his chambers, hanging up without comment when she finished, giving no indication whether he would back her up or throw her under the bus.

She didn't want to think about the judge's photograph of her kneeling over Dwayne Reed's body. With everything else that had been happening, she'd had no time to deal with it, flashing on an image of Judge West handing it to Rossi, clenching her eyes until the image faded in an explosion of starbursts. Even if the photo was a fake, by the time she proved it, all anyone would remember would be that damning pose.

It was harder still not to think about the conversation she had when Bonnie called her after returning from the hospital and finding the note Alex had left for her. It was brief, but that hadn't made it easy.

"Come home," Bonnie said.

"I can't."

"Why not?"

"You read my note. You know why."

"Don't do this, Alex. Please. We'll figure something out."

"Remember the first time you took me to the ER? You showed me around, showed me all the crash carts and other equipment and introduced me to all the doctors and nurses and staff?"

"Of course I remember."

"And there was that guy, the chief or head of the ER, what was his name?"

"Adelson. Barney Adelson."

"Right. So you're showing me all of that and bragging about what a great job the trauma unit does, and Dr. Adelson interrupts and says something that I've never forgotten. Do you remember what he said?"

Bonnie sighed. "Some things can't be fixed."

Desperate to find another way but certain there wasn't, Alex cried, choking as she spoke.

"And this is one of them. I'm sorry. Good-bye."

Alex had ignored Bonnie's steady stream of texts and voice messages since then, and when her phone buzzed with yet another, she turned it off, stuffed it in her pants pocket, and resumed staring out the window.

A mountain of work was sitting on her desk, correspondence to answer, motions to respond to, drafts of pleadings to review, and research to read. She'd thought that plunging into work would get her focused on something productive, but she'd been wrong. The best she could do at the moment was to stare out the window, unfocused and unseeing.

Grace Canfield broke the spell, rapping her knuckles on Alex's open door, a file folder in one hand.

"I'd say I was sorry for interrupting, but I'd be lying," Grace said. "You think all that work is going to get done by itself?"

Alex swiveled her chair around and gave Grace a weak smile. "A girl can dream, can't she?"

Grace shook her head. "Unh-uh. Look at you, all down in the mouth. What happened to Little Miss Piss and Vinegar from last Friday? You were all dolled up and ready for the ball and now you got your lip stuck out like your dog died."

"My dog is fine."

"But you aren't. You and Bonnie have a fight?"

Alex leaned her head to one side, sighing. "You could say that. We broke up."

Grace took one of the chairs in front of Alex's desk. "Oh, honey, I'm so sorry. You two were so good together. Isn't there something you can to do to patch things up?"

Alex shook her head. "No. It's time to move on, and you're right about the work."

"Is that your way of telling me it's none of my business and to butt out?"

"Yeah. I'd appreciate that."

"You can appreciate it all you want, but I'll tell you one last thing. I haven't seen two people more in love or better suited to each other than you and Bonnie, and that's something worth fighting for. I don't care what happened between the two of you; it's nothing that can't be fixed."

"That's actually two things, maybe three, but thanks. What's up?"

Grace shoved the piles of paper on the desk out of the way, making room for the file she'd been carrying, then setting it in front of Alex.

"Here's what I found on Joanie Sutherland. She's been in the system since she was thirteen. She specialized in the *P*s."

"Possession and prostitution," Alex said.

"You got it. She's been in the county lockup half a dozen times but never gone away."

"If she was a prostitute, that could help us on the rape charge. The coroner says he found genital trauma and Jared says their sex was consensual. So maybe Joanie had rough sex with one of her other johns earlier that evening. You think you can talk to some of the women who work Independence Avenue, maybe get a line on any of her johns?"

"My church is doing outreach to those girls. I'll find out who to talk to."

"Grace, you are too good for words. I don't know another investigator who could turn her church into a source. What else did you find out about Joanie?"

"She was twenty-eight years old. Been to rehab a couple of times. Grew up in Northeast."

"Where was she living?"

"She spent a lot of time on the street, but she stayed some with her sister, Bethany, in a mobile home park just off of Blue Ridge."

"Where's that?"

Grace opened the file and pointed to the address. "Pull it up on Google Maps."

Alex punched in the address, hunching her shoulders and leaning toward the monitor as she zoomed in and out.

"How about that?"

"How about what?" Grace asked.

"The mobile home park is a little east from where her body was found, maybe a couple of miles," she said, pointing to the map.

"So you're thinking Joanie was familiar with the area?"

"Makes sense. I don't think she met Jared on Match.com." She scooted her chair away from the monitor. "What do we know about the sister?"

Grace turned to another page in the file. "Here's a copy of her driver's license. She's had a couple of speeding tickets but nothing more than that. She works at the Clay County courthouse."

"North of the river, huh. What's she do up there?"

"Cleans."

Alex picked up the copy of the driver's license, studying the photograph. "This is a lousy picture, and the photocopy makes it worse, but…"

"But what?"

"I may have run into her last Friday," she said, telling Grace about the little girl in the creek and the woman driving the Impala.

"Well, now we've got an address, we can find out for sure. You want me to go see her?"

"No, I'll go, but I want to talk to Jared first. It's time he filled in some blanks for me."

THIRTY-THREE

"How's the neck?"

They were back in the same closet-sized room, the air sour from the day's earlier meetings. It was warm enough that she took off her jacket. She wished she'd chosen short sleeves with her khaki pants instead of a sweater.

The more violent her client's offense, the more claustrophobic the room felt. But Jared was too mellow to trigger that vibe, as he fingered the bandage on his neck.

"Okay, I guess. First time I've ever been stabbed."

Alex's hand went to her neck, a sympathetic reaction, her fingers tugging at her flesh.

"Tell me what happened."

He furrowed his brow. "Didn't nobody tell you?"

"I'd rather hear it from you."

"This old dude, he come up from behind and jumped me for no reason. I threw him off of me and the guards hauled him away. That's all I know."

"Did you find out who he was?"

"Somebody said his name was Wood or Woody, something like that."

"His name was Mathew Woodrell. Does that name mean anything to you?"

Jared's eyes fluttered for an instant as he made a fist and pressed it hard against his mouth.

"I knew a Woodrell in the army, but it wasn't him," he said, his fist muffling his answer.

"No. It wasn't him. It was his daughter, McCallister."

He ground his fist against his teeth, his face flushing; then he pulled his fist away, his knuckles gouged and red.

"Yeah, I knew her," he said, his voice thickening.

Alex knew she was on fragile ground. She kept her tone soft and easy.

"Everyone called her Ali."

He nodded.

"One of the COs told me that sometimes you wake up during the night calling her name. Why is that?"

He pressed his fingers against his eyes, dragging his hands across his cheeks. He ducked his chin and turned his head from side to side, moving his lips like he was having an argument with himself about what to say. Then he sniffed, wiped his moist eyes with the backs of his hands, and shook his head again, finally squaring up and looking straight at Alex.

"'Cause I killed her. That's why her father jumped me, isn't it?"

Alex sucked in a breath. She knew how hard it was to admit to such a thing.

"That's what he says. Tell me what happened, Jared."

He raised his head to the ceiling, one hand covering his eyes, breathing deeply before coming back to her, his face pinched.

"I didn't mean for it to happen."

"I'm sure you didn't. Things sometimes get out of hand."

"Ali was so pretty and so kind. All I wanted was to be around her, even if she never give me the time of day."

"How did that make you feel?" Alex asked.

He sighed. "Like I was nothing, like I didn't deserve her, but I knew I did. I was as good as she was. I kept telling her if she'd just give me a chance, we could be real good together."

"And what did she say about that?"

He clenched his eyes, ticktocking his head back and forth.

"She said, 'Not in my lifetime, soldier.' That's what she called me, soldier, even though I wore a name tag like every other grunt."

"Did that make you angry?"

"A little bit, I suppose, but I couldn't stay mad at her, not the way I felt about her. I just told myself, Jared, you stick with it, give her a reason, and she'll come around."

"How did Ali feel about all the attention you paid her?"

He shrugged, eyes down. "I dunno."

"Did she complain to her superiors that you were harassing her?"

He pressed his palms against his thighs, straightening his back.

"I wasn't harassing her. I just wanted to, you know, talk to her, be friends. That was all."

"You must have been angry, then. Is that why you killed her?"

"I was scared, but I wasn't angry," Jared said.

"What were you scared of?"

"Getting caught."

"For killing Ali?"

He shook his head. "No. I was scared of us getting caught by the Taliban."

Alex squinted at him, trying to make sense of what Jared was saying. "I'm not following you."

He wiped his face with his sleeve and took a breath. "All that time I was trying to get her to like me and getting nowhere; then one day out of the blue, we get assigned to the same detail and we're riding in a jeep together, in the middle of a three-vehicle convoy, trucks carrying supplies in front and behind. Anyway, we're in this little convoy and the truck in front of us hits an IED, gets blown all to hell. Then the truck behind us takes fire and it runs off the road. Next thing I know, we're surrounded and they dragged me and Ali out of the jeep. I coulda swore they got rid of the others just to capture us."

"Why would they do that? Why not kill you guys too?"

"Oh, they were going to kill us all right, but not till after they were done with Ali."

Alex nodded. "Then what happened?"

"Well, I was right, 'cause one of them towelheads put a gun on me while the others held Ali down and…" He choked on the words, unable to get them out.

"Raped her."

He bobbed his head up and down, his voice breaking. "Then they hauled her up to her knees and that was the first and only time she called me by my name. 'Jared,' she said, 'help me.' But all I did was stand there and watch one of those fucking haji shoot her in the head. They'd have shot me next except an Apache helicopter found us and opened up on them. I hit the dirt and they run off." He dropped his head, crying. "God, I wish they'd killed me too."

Alex swallowed the lump in her throat.

"But you didn't kill her; the Taliban did."

He lifted his head, red-eyed. "It's the same thing, 'cause I should have saved her and I didn't. That's what you do for someone you love, and I didn't even try."

Listening to Jared's story, seeing how his guilt and pain contorted him, Alex realized why he'd confessed to killing Joanie Sutherland. She was a stand-in for Ali. That's why, the first time they talked, Jared had told her that his arrest was a long time coming. Joanie was a stand-in for the relationship he'd wished he had with Ali. Whatever had happened between them, as far as Jared was concerned, he hadn't raped Joanie Sutherland. He'd made love to Ali Woodrell. That was why he hadn't confessed to raping Joanie, though Alex had no way of knowing whether that was how Joanie saw it. At least Alex understood Jared better, even if she was still uncertain of his innocence.

"Did you kill Joanie Sutherland?"

He stopped rubbing his palms against his thighs, sitting still, looking straight at her. "No, ma'am, but after what I done, I deserve to be in prison or executed, whatever they decide. It don't matter to me."

"Well, it matters to me, and trust me, it will matter more to you when you stop feeling guilty for Ali's death. I see how painful it was for you to tell me about Ali, but what happened to both of you is very important for your defense, so I've got to ask you a few more questions, if that's all right with you."

He cleared his throat. "Okay."

"How did you get to know Joanie?"

"She was a hooker that worked Independence Avenue. I seen her there a few times."

"Were you attracted to her?"

He blushed, turning and looking away. "Yeah, I guess so."

"What was it about her that attracted you?"

He couldn't face Alex. "I dunno. Everything, I guess."

"Ali must have had long dark hair, kind of an oval face, and a good figure."

Jared swirled around, hands on the table. "How did you know that?"

"Because Joanie did. Were you drawn to Joanie because she reminded you of Ali?"

Jared clenched his jaw. "Ali wasn't a whore!"

"And I'm not saying she was. But Joanie was a whore who happened to look like Ali. When you talked to Joanie, I bet she didn't make you feel like nothing."

Jared hesitated, his eyes glazing over as if he had gone somewhere else, and Alex was uncertain whether he was still with her or back in Afghanistan with Ali. She rapped her pen on the table.

"Jared? Are you with me?"

He blinked, focusing, his voice soft. "Yeah."

"Did Joanie make you feel like nothing?"

"No, she didn't."

"She was probably the one who asked if you wanted to have sex."

He nodded.

"But you didn't have any cash, did you?"

He shook his head.

"But you had all that jewelry you'd picked up along the way, and every woman, even a whore, maybe especially a whore, likes jewelry."

"They do. Even the ones that got enough of it."

"So you offered to pay Joanie with jewelry. But that meant she had to come to your tent."

"She didn't mind. I told where I was camped out and she laughed, said she used to play down there all the time when she was little. Knew right where it was. Said it was practically on her way home and that she'd meet me there."

"What time was it when she got to your tent?"

"I'm not real sure since I don't have a watch, but it had been dark for a couple of hours."

"That's pretty early in the evening for a working girl to get off the street. How much jewelry were you going to give her?"

He chuckled. "It wasn't like that. I mean, yeah, I was going to give her something. I was even going to let her take her pick. She said she was meeting someone later on and wanted to go home and clean up first and she wanted a nice piece of jewelry to wear when she went back out."

Alex leaned in hard against the table, trying not to get too excited. "Did she say who she was going to meet?"

Jared shook his head. "No, and I didn't ask. I didn't want to hear about her being with someone else even though I knew that's what she did."

"So you had sex with her in your tent."

He blushed again, dropping his gaze to the floor. "Yeah."

"And afterward, did she pick out a piece of jewelry?"

He nodded.

"What did she choose?"

"The gold cross I took off her when I found her in the creek."

"Why did you take the cross?"

"'Cause I wanted it for Ali."

"Then why did you let Joanie take it in the first place?"

He raised his hands chest high, waving them back and forth, his eyes fluttering. "I dunno." He took a deep breath, shaking his head. "I dunno. I guess maybe 'cause, like you said before, she reminded me of Ali."

Alex studied him, looking for something that would expose him as a liar, rapist, and murderer, but it wasn't there. He believed what he was telling her regardless of whether it was true. Mathew Woodrell had been just as certain.

"And was that the last time you saw Joanie alive?"

He raised his head, looking squarely at Alex, not blinking. "Yes, ma'am."

THIRTY-FOUR

Rossi didn't like going to the courthouse because it usually meant that he was going to have to testify in one of his cases, and that always meant that a defense attorney was going to second-guess his investigation and twist his testimony to create reasonable doubt where there was none. He got the whole innocent-until-proven-guilty thing and he wasn't so full of himself that he thought he was infallible, but smarmy defense lawyers and their smirky clients made him long for frontier justice.

He'd been a witness in Judge West's courtroom dozens of times, always appreciating how courteous the judge was to him and enjoying each time the judge jammed his gavel up defense counsel's puckered ass. The days of frontier justice weren't coming back, but every cop knew that Wild Bill's courtroom was the next best thing.

So he had mixed emotions about starting his Monday by bracing his favorite judge. He couldn't fathom how the judge could have gotten tangled up in either Robin Norris's murder or Jared Bell's case, and that was enough to make him cautious. Not because he might ruffle the judge's feathers but because hard experience had taught him that the quickest way to miss something important was to rule out the improbable. And while he doubted that Judge West had anything to hide, he couldn't ignore the threads that tied the judge and Alex Stone together.

Lawyers, litigants, and potential jurors were crowded outside the judge's courtroom, typical for a Monday morning, when new trials were starting. Rossi threaded his way past them and into the office outside Judge West's chambers. His secretary was on the phone but the door to the judge's chambers was open. Judge West looked out into the office as he slipped into his black robe, recognizing Rossi and waving him into his chambers.

"Morning, Your Honor," Rossi said, shaking his hand.

"What brings you over here, Detective? I'm starting a civil case this morning, not criminal."

"And I won't keep you from that," Rossi said. "I just need to ask you a couple of questions."

"About what?"

One of Rossi's rules about questioning a witness was to establish control. His badge was usually enough to do that, but he knew it wouldn't have any effect on Judge West. Another rule was to slow it down, because most people couldn't wait to get the questioning over. Making them go at his pace was one more way of letting the witness know who was running the show. Judge West was in a hurry. Rossi wasn't. He looked over his shoulder at the open door.

"Mind if I close this?"

"Go right ahead," West said, looking at his watch. "But let's be quick about it. I've got a bunch of people dying to get out of jury duty and I want to disappoint them just as soon as I can."

Rossi closed the door. "I've got to tell you, Judge. I kind of sympathize with them. Every time I'm in your courtroom, I can't wait to get out either."

Both men chuckled, though the judge didn't say anything. He was waiting for Rossi.

"Mind if we sit down, Your Honor? It's easier for me to take notes that way."

Rossi pulled a small spiral notepad from his pocket to make the point.

"Do we really need to do this right now? I've got—"

"A jury and a trial, I know, Your Honor. But I wouldn't be here taking up your time if I didn't have to. I've just got a few questions about a case I'm working on."

"How could I possibly know anything about one of your cases unless it was in my court? And if you want to talk to me about one of my cases, you'll have to go through the prosecutor's office. I don't want to give defense counsel any grounds for claiming judicial misconduct by claiming I was helping the prosecution."

Rossi sat in one of the chairs in front of the judge's desk. "That's the last thing I want to happen, but I talked to the prosecutor and she suggested I come see you."

The judge didn't move. "Which prosecutor is that?"

"Kalena Greene."

West raised his eyebrows. "And which case?"

"Actually, it's three cases. One of them is in your court, *State v. Jared Bell*. It's a murder and rape case."

"I know the case, Detective."

"The second one concerns the death of Robin Norris."

"The newspaper said that was an accident."

"We've reason to believe she was murdered."

Judge West's jaw dropped, and he took a deep breath, letting it out slowly. He unzipped his robe and sat in his desk chair. "Murdered. How? By whom?"

"Run off the road up in Clay County, which puts it out of your jurisdiction, so there's no chance the case will be in front of you. As for who did it, we don't know."

West swiveled his head slowly from side to side. "Murdered. What possible reason would anyone have to murder that woman?"

"Like I said, we don't know."

"You said there were three cases."

"The third involves a man named Mathew Woodrell. He robbed a liquor store yesterday. He was caught and put on the seventh floor of the jail. First thing he did was stab Jared Bell in the neck with a shiv he made out of the frame for his glasses. Bell's okay and now Woodrell is facing two felonies."

"Well, Detective. I can't help you with that one. I don't know anything about Mathew Woodrell."

Rossi sat back in his chair, notepad on his thigh. "Actually, Your Honor, you do."

Judge West squinted at him. "How's that?"

Rossi pulled up Woodrell's booking photo on his cell phone and showed it to the judge. "You recognize this man?"

West studied the photograph, eyes opening in recognition. "This man was waiting for me in my chambers last Wednesday when I got off the bench. What's his connection to Jared Bell?"

"He says Bell raped and killed his daughter while they were in the army stationed in Afghanistan."

"Did he?"

"According to Woodrell, the army says no but Woodrell doesn't buy it. When he found out Jared had been arrested for raping and murdering someone else, he drove here from Ohio to tell you what happened to his daughter so you wouldn't let Jared off on a technicality. What happened when you saw him in your chambers?"

"I asked him who he was and he said he'd made a mistake and was in the wrong place and he apologized and left."

"Did he tell you who he was or why he wanted to talk with you?"

The judge scooted his chair toward his desk. "Detective, I just told you everything the man said to me."

Rossi nodded. "Just wanted to be sure, Your Honor. Was anyone else in your chambers at that time?"

"Alex Stone. She was also waiting to talk to me. I believe you're familiar with her."

The judge was smooth. He'd denied knowing Woodrell until Rossi showed him the photo, covering the denial by admitting the man had been in his chambers but he hadn't known the man's name. He'd handled Alex Stone the same way, not making Rossi work for answers to his questions. That's what someone did who either had nothing to hide or who was well prepared.

"That I am. Why was she in your chambers?"

"She wanted to talk to me about deadlines in cases where the PD's office was representing the defendant. She said that with Robin Norris's death, they may need some more time."

Another match, but Rossi would have bought it more easily had the judge stumbled on that one. It was rare for two people to tell the same story down to the smallest details. And although there weren't a lot of details in these stories, there was something about the telling that didn't sit right with Rossi. Alex had struggled to get her legs under her before she gave her version, but the judge was right there with her, word for word, beat for beat.

"And what did you tell her?"

"I told her that I'd entertain any motions her office might file but that I couldn't discuss any particular case in which she was not counsel of record and that those discussions would have to include opposing counsel. Now, is that all?"

"One last thing, Your Honor. Kalena Greene tells me that someone gave Robin Norris an advance copy of the police department's investigative report on Jared Bell—my report, as it turns out—and the criminal complaint. Her office provides that to defense counsel at the initial appearance, but Alex Stone already had a copy. I'm wondering if you might know how that happened."

"What difference does it make when defense counsel gets those documents? They're certainly entitled to them."

"As I said, it's the prosecutor's policy not to provide it before the initial appearance."

"Fuck the prosecutor's office."

Rossi grinned. "You might have to get in line to do that, Your Honor, but that doesn't answer my question. Do you know who sent that file to Robin Norris?"

Judge West leaned back in his chair, hands clasped over his belly. "I did."

"Mind if I ask why?"

"She asked me for it. She called me the day Bell was arrested. She knew about the case from all the press coverage, figured Bell would need a public defender, and said she'd like to get a head start on it. When I suggested she get the file from the prosecutor's office, she told me about their policy and I said I'd be glad to send the file over to her."

"Did the two of you discuss which lawyer in her office would handle the case?"

"She mentioned that she was going to assign the case to Alex Stone, but we didn't discuss it."

"What was your reaction to that?"

"Reaction? I didn't have one. Now, I've been very patient with you, Detective, even if I do have a full courtroom waiting for me. I've answered your questions, and now you can answer mine. What the hell does any of this have to do with me?"

Rossi smiled as he stood. "Just going where the case takes me, Your Honor."

"Which case? You're asking me about three different ones."

"All of them," Rossi said, sliding his notepad into his pocket.

Judge West rose, closing the zipper on his robe. "I take it, then, that we are done."

"We are." Rossi turned toward the door to the judge's outer office, stopping with his hand on the knob, looking back at West. "Except for one thing. What's the nature of your relationship with Alex Stone?"

Judge West held his look but couldn't help the way his eyes narrowed, his nostrils flared, and his fists clenched. Rossi knew the judge might not even be aware he'd done any of those things, but Rossi picked up on all of them, knowing he'd touched a nerve. This was Judge West unplugged and honest. The judge opened his mouth just enough to let his words out.

"She's a lawyer who appears in my court."

"What do you think of her…as a lawyer who appears in your court?"

"She's very good at what she does."

"Can't argue with that. After all, she gunned down her client and got away with it in your courtroom."

Judge West glared at him, Rossi giving him a flat look in return, neither moving the other.

"Yes," Judge West said. "She did."

THIRTY-FIVE

Rossi walked down the courthouse steps, satisfied that he'd accomplished one of the basic objectives of any interrogation. He'd confirmed another witness's story. Both the judge and Alex gave the same explanation for why she wanted to talk to him, meaning either they were telling the truth or they'd gotten their stories straight before he got to the judge.

If it were anyone other than Alex Stone, he'd give a heavy lean to the first option, particularly since both also confirmed Mathew Woodrell's story about their encounter in chambers, but he couldn't do that with her. And that left him wondering what could possibly be going on between them that would prompt both of them to lie.

He was also pleased that he'd accomplished a second goal of interrogation, pissing off the witness, because pissed-off people make mistakes that can turn into breaks that solve cases. The judge was annoyed that Rossi was keeping him from his courtroom, but annoyed people don't give him the bull-about-to-charge look that West flashed at him when he asked the judge about his relationship with Alex. And when he said that Alex had not only gotten away with killing Dwayne Reed but that she'd gotten away with it in his courtroom, the look the judge gave him was more executioner than judicial.

All of which made him think that whatever was going on between the judge and Alex had to do with Alex killing Dwayne Reed. The judge might have reacted that way because he'd been forced to acquit her because the prosecutor didn't have enough evidence to make the case. Given West's hanging-judge reputation, Rossi could understand how that would chap the judge's ass. But there were two other possibilities that were more intriguing.

The first was that Alex had something on the judge that she used to pressure him into the acquittal, but the judge didn't strike him as someone who would let himself be blackmailed. The second was that Alex and the judge had conspired to get her off, but that made less sense to him than the blackmail scenario. Neither theory got him closer to the truth—not yet—but if he kept pissing off enough people, he knew he'd get there.

"In here, Rossi," Mitch Fowler said from his office when Rossi got back to the homicide unit.

Rossi stood in the doorway. "What's up?"

Fowler looked up from a stack of reports on his desk. "You've got a visitor."

Rossi glanced around the empty bullpen. "Where?"

"Interrogation Two. She said she wanted to have a private conversation with you."

"Who is she?"

"Sonia Steele. Says she's a lawyer but I didn't ask to see her bar association card."

"Why not?"

"Didn't have to. She had *arrogant ballbuster* written all over her face. You know her?"

"Enough to say hello."

"If she's representing someone who's getting ready to sue your ass and the department because of some bullshit you pulled…"

Rossi held up one hand. "Easy, boss. She's representing Robin Norris's kids. Wheeler and I met her at the Norris house Friday night. I haven't had time to pull any bullshit on her, but I'll see what I can do."

Wheeler's mouth turned down like he got a bad taste of something. "I'm tired of you fucking with me, Rossi."

Rossi grinned. "Don't worry, boss. You'll get a second wind."

Sonia Steele was seated at the interrogation table, her briefcase at her feet, her backbone straight, tapping away on her smartphone when Rossi walked into the room. She was wearing slacks and a sleeveless scoop-neck blouse under a jacket she'd set on the back of her chair. The blouse showed off her buff arms and shoulders. She was in her fifties but in better shape than women—and men—ten years younger. Having met her twice, Rossi was impressed with more than her good looks. He liked the toughness in her muscle message.

"Mrs. Steele," Rossi said, taking a seat opposite her and gesturing at the scuffed table. "This is what passes for a homicide cop's conference room. I'm sure you're used to better."

She smiled at him with perfect teeth. She may have had them whitened, but the rest of her face was original equipment, down to the crow's-feet in the corners of her eyes and the laugh lines at her mouth.

"I've never seen a table that could get a deal done. It always comes down to the people sitting around the table."

"So what kind of a deal are you interested in?"

"That's not why I'm here, Detective."

Rossi spread his hands wide. "Then what can I do for you?"

She took a breath, pursed her lips, and let it go, her posture softening to rounded shoulders, the confident sheen she'd had when he walked in the room fading. He might have been wrong about the toughness thing, working out taking her only so far.

"I don't really know. I mean, you can't do anything for me." She sat back, chewing her lower lip and shaking her head. "I'm sorry. It's just that I'm really out of my element here," she said, pointing to the mirrored wall. "Is that one of those two-way mirrors I see on *Law and Order* and all those other shows?"

"Yes."

"So you really do that? Watch people while they're being interrogated."

"If we could sell tickets, we'd make a bundle."

She didn't say anything. She was stalling, but it was her meeting, so Rossi let the silence do its work. She pressed her palms flat on the table and took another deep breath.

"Okay. I'm just going to tell you what I came to tell you and I'll leave the rest up to you."

"And what's that?"

She reached into her briefcase for a manila envelope, placing it on the table in front of her. It was the kind of envelope that was held closed by a metal clasp inserted through a hole in the flap. She toyed with the clasp, opening and closing it.

"It's just that Ted is still the father of those kids, and even though he's been a lousy father—and that's putting it mildly—he's still their dad, and with Robin gone, well…I hate to do anything that might hurt the kids even more. Especially if I'm wrong."

"Wrong about what?"

She looked at him, her fingers on the clasp, deciding. "It's possible Ted killed Robin. I mean, I don't know that for certain. I don't have a smoking gun or anything like that. In fact, what I have is strictly circumstantial and can probably be explained. I haven't said a word to Ted or my husband or—God forbid—the children, but I couldn't stop thinking about it all weekend. Not after you told us what happened to Robin."

"How about this," Rossi said. "You tell me whatever it is you came to tell me and show me whatever is in that envelope, and I'll figure out what to do with it. If it raises any questions about Mr. Norris, I'll look into it."

"But what about the children? Will they have to know?"

"It depends on what I find out. But you have to tell me first."

She nodded. "I know. Robin and I have been friends since law school. I remember how we talked back then about all the things we wanted to do in our lives, but I never thought it would come to this. I represented Robin in her divorce. That was years ago before I began specializing in estate planning. It was an ugly breakup. Ted was drinking heavily and cheating on her. He started threatening Robin that he was going to get even with her, that sort of thing, nothing real explicit but enough that we got a restraining order against him."

"Did he ever act on any of those threats? Did he ever hit her?"

"No, nothing like that. Mostly calling her in the middle of the night screaming what a bitch she was and how he was going to make her life a living hell. It was probably the booze more than anything else. One of the conditions for him seeing the kids was that he go to AA, which he did. He sobered up and stayed sober, most of the time, until the last few months."

"What happened then?"

She tilted her head, shrugging her shoulders. "Well, he got laid off from his job selling restaurant equipment, and then he started drinking again. And then he started calling Robin, asking her for money, and she told him no. When he threatened to make her pay, she told me what was going on and I said we should go back to court for another restraining order, but she didn't want to because of the kids and because she thought Ted was all talk, just like before, until the thing in the parking lot."

"What thing?"

"Ted was stalking her, following her to work and back home, sitting in his car on her street. Then a couple of weeks ago, he rear-ended her in the Costco parking lot, you know the one off of Linwood?"

Rossi nodded. "That's where I get all my canned tuna."

She arched an eyebrow. "Is that supposed to be funny, Detective? Because I don't find any of this amusing."

Rossi wasn't trying to be funny. He wanted to see how she'd react to an out-of-place wisecrack. If she joined in the fun, he'd question her sincerity. If he offended her, she'd go up a notch on his credibility meter.

"You're right. I'm sorry. When did this happen?"

"A couple of weeks ago. She called me, hysterical, and I said enough was enough and that I was going to file for the restraining order, but she begged me to wait because of the kids. So I did. But I drafted the motion and had her sign an affidavit so everything would be ready to go. And then she called me last Wednesday and said he was following her again and to go ahead and file it."

She opened the envelope and pulled out a copy of the motion and handed it to Rossi. Robin's affidavit, notarized by Sonia, was attached, detailing Robin's allegations. There was also a copy of the court's ex parte order of protection. The court clerk's file stamp showed that the motion was filed at nine a.m., Tuesday, September 14 The order of protection was filed an hour later, ten hours before Robin was killed. It was a classic domestic violence timetable, the system playing a fatal game of catch-up.

"Were you able to serve the order on Mr. Norris?"

She shook her head, her eyes watering. "No. I went straight from the courthouse to his apartment, but either he wasn't there or he saw that it was me and wouldn't answer the door. I went back to my office and hired a process server to keep after him, but they couldn't find him either." She paused, chest heaving. "Then Donny called me in the middle of the night to say that Robin was dead and it didn't matter anymore." She took a tissue from her purse and wiped her eyes. "The police said it was an accident, so I didn't mention anything about Ted because I didn't want to upset the kids any more than they already were. But then last Friday night, you told us Robin had been murdered, and," she said, hands fluttering, "well, here I am, and I don't know whether to wish that I'm right or wrong."

Rossi studied the documents, pausing when he came to Ted Norris's address.

"This says he lives on Roanridge Road. Where's that?"

"North of the river, just off Barry Road," she said.

THIRTY-SIX

Alex drove toward the Blue Ridge Mobile Home Park, thinking about how to approach Bethany Sutherland. Their encounter last Friday hadn't gone well. Bethany had denied knowledge of the murder and had said nothing about her relationship to Joanie Sutherland. And she had sidestepped Alex's questions about the girl.

Alex had given Bethany the benefit of the doubt. Even if the little girl knew something, that didn't mean Bethany did, and since the victim's next of kin hadn't been notified, Bethany might not have known her sister was dead. She hoped that Bethany knew by now, not wanting to be the one to tell her.

Nor did Alex blame Bethany for not answering her questions about the girl, whom Alex assumed was her daughter. What mother wouldn't shield her child from being drawn into a murder investigation?

Knowing that Alex was defending the man accused of murdering her sister, not some stranger, would make Bethany less cooperative, particularly regarding the little girl. Still, she had to try.

Bethany's trailer was parked in the shade of two towering oak trees in the middle of a long row of mobile homes. It was an old Jayco White Hawk, cream-colored paint faded by years in the sun, pockets of rust visible on the undercarriage. The trailer sat on a concrete slab made out of sections pieced together like a jigsaw puzzle. There was a four-by-eight-foot flat-roofed metal storage shed next to the back end of the trailer, a pair of outdoor folding chairs in front of it, a couple of coolers, a bicycle, and a spare tire wedged between the shed and the chairs. The trailer might have been mobile, but its occupants had put down roots. This was home.

Alex parked on the street in front of the trailer. There was no sign of the Impala. She got out, scanning the area for Bethany and the girl, finding neither. Nor did she see any neighbors, though she imagined at least a few were watching her from inside their trailers. *Act like you belong*, she reminded herself, walking briskly to the trailer and rapping on its tinny door, not surprised when no one answered, then turning toward the street when she heard the Impala approach.

Bethany jerked the car to a stop, nose to nose with Alex's, and got out with a bag of groceries in one hand, eyes narrowed, mouth set, her face creased with caution. The girl climbed out of the passenger side, following Bethany while keeping her distance, clutching a plastic spatula.

"How'd you find me?"

"I didn't. My investigator did. She's good at that. I'm sorry about Joanie."

"You say that, but you're the lawyer for the one that killed her."

"He's accused of killing your sister. That doesn't mean he's guilty and it doesn't mean I'm not sorry for your loss."

"Well, I got nothing to say to you."

"I just want to talk with you for a few minutes."

Alex kept her tone neutral but didn't move from her position in front of the trailer door. She kept her arms at her sides and her stance casual, not wanting to appear threatening, while letting Bethany know that she wasn't going anywhere. Bethany called her bluff, coming toward her, chin and chest thrust out, tugging the girl along with her, stopping when they were two feet apart.

"Well, I ain't interested."

Alex couldn't let Bethany intimidate her. Neither could she ignore how the veins in Bethany's neck were throbbing against her skin, her flight-or-fight instinct about to settle on kicking some ass. Alex diffused the tension by taking half a step to one side and squatting down until she was eye level with the girl, giving her a big smile.

"Hi, there. I'm Alex. What's your name?"

The girl didn't answer, instead drawing back and looking away. Her hair was pulled back in a long ponytail secured by a clasp adorned with an oversized butterfly. She was wearing jeans torn at the knees and a frayed One Direction T-shirt. Alex looked up at Bethany.

"She's a quiet one."

"She don't talk."

"Shy, huh? That's okay," Alex said, grinning again at the girl and tousling her hair as she stood, the girl crying out as if she were hurt, pounding the air with her spatula.

"She don't like to be touched."

"I guess not. Is she your daughter?"

"She's mine."

"When I asked you about her the other day, why'd you pretend you didn't know who I was talking about?"

"There's more than one little girl in this world, and why would I tell you anything about mine?"

Alex didn't argue. She was right on both counts.

"What's her name?"

"Charlotte."

"I'll bet she talks a blue streak when it's just the two of you."

Bethany gave her a warm look and a sad smile. "I wish she could."

Alex grimaced at the awkward situation she'd created.

"I'm so sorry. I didn't realize she was deaf."

"Oh, Charlotte's not deaf. She's autistic. The doctor at Children's Mercy said some autistic kids never talk."

"How do you communicate with her? Do you use sign language?"

"She understands me as long as I'm real clear. The doctor told me autistic kids take things real literal, like if I say hold your horses, she's gonna look around for a horse, so instead I got to say slow down or stop. And don't try to tell her a joke, 'cause she won't get it."

"But how does she communicate with you?"

"She'll take my hand and pull me over to something she wants or shake her head, things like that. We've kind of worked out a system. Sometimes she throws a fit and I just have to wait till it passes. And if she gets scared, she screams bloody murder and there's no stopping her till she calms down."

They were talking now instead of trading punches. Bethany's posture was more relaxed, making Alex hopeful that Bethany would open up.

"Why isn't she in school? There are special education programs for kids like her."

Bethany recoiled, squinting at Alex, their cease-fire over. "What are you? Her truant officer? Now, get off my property while you still can."

Friendly but firm hadn't worked, so Alex switched gears.

"Who needs a truant officer when I can get someone from Child Protective Services out here in an hour to find out why Charlotte's not in school and when she last had a decent meal, a bath, and clean clothes."

"Don't even think about doing that," Bethany said, setting down the bag of groceries and balling her hand into a fist. "Nobody's takin' this child away from me."

Alex took her phone from her pocket. "I've got their number in my phone. I see a lot of this kind of thing." She scrolled through her contacts, clicking on a number, holding the phone to her face. "This is Alex Stone from the public defender's office. I need to report a possible child neglect case."

Bethany gritted her teeth. "Okay! Okay! What do you want?"

"I'll have to call you back," Alex said, clicking off the call. "I want answers."

THIRTY-SEVEN

Alex followed Bethany into the trailer. It was twenty-four feet long and eight feet wide, not counting the pop-out dinette, which was like a restaurant booth with a cushioned horseshoe-shaped bench. A sleeping bag and pillow were laid out on the bench, turning it into Charlotte's bedroom. There was an unmade sofa sleeper at one end of the trailer flanked on each side by a small wardrobe closet. A Murphy bed was mounted in the wall above the sofa, Alex guessing that Bethany got the sofa sleeper, leaving the Murphy bed for Joanie. The bathroom and shower were at the back of the trailer. Kitchen appliances were mounted on both sides in the middle, an ironing board leaning against the dishwasher, the iron on the floor. The air was stale with fast food and dirty laundry.

Charlotte scrambled onto the dinette bench, pushing the sleeping bag into a corner and hugging her spatula to her bony chest. Bethany set the grocery bag on the narrow kitchen counter.

"I gotta use the john," Bethany said.

Alex leafed through a stack of mail on the kitchen counter, finding an open bank statement from the month before. She ran her finger down the transactions, noting the direct deposit of Bethany's modest paychecks from Clay County and an ending balance of twenty-eight dollars. Beneath that she found an open envelope filled with cash, the top edge of a hundred-dollar bill sticking out. She picked the envelope up, doing a quick count that totaled five thousand dollars. She put the envelope and the bank statement back where she found them when she heard the toilet flush, glancing at the girl, who was watching her, expressionless.

Alex smiled, giving her a thumbs-up, smiling again when Charlotte balled her fingers together, her thumb poking up. Alex nodded, touching her forefinger to her thumb in the universal okay sign, clapping when Charlotte did the same. Encouraged, Alex shrugged, opening her palms out, as if to say, *What else?* Charlotte didn't hesitate, giving Alex her middle finger.

Bethany came out of the bathroom. "Don't worry. She doesn't know what that means. She picked it from me flipping people off all the time."

Alex laughed. "Thanks. I'd hate to think I made such a bad impression. Have you gotten Charlotte any therapy? There's been a lot of progress treating kids with autism."

Bethany shook her head. "Not that I don't want to, but when am I gonna do that? I leave here at three thirty to get to work, and I'm there from four to midnight. By the time I get home and get some sleep, I hardly have time to do what I need to get done before I got to get back to work. And how am I gonna pay for it? The county's insurance don't cover it, and I ain't poor enough for Medicaid."

Alex wanted to tell her to use the five thousand bucks sitting buried in her stack of mail but was afraid Bethany would throw her out for pushing too hard and for snooping. She'd have to make that call to Child Protective Services after all, opting for sympathy for the time being.

"That's a shitty crack in the system to fall through."

"Tell me about it. But you didn't come here to listen to my troubles. I guess you want to talk about Joanie."

"If you don't mind."

Bethany cocked her head to one side. "Quit pretending that I've got a choice. Let's go back outside. I need a cigarette."

They sat in the folding chairs. Bethany lit up, exhaling a long plume of smoke.

"See there? I don't smoke in the trailer because I know that's bad for Charlotte."

"Good for you. When did you find out about Joanie?"

"Friday afternoon, just after I got to work. The supervisor called me in to her office. There was a detective waiting for me and he told what happened and asked me to go to the morgue to identify Joanie's body."

"That must have been quite a shock," Alex said.

"Not so much. With her, it was always a matter of when, not if, she'd end up like that. I told her so till I was blue in the face, but she wouldn't listen. She'd get that drug addict's dreamy look and say someday she was gonna find a guy who'd take her away from all that, and I'd ask her how that was gonna happen when all the guys she met just wanted her to suck their dicks, swallow, and get the hell out of their cars."

"Sounds like you two argued a lot."

"Pretty much all we did. I shoulda thrown her out twenty different times, but she was my sister and no matter what she did, I couldn't turn my back on her. "

"Must have been hard on Charlotte."

Bethany nodded and took a drag on her cigarette. "Hard on all of us."

Whatever grief Bethany felt was too tied up in anger and resignation to find its way to the surface, but Alex could see hints of it in her unsteady hands and glistening eyes.

"How did Joanie end up on the street?"

"You want the whole father-raped-her-strung-out-junkie sob story or you want me to just cut to the chase and tell you that selling her pussy and trading blow jobs for crystal was the only thing she was ever halfway good at?"

"I get the picture. Did she ever try rehab?"

Bethany laughed. "Shit! Whenever it was too cold to be outside and she was too mad at me to come home."

"How'd she pay for that?"

"Medicaid, except for when she did a stint at Fresh Start, that fancy place up north of the airport."

Alex was familiar with it. Fresh Start was the closest thing to the Betty Ford Clinic in the Kansas City area, drawing an affluent clientele from around the region. Medicaid patients didn't fit their preferred patient profile.

"How'd she pay for a place like that?"

Bethany took another drag on her cigarette, lifting her chin and blowing out the smoke. "I wouldn't know."

Alex didn't believe her, not the way Bethany looked away and her voice took on a phony nonchalance. Rather than press the point, Alex filed it under leads to follow up on, knowing she could subpoena Fresh Start for the information."

"When was the last time you talked to her before she died?"

"The day she was killed. She called me all excited that she had some big date that night."

"Did she say with who?"

"No, and I didn't ask. I figured it was more of her bullshit."

"If she did have a date with someone special and she wanted to get all dressed up, would she come here to shower and change?"

"I don't know where else she'd go."

"Did the detective tell you that Joanie wasn't wearing anything when her body was found?" Bethany nodded. "Do you have any idea what she might have worn if she was going out for a special evening?"

"Only thing she had was a satiny black dress she said always showed off her tits and ass real nice."

"Do you know if that's what she was wearing that night?"

"Must have been because when I came home from the morgue, I gathered all her things and took them to Goodwill and I didn't see that dress."

Rossi's investigative report didn't mention finding the dress or any other clothing belonging to Joanie.

"Did the detective ask you about what Joanie might have been wearing?"

"No. Only thing he asked me was if it was Joanie lying in the morgue. When I told him it was her, he said not to worry 'cause they got the guy that did it."

Bethany took a final pull on her cigarette, the smoke curling around her until a wisp of air coming through the trees blew it away. She turned in her chair, facing Alex, her brow furrowed.

"You think maybe she really did have a date that night and was wearing that dress when she was killed?"

"Maybe."

"That fella they arrested, what'd he do with the dress?"

"I don't think he did anything with it. He was living in a tent down in Liberty Park. That's where they had sex, but he says he didn't rape her. She told him that she had to go home to get cleaned up for some big date. That was the last time he saw her."

Bethany gave her a long look. "So you really think he's not the one who killed her?"

"I haven't seen all the evidence the police have against him, but at least that part of his story matches up to what Joanie told you."

Bethany dropped the cigarette on the ground and clasped her hands in her lap.

"Joanie always did look good in that dress."

She lowered her chin, quiet at first. Her chest began to swell, her shoulders heaving. She snaked her arms around her middle, trying to hold back her grief, then giving in and sobbing.

"I shoulda been there. I shoulda been there."

Alex put her hand on Bethany's shoulder. "Been where?"

Bethany lifted her head, tears streaming down her face. "In the garage the first time our daddy raped her. On the street the first time she traded her pussy for dope. I shoulda been there, but I wasn't. She was my baby sister and I shoulda been there. I shoulda saved her."

She began to cough, a convulsive smoker's hacking that forced her to stop crying. When the cough subsided, she stood, red-eyed and out of breath, ashamed that she'd broken down in front of Alex. She lit another cigarette, putting her armor back on.

"You can go. We're done here."

"Almost. Who stays with Charlotte when you're at work?"

Bethany folded her arms against her breasts. "That child is ten years old. She don't need nobody to stay with her."

"Of course not."

Alex walked away, stopping and turning around when she reached the end of the concrete slab. Bethany was standing at the trailer door, one foot on the step, watching her.

"You've got five thousand dollars sitting on your kitchen counter. That would buy a lot of therapy for Charlotte."

Bethany glared at her, drawing deeply on her cigarette and exhaling the smoke through her nose.

"You come snooping around here again, you'll wish you hadn't."

"Is that money yours or Joanie's?"

Bethany flicked the butt on the ground and opened the door to the trailer.

"Doesn't matter anymore, now, does it?"

THIRTY-EIGHT

Pieces were lining up, even if they weren't quite falling into place for Alex as she drove away. Joanie Sutherland had a benefactor concerned enough about her to pay for a rehab stint at an exclusive treatment center. She was excited enough about meeting someone special the night she was killed to put on her one good dress. And Bethany had five thousand dollars in crisp hundreds sitting on her kitchen counter. Chances were those dots connected in a straight line to Joanie's killer.

Her benefactor may have started out smitten, pretending he was Richard Gere in *Pretty Woman* or, if he was old and proper enough, Rex Harrison in *My Fair Lady*. Joanie latched onto him, street-smart enough to know a good thing when she saw one, leveraging sex for rehab, then tacking on a premium to keep their relationship a secret, adding blackmail to prostitution. Her benefactor ran a cost-benefit analysis and decided he could no longer afford her. End of a sad but familiar story. The good news was that, if Alex was right, Jared Bell was innocent.

Had Rossi not made up his mind that Jared was the killer, he might have actually done an investigation that would have painted the same picture. But he didn't, which brought Alex back to the night in Judge West's barn when he told her that Jared was her new client. She suspected then that the judge was fronting for someone who wanted this case closed in a hurry, and now she wondered whether Rossi's decision not to look past Jared for a suspect was part of that effort. She couldn't picture Rossi conniving with the judge, but a year ago she would have said the same thing about herself.

Proving all of that wouldn't be easy. Judge West wasn't going to find religion and confess his sins, and he wasn't going to give up whomever he was protecting. The same was true for Rossi if his hands were dirty. Bethany knew more than she was willing to say, maybe even knowing who killed her sister. But five thousand dollars was a lot of money, and if there was more where that came from, it might be enough to soothe her grief and guilt over her sister's death.

Alex called Grace Canfield, leaving a message with a to-do list when Grace didn't pick up. Subpoena Joanie's records from Fresh Start and find out who paid for her treatment. Check Joanie's rap sheet to find out who posted her bail. Track down her street sisters and ask them if they knew Joanie's sugar daddy's name.

If none of that panned out, there was still Charlotte. Like a lot of autistic kids, the girl was a wanderer. A couple of years before, Alex had defended a father who was charged with felony child endangerment for not preventing his autistic son from sneaking out of the house at night. The boy was found at the bottom of a neighbor's swimming pool. The boy's doctor testified that nearly half of parents with an autistic child aged four or older said their child had tried to leave a safe place at least once and one in four said their child had disappeared long enough to cause concern.

Bethany must have been searching for Charlotte the day Alex found her playing in Rock Creek. That she was playing in the exact spot where Joanie's body had been found could have been a coincidence, but Alex didn't have faith in random chance on that order of magnitude. Since Bethany left Charlotte alone when she went to work, Charlotte might have gone out the night Joanie was killed and might have been playing in Liberty Park, maybe even in the creek, when the killer dumped Joanie's body.

If so, Charlotte might be able to identify the killer, assuming Alex could get her to talk.

It was midafternoon and Alex was famished. She headed to Hamburger Mary's near the southwest edge of the downtown. The chain was known for its gay founders, openness to diversity, and knockout burgers, though Alex favored the GLBT, which added guacamole to the traditional BLT in a tasty salute to her world.

Her cell phone rang as she pulled into the parking lot on Southwest Boulevard, but it wasn't the phone resting in the cup holder next to the steering wheel. It was the burner phone she'd set in the console between the driver and passenger seats, the caller ID displaying *Unknown* instead of a name.

She picked up the phone, unable to tell whether her hand was shaking because the phone was vibrating or because her insides were quaking. Judge West and his wife, Millie, were the only people who had the number for the burner phone. Millie had no reason to call. When the judge called her from his office, the familiar phone number showed up on caller ID, and when he called her from his home, his name was displayed.

Either the caller had misdialed or someone else had her number, and she didn't want to answer without knowing who that might be. She hadn't set up voice messaging for the phone, and since the caller was unknown, the phone wouldn't capture the caller's number. She stared at the phone, transfixed, waiting for it to stop ringing. Most people's phones had voice mail. If it was a wrong number and there wasn't an option to leave a message, odds were the caller would realize her error and not try again. If it wasn't a wrong number, the caller would keep trying.

The phone quieted. Alex silently counted to ten, easing the phone back onto the console like it was fragile, jolting so hard when it rang again that she banged her head against her seat's headrest and dropped the phone on the floor of the car. Unlatching her seat belt, she leaned forward, groping with one hand around her feet, accidentally kicking the phone beneath the seat. Cursing, she opened the car door, slid onto the asphalt parking lot on her knees, and stuck her head inside the car, peering under the seat. She grabbed the phone and answered.

"Who is this?"

"Why is Rossi asking me about our relationship?" Judge West asked.

Alex began to shake, her voice uneven. "I have no idea."

"Don't forget that if I go down, you go down with me."

Alex heard footsteps approaching from behind her. "Like that's news. I gotta go. Someone's coming."

The footsteps stopped. She could feel someone standing over her.

"Are you praying, throwing up, or just hiding from me?" Bonnie asked.

Alex shoved the phone under the seat and grabbed the inside of the car door, pulling herself up, her gut in full-tilt trampoline mode, a hot flash racing through her.

"I dropped my phone."

Bonnie pointed to the phone in the cup holder. "There's your phone. Is that the best you can do?"

Alex's face was so warm she thought her eyeballs would catch on fire.

"And yes," Bonnie added. "You're blushing like your mother just caught you playing with yourself."

"I can explain."

"Me first. Sit down. In the car, not on the pavement."

Bonnie walked around to the passenger side and got in. Alex stared at her. She wasn't wearing makeup. Her eyes were red and puffy. Her hair was pulled back, held in place by a black headband. She was wearing faded jeans and a heavily pilled crewneck sweater. The only other time Alex had seen her leave the house looking like that was when they had to evacuate in the middle of the night because of a gas leak.

"You wouldn't answer my calls, so I had to track you down. I looked at your credit card charges online to find out you were staying at the Residence Inn at Twenty-Ninth and Main."

"You did what?"

"Don't be so surprised. Did you think I was just going to sit back and do nothing? And in case you forgot, I know where you keep your list of passwords. I wanted to know where you were staying so I wouldn't worry as much. I hear that Residence Inn is nice. It's across the street from Penn Valley Park. I know you love to run there, but please don't go at night. It's not safe."

Alex blinked, her mouth half-open, dumbfounded. "It's okay."

"I drove by a couple of times but I was afraid to knock. I didn't want you to think I was stalking you."

"You mean you didn't want me to know that you were stalking me."

Bonnie took a breath, smiling. "Yeah. That. And I thought you needed time and space, but that was Saturday and this is Monday and I talked to Grace and she said she didn't know where you were, but I know how much you like to eat here so I took a chance and I've been sitting at a table in the front window since eleven this morning and—"

Alex stopped her. "I'm not coming back."

Bonnie sniffed. "I know. Not now anyway. Maybe never. But you can't just walk out like that without…without me telling you something."

"I know you love me. I love you too, but that's not what this is about."

"I do know that, but you've got some crazy idea what loving someone means, so just be quiet and listen for a minute."

Alex nodded. "Okay."

"I'm glad you told me everything. I know you think you did some terrible things and I'm not saying you're wrong about that, even if I'd like to think I'd have shot Dwayne Reed if it had been me instead of you. And the whole thing with the judge and your clients, well, I won't lie. That's…" She shook her head. "That's a real mess. And shutting me out, that's a huge problem in the trust department even if I get why you did it." She made a quarter turn, facing Alex. "You carried all this crap by yourself for the last year and you can see how well that worked out, but you can't fix it now by running away from me, from us. I don't know anything about the law or what you have to do to set things right or even if you can. I don't know if you'll lose your job, your law license, or go to jail, and I don't care. All I know is that I love you and I'll be by your side every step of the way if you'll let me. And if you don't come home, I'll find you no matter where you go."

She leaned over, kissed Alex on the cheek, got out of the car, and walked away, not looking back.

THIRTY-NINE

Interrogating a suspect was like putting on a play where everyone but the suspect knew their lines. The other actors had to be rehearsed and ready and the stage had to be set to keep the suspect unbalanced, desperate to catch the right cue.

Rossi liked flashing his badge in front of the suspect's family, coworkers, or nosy neighbors and asking if there was someplace private they could talk. Catching suspects cold, he'd watch them stammer and stutter, littering their stories with tissue-thin lies that would trap them later.

Knocking on a suspect's door and telling him they were going downtown for questioning could be just as effective. Whether the suspect spent the ride asking his own questions or stewing in silence, the uncertainty softened him up. And if it didn't, the perp walk from the car to the interrogation room with cops holding each arm and dozens of heads tracking every step made all but the most hardened thug afraid they would mess themselves. And having met him at Robin's house, Rossi knew there was nothing hardened about Ted Norris.

Rossi wanted to know as much as he could about Norris before he asked the first question. He wanted to know his work history, his criminal history, and his financial status. He wanted to have copies of the restraining order from the divorce and the one Sonia Steele had obtained, for the moment when Norris denied ever threatening her. He wanted surveillance video from the parking lot where Norris rear-ended Robin's car, for when he claimed that never happened.

More than anything else, he wanted Norris's car. He pulled Norris's license and vehicle registration records. The car was a black six-year-old Camry, not the white Ford Escort Norris had been driving when Rossi escorted him out of Robin's house a few days ago.

Putting all of that together took time, so Mitch Fowler grudgingly assigned a couple of detectives to sit on Norris and make sure he didn't run, warning Rossi that Norris better be their guy or the overtime was coming out of Rossi's paycheck, an empty threat Rossi ignored. By Tuesday morning, less than twenty-four hours after he met with Sonia Steele, Rossi had everything he wanted except for Norris's car.

The surveillance video from the parking lot confirmed that Norris had been driving the Camry when that accident happened. The detectives babysitting Norris reported seeing only the Escort, so Rossi had dispatch issue a be-on-the-lookout for the Camry. When the BOLO didn't turn up anything overnight, Fowler ordered Rossi to bring Norris in for questioning.

The detectives watching Norris banged on his door Tuesday morning at seven o'clock. They hammered loud and long enough to rouse the neighbors on either side before Norris opened up. They let him throw on some clothes and brought him in, bleary-eyed and hungover, depositing him in an interrogation room. Rossi watched him through the two-way mirror. Unshaven and disheveled, Norris gazed around the room, drummed his fingers on the table, and then laid his head down using his folded arms as a pillow. Rossi poured a cup of coffee and joined him.

"Good morning, Mr. Norris."

Norris raised his head, squinting at Rossi. "You're the cop from the other night?"

"Detective Rossi. Thought you could use this. It's not exactly hair of the dog, but it's the next best thing."

Rossi put the cup of coffee on the table in front of Norris, who raised it to his mouth, inhaling the aroma before taking a sip.

"What am I doing here? The other guys, all they'd tell me is that it was something to do with Robin."

"That's right. We're making progress in our investigation, but we need your help to clear up a few things."

Charlie Wheeler knocked on the door and stepped inside, right on schedule.

"Mr. Norris, I'm Detective Wheeler. I did the reconstruction on your ex-wife's accident. Sorry to interrupt, but I need to talk to Detective Rossi for a minute. Won't take long. Do you mind waiting?"

Norris took another sip of coffee. "No. Take your time. You got a newspaper or something?"

"I'll see what I can do," Wheeler said.

Mitch Fowler met Rossi and Wheeler out in the hall.

"How long are you going to let him sit like that?" Fowler asked.

"Couple of hours at least," Rossi said. "I'd like to find his car before I go at him."

"Still nothing on the BOLO," Wheeler said. "Airport police are still checking all the lots in case he stashed it out there, but there are thousands of cars for them to look at."

"Why would he leave the car at the airport?" Fowler asked. "Why not take it to a body shop and get rid of the evidence?"

"Because he knows we'll check the body shops and they all take before-and-after photographs for insurance purposes," Wheeler said. "He could take it to a chop shop that handles stolen cars if he knew where to find one or he could sell it to a salvage yard for scrap, but they'd probably just take his money and sell it to someone else since it's worth more as a used car than a hunk of steel. So hiding it in an airport parking lot until he can figure out how to get rid of it isn't a half-bad idea."

"Checking all those parking lots could take a couple of days," Fowler said. "And if he didn't leave it there, he could have parked in any number of garages or lots on either side of the state line. Are you going to search all of them?"

"If we have to," Rossi said. "But I like the airport because once he ditched the car he could take a shuttle to the terminal and a different one back into town."

"What about the Escort?" Fowler asked.

"I ran the tag. He rented it from Enterprise. They delivered it to his apartment the morning after Robin was killed."

"And if he left the Camry at the airport," Wheeler said, "there may be video of him driving into the lot and getting out of the car."

Fowler thought for a moment. "Okay. I'll send some uniforms to the airport to help out. You can let him sit for two hours, but then you go at him, car or no car. If you don't have enough to hold him, cut him loose. I don't want any more goddamn harassment lawsuits."

Two hours later, Rossi and Wheeler went back to the interrogation room. Norris was standing in front of the two-way mirror, cupping his hands around his eyes, staring at the glass. He turned around when the door opened.

"You guys get off watching me sitting in here, scratching my nuts waiting for somebody to tell me what the hell I'm doing here?"

"Sit down, Mr. Norris," Rossi said.

"I'm not doing shit until you tell me what's going on."

"What's going on is that you are going to sit down and answer our questions."

"Maybe I should call my lawyer first."

"That's your right at any time, but it would sure make me wonder why you'd think you need a lawyer before you even know what we want to talk to you about. Wouldn't that make you wonder, Detective Wheeler?"

"Sure would, unless Mr. Norris is hiding something."

Norris raised both hands above his waist, palms out. "Hey, I'm not hiding anything. You guys wake me up at the crack of dawn and drag me down here, leave me sitting here for half the morning…anybody would want to know what it's all about. Doesn't mean I'm hiding anything, 'cause I don't have anything to hide."

"Good," Rossi said. "So there's no reason you can't sit down and answer our questions."

Norris shrugged and took a seat. "Fire away."

FORTY

"Where's your Camry?" Rossi asked.

Norris flinched, his eyebrows bouncing. "My Camry?"

"Yeah. The one you were driving when you rear-ended Robin a couple of weeks ago."

Norris leaned back in his chair, arms folded over his chest. "That's what this is about? Hey, I can explain. That was an accident. My fault, that's for sure, but it was an accident. I was looking at my phone and the next thing I know, boom, she stopped in front of me and I ran into her."

"Answer my question. Where's your Camry?"

"Did my oldest, Donny, put you up to this? His mother is dead and he's jerking me around to pay for the damage to her car from that parking lot fender bender even after her car was totaled in the accident when she was killed? Unbelievable! I told him I didn't have insurance."

"Donny has nothing to do with this, Mr. Norris. I'm going to ask you one more time, and if you don't answer me, Detective Wheeler and I will be back to wondering why you're refusing to cooperate with us. Where's your Camry?"

"Refusing to cooperate? Are you kidding? I'm here, aren't I? I didn't call a lawyer, did I?"

"But you're trying awfully hard not to answer what should be a very simple question, which doesn't put you in a good light."

Norris slid down in his chair, scratched his nose, thumped his fingers on the table again, and sat up. "Okay, okay. Somebody stole my car."

"When?"

Norris tugged at his chin, thinking. "Last week. Must have been Wednesday night. I came out of my apartment Thursday morning and it was gone."

"Did you file a police report?"

Norris shook his head. "No. No police report."

"Why not?"

Norris turned away, staring at the two-way mirror, squirming in his chair. He took a deep breath. "Look, if I tell you, you gotta help me out."

Rossi leaned forward, hoping Norris was about to confess in record-breaking time.

"I'll do whatever I can to help you, but you have to help yourself by telling me what happened to the car and why you need my help."

Norris's eyes darted back and forth from Rossi to Wheeler and back again until he slapped one hand on the table. "Shit! I knew it was a mistake to get involved with that guy. I knew it. I knew it. I knew it. I'm such a fucking moron!"

"What guy?"

"Richie Vigliaturo."

Rossi sat back. "Richie the Vig? The loan shark?"

Norris scrunched his eyes and rubbed the sides of his face with both hands. "Yeah. I was broke and a friend of a friend hooked me up with Richie. He loaned me a few bucks and I gave him the title to my car as security. He said if I got behind, he'd take my car before he broke my legs."

"And you got behind."

"Yeah. I owed him every Monday, but I missed last Monday, so he took my car. That's why you gotta help me out. I missed this Monday too, and I don't want my legs broken."

"Wait here," Rossi said, signaling to Wheeler. "We'll be back."

"Hey, you think you can help me?"

"I think that if Richie repossessed your car, you're the luckiest guy in the world."

Rossi and Wheeler retreated to the break room, each pouring a cup of coffee.

"What do you think?" Wheeler asked.

"I think if Richie boosted the car before Robin was killed, he won't mind telling us, and if he took it after she was killed, he'll give it up in a heartbeat to prove he had nothing to do with her death. He's not interested in that kind of trouble."

"Yeah, but if he took the car last week, what are the odds he still has it this week?"

"Next to zero. I'll give him a call."

"What, you got him on speed dial?"

Rossi grinned. "Let's just say he'll take my call and leave it at that."

"Hang on. Let's say Richie didn't take the car and we find it out at the airport or wherever and we can prove that it's the car that knocked Robin off the road."

"Then we charge Norris with first-degree murder."

"I know, but—"

"But what?" Rossi asked.

"How did they end up out on that stretch of road? I know that Norris lives off of Barry Road, but that raises more questions than answers. Was Robin at his apartment? What was she doing there? According to the kids, their folks went out of their way to avoid each other. And if she was there, what happened? Did they have a fight and she ran out and he chased her out to the boonies? Or did Norris just happen to see her driving around his neighborhood and decide to run her off the road?" Wheeler scratched his head. "I don't know. It doesn't feel right to me."

"All we have to do is prove it was Norris's Camry and that he was behind the wheel. How and why they ended up out there doesn't change the fact that they did. I'm going to call Richie."

Wheeler's cell phone pinged with a text message before Rossi punched in Richie's number. Wheeler opened the message and looked at Rossi.

"Don't bother. They found the car at the airport. Take a look at this."

He passed the phone to Rossi. Photographs of the car from all four sides were attached to the text message. The license tag matched the registration records Rossi had in his file. The front end was creased and dented, though the extent of the damage wasn't clear from the photograph.

"I've got to get out there," Wheeler said. "I don't want anybody touching that car until I've gone over every inch. Then I'll have it towed to our garage so I can see if the damage pattern fits with the damage to Robin's car."

"Will you be able to separate the damage from the parking lot accident from the Barry Road collision?"

"Won't know until I get a look at it." Wheeler's phone pinged with another text. "Airport security says we can have a look at their video whenever we're ready."

"I'm like lunch meat," Rossi said. "I'm always ready. You take the car and I'll check out the video."

"What about Norris?"

"Have somebody bring him a newspaper."

FORTY-ONE

Kansas City International Airport was twenty minutes north of downtown, enough time for Rossi to think about what Wheeler had said. Figuring out how Robin and her ex ended up where they did was an important part of the case, but only if Rossi could prove that Norris had run her off the road. He'd get to the how and why later.

The airport was laid out in three terminals, A, B, and C. Airport police headquarters was in Terminal A. Rossi's cell phone rang as he pulled into a parking place across from the terminal. When he saw Bonnie Long's name displayed, he broke into a grin.

"Dr. Long, what can I do for you?"

"We need to talk."

"About what?"

"I think you know. Tell me where and when and I'll be there."

"I'm a little busy at the moment."

"It's important. Please."

"Okay, there's a bar not far from—"

"No. Not at a bar or at the hospital or at police headquarters. Someplace private, just you and me."

"Okay. You got any suggestions?"

Bonnie was silent for a moment. "Be at my house at five o'clock."

"I'll do that."

Rossi clicked off the call. He'd driven a wedge between Alex and Bonnie, not knowing whether it would pay off, congratulating himself now that it had. He hadn't been able to get the truth from Alex, but hearing it from Bonnie would be the next best thing. From the start, he'd focused on proving Alex had murdered Dwayne Reed, uncertain what he'd do next. Now he knew. He'd find out whether Alex and Judge West had made some kind of deal to ensure her acquittal. If they had, he'd put her away for as long as he could for obstruction of justice.

He was still grinning when an airport police officer escorted him into the video monitoring room and introduced him to Sergeant Libby Hellmann.

"You're looking pretty happy," Hellmann said.

"Just got some good news on another case."

"Well, let's see if we can make it two in a row. Your suspect's vehicle was found in the Economy B parking lot. Our cameras cover the entry to the lot and each aisle, looking north, south, east, and west."

"Can you track the car from when it entered the lot until it was parked?"

"We pieced it together from different cameras. I did a quick-and-dirty edit, so its kind of herky-jerky. I can put together a more seamless video once I know exactly what you need."

"Great. Let's have a look."

They sat in front of a monitor as Hellmann cued the video. The images were dark and grainy, but the lights in the parking lot provided enough illumination to make them out.

"See there," Hellmann said, freezing the screen. "That's your guy getting his ticket at the entrance to the lot. The time stamp shows it was ten thirty-five and eighteen seconds when he rolled in."

Robin Norris had called Alex Stone at ten fifteen, the instant before her car was struck. Ted Norris could have easily made it to the airport from the scene of the wreck in twenty minutes.

"That's a view of the driver's side of the car. How do you know it's the right one?"

"Once we confirmed the license tag, I worked backward from where he parked the car. I can show you the whole thing in reverse if you want."

"After I see it this way first. Can you zoom in on the driver? I can't make out much of his face."

"Sure."

Hellmann tapped on the zoom feature, but the larger the image got, the more indistinct it became, until it was just a jumble of pixels. She played with it until she found the right balance. The driver was wearing a ball cap pulled down low on his face. He was looking straight ahead, not at the camera.

"That your guy?"

Rossi took his time. "Can't tell. Run the rest of it."

The video tracked the car from the gate to a spot near one of the stops where shuttle buses picked up passengers and took them to the terminal. The driver parked the car between a tall SUV and a minivan but didn't get out of the car.

"What's he waiting for?" Rossi asked.

"You'll see."

Two minutes passed. Then a shuttle bus appeared. The driver got out of the Camry, head down and carrying a small duffel bag. He dropped something, bending down and out of the camera's range to pick it up, before walking to the bus and climbing on, never looking up so that a camera could capture his face. Hellmann froze the screen again.

"Son of a bitch," Rossi said. "It's like he had the whole thing planned. He picked the perfect parking place. The SUV and the minivan blocked the cameras. He waited for the shuttle to keep his time outside the car to a few seconds, and he never looked up. How did he know he'd find such a perfect parking place?"

"It's a big lot. With all those cars and all those bus stops, his chances of finding a parking place like that were pretty good."

"But he wouldn't have known that."

"Unless he was used to parking there. That lot is for Southwest, and they've got more flights out of here than any other carrier."

"Okay, run it in reverse."

Hellmann played it backward several times.

"That help any?"

"No. What about the bus? Can you track it?"

"Not all the way. We have cameras at the lot and at the terminal, but not in between. But we know how long it takes the driver to reach the terminal after leaving the lot, so I was able to pick the bus up again when it got there."

Hellmann resumed the video, following the bus as it stopped at the terminal.

"Usually there's not that much shuttle traffic at that time of night," she said, "but a couple of incoming flights had been delayed by bad weather, so there was a crowd waiting for the bus to pick them up and take them back to the economy lot."

Rossi watched as the bus stopped and people swarmed on and off, heads bobbing and weaving. Several people were wearing ball caps, and it was impossible to identify one from another. They played the sequence over and over so that Rossi could follow each person wearing a ball cap as he or she moved through the crowd. None of them matched the person who'd gotten out of the Camry, and none of them were carrying the same duffel.

"How could he just disappear like that?" Rossi asked.

"Beats me."

"Go back to the parking lot and zoom in on the duffel bag. Maybe we can pick something up that would identify it."

Hellman found the frames with the duffel bag, enlarging each one as much as possible without losing the image.

"It looks like there's some lettering and some kind of logo on the bag," Rossi said. "Can you make that any bigger?"

"Sure."

Hellman bracketed the side of the bag until they could make out the logo.

"I recognize that," she said. "I've got a bag just like it from Lands' End. The word on the bag is *solutioneering*. I use the bag for my workout gear when I go to the gym."

"What's it made out of?"

She shrugged. "Some kind of polyester."

"I want to talk to the driver. Maybe he remembers something."

"I'll have to find out who the driver was and when he has his next shift. We'll have him come in early so you can have some time with him. I'll call you when I know something."

"What about the shuttles that take people into town, to the hotels? Where do they pick up passengers?"

"Two lanes of traffic run past the terminal. The lane closest to the terminal is for people dropping off or picking up passengers and for the parking lot shuttles. There's a median that separates that lane from the outer lane. Hotel and rental car shuttles pick people up on that curb."

"Do your cameras cover that area too?"

"Right down to your shoelaces."

"Great. Show me the video from the outer curb at all three terminals for two hours beginning when the parking shuttle stopped at Terminal B. I want to see if whoever got out of the Camry took a shuttle home. And if you don't see anyone carrying that duffel, check every trash can and bathroom in the terminal."

"That will take a while even if I fast-forward. How much time do you have?"

Rossi looked at his watch. Ted Norris was waiting for him in the interrogation room and he had to be at Bonnie Long's house by five.

"Not enough to spend it here with you. Can you put together a tape that just includes anyone getting on a shuttle in that time frame?"

"Sure. I can e-mail it to you along with the video we just looked at, and I'll let you know if we find the duffel bag."

Rossi handed her a business card and stood, shaking his head as he stared at the screen. He'd expected to hit the jackpot and had shot craps instead.

"Thanks. My e-mail address is on the card."

"You lost your grin."

"Don't worry. I'll get it back."

FORTY-TWO

Grace Canfield was waiting in Alex's office when she arrived Tuesday morning.

"I'd say that you looked like something the cat dragged in, but you'd probably think it was a compliment," Grace said. "When are you going to get some sleep and comb your hair?"

Alex ran her fingers along her scalp. "Best I can do."

"You could put something on nicer than that army surplus you're wearing."

"These are cargo pants, not army surplus."

"Why can't you be one of those lipstick lesbians that dress nice, like Bonnie does?"

"Bonnie wears pants."

"Men's pants?"

"If you think all lesbians should look alike, why don't you look like Oprah Winfrey?"

"'Cause I don't have a hundred million dollars to help me get dressed every day, that's why."

Alex laughed.

"You are something else, Grace, you know that?"

"I'm just glad to see you smiling." She paused. "Did Bonnie get ahold of you?"

Alex sat at her desk. "We ran into each other yesterday."

"And?"

"What are you? My investigator or my mother?"

"What difference does it make? You need both."

Alex sighed. "I suppose you're right. We talked. Actually, Bonnie talked and I listened, and then she...she left."

"So are you two going to get back together?"

Alex pointed to the file Grace had in her hand. "I'd rather talk about whatever is in that file."

"Soon as you answer my question."

Alex scowled at her. "Grace..."

"Don't *Grace* me. Are you two getting back together?"

Alex sighed again. "We'll see."

Grace lit up. "Well, that's better than yesterday's 'never.' I served a subpoena on Fresh Start like you asked me. They told me that it takes a month to get copies of medical records and that they need a release signed by the patient. I told them they'd have to settle for a subpoena since the patient is dead and that I was going to haunt them every minute of every day it took to get those records, and they said we'd have them by tomorrow."

"I'm glad you're on my side. What about the rest?"

"I had one of my church ladies who's doing the street outreach go with me last night to talk to some of those girls since none of them know me. One girl, name of Chantelle, told us that Joanie did have a special friend, the way she put it."

"Did she have the special friend's name?"

"No. Only thing she knew was that this guy has been helping Joanie a long time."

"Helping her? Like something besides paying her for sex?"

"That's right. She said it wasn't a sex thing at all. More like a father thing."

"Did she know anything about Joanie meeting this guy the night she was killed?"

"Maybe. She said Joanie had trouble with a john earlier that day. Said the guy hurt her the way he..."

"Fucked her?"

"I wasn't going to use that language, but yes. Anyway, Joanie came crying to Chantelle and Chantelle told her it goes with the territory and Joanie said not for much longer 'cause she was getting off the street. Chantelle didn't think much of that because all the girls talk that way."

"Go back to Chantelle and see if we can get a line on this john. If he hurt her, that could explain the vaginal bruising the coroner found."

"I'll go back down there tonight. And I checked Joanie's arrest record. Most of the time, the judge let her go on her own recognizance. When she did have to post bond, she had enough cash that she didn't need help."

"How many prostitutes can post their own bond?"

"Just the ones that are making enough money and keeping it from their pimps."

"Do we know if Joanie had a pimp?"

"Chantelle said Joanie didn't have one as far as she knew."

"So Joanie's arrest records are a dead end."

"Maybe, maybe not. The first time she was arrested was eleven years ago. It was for possession with intent to sell."

"Which court was she in?"

"Clay County, up in Liberty. That's where she grew up. The prosecutors up there like to ask for shock jail time for first offenders and the judges are known for going along with that. Only Joanie got put in a diversion program over the prosecutor's objection."

"She must have had a good lawyer."

"That's the funny thing. She didn't have a lawyer."

"How could she be put in a diversion program without having a lawyer?"

"According to the court file, she entered a guilty plea at her arraignment and the judge put her in the diversion program. She stayed out of trouble for two years until she was arrested in Jackson County for prostitution."

"Who was the judge who put her in diversion?"

Grace opened her file, flipping through the pages. "Judge Anthony Steele. He moved up to the Court of Appeals not too long ago."

"Hmm. I wonder why he did that."

"You can ask him."

"Maybe I will. I'll call his office and see if I can get an appointment for today or tomorrow."

"You won't need an appointment."

"Why not?"

"Girl, don't you read your e-mail? Our big boss in the state capital decided she wanted to have a get-together honoring Robin's memory. It's this afternoon at four."

"Where?"

"Judge West's courtroom. And Judge Steele is going to speak. Meg Adler says we all got to be there."

"I wouldn't miss it."

FORTY-THREE

Alex walked down the hall to Robin's office. Meg Adler was there, packing up Robin's personal possessions, depositing her photographs of family and friends into a cardboard box. Buried on Sunday. Expunged on Tuesday. She cringed at how swiftly the world left the dead behind.

"What are you doing?"

Though it was obvious and Alex knew it had to be done, she had to ask, registering a small protest with her question, clinging to Robin however she could.

Meg looked up. "We need this office. I called Robin's oldest, Donny. He seems to be the one handling things for the family. I asked him what he wanted us to do with Robin's things and he said to box them up and send them to the house."

Alex nodded. "I can drop them off."

"That would be great. Have a seat. There's something I want to talk with you about."

Alex took a chair across from Robin's desk. "What's up?"

"They want me back in St. Louis next Monday."

"Okay. Is the director sending in another interim?"

"She'd like to avoid that. We're short staffed in every office as it is. But she has to conduct a search to fill the position and that's going to take some time."

"So what's the plan?"

Meg smiled. "The director would like you to be the interim."

Alex's jaw dropped. "Me? Are you kidding? I'm a trial lawyer, not an administrator."

"So was Robin before she started running this office. Turns out that Robin was planning on retiring at the end of the year and she'd already recommended you as her replacement. I've talked to everyone around here, and they'd like to see you in the job."

Meg's offer came at Alex faster than she could process it, as if she was hearing part of the discussion instead of getting the big picture. She was flattered but didn't like that Meg had floated her name without her permission, making her feel like she was trapped.

"You asked them before you asked me if I was even interested? What if I'm not? If I say no, everyone will think I let them down, and if the new boss is a jerk, they'll blame me for not taking the job."

"It wasn't like that at all. My first day here, I said I was going to talk to everyone to get a feel for the office. I asked them what kind of person they wanted to run the show and whether there was anyone they'd recommend. I never suggested you because I didn't want to bias what they told me, but you were the clear favorite. I would have asked you too, but you've been pretty scarce."

Alex stood and looked out the window, past the office towers, past the Missouri River, past the horizon. Her life had never been more unsettled, and Meg's offer had knocked one more pin out from under her.

"I don't know what to say."

Meg joined her at the window, putting her hand on Alex's shoulder. "Say that you'll do it. And say that you'll apply for the permanent position. That will make the search go a lot faster and reassure the lawyers and the staff."

Alex forced a weak smile. More pressure, just what she needed.

"Can I think about it for a few days?"

"Of course. Let me know by Friday. If you're not interested, I have to tell St. Louis that I'm staying and then I have to go buy more underwear. And you might as well take that box. I'm done with it."

FORTY-FOUR

Judge West's courtroom was crowded, a few bodies shy of shoulder to shoulder, a testament to how well liked and respected Robin was. From the number of lawyers and judges milling around, Alex figured the wheels of justice had ground to a halt.

Off to one side, she saw Kalena Greene and her boss, Tommy Bradshaw, chatting with Lee Goldberg, who ran the local Innocence Project. Goldberg was his usual histrionic self, arms flapping as he spoke. Kalena caught Alex's attention, rolling her eyes at Goldberg, and Alex pointed to a vacant spot at the back of the courtroom, gesturing to Kalena to join her. Kalena mouthed a thank-you and broke away.

"You rescued me," Kalena said. "As far as Goldberg is concerned, the jails are filled with innocent people."

"Including Jared Bell."

"You're worse than Goldberg. That case is tight."

"The only reason it's tight is that Rossi didn't look past Jared."

"You mean he didn't look past your client after he confessed and after he was found in possession of a crucifix the victim was wearing when she was murdered and after the coroner found evidence of rape and after your client admitted having sex with her."

"Consensual sex. He paid her with the crucifix, which I admit sounds creepy, and he took it back after he found her body because he intended to give it to Mathew Woodrell's daughter, which I admit sounds even creepier."

"Or crazy and crazier. Was Woodrell telling the truth about what happened to his daughter?"

"Let me put it this way. Jared told me the same story the army told Woodrell, and I believe Jared. He's so fucked-up from the war he thought Joanie was Ali Woodrell. He was in love with Ali and never would have hurt her."

"So what are you going to do? Use a post-traumatic stress disorder defense?"

"Only if I have to. He didn't rape or kill Joanie Sutherland, which is why you're going to end up dismissing the charges."

Kalena laughed. "I think I was better off listening to Goldberg."

"Laugh all you want now, because you won't be laughing when I get your case tossed out at the preliminary hearing."

"And why will Judge West, of all judges, toss my case?"

Alex preferred not to share her theories or her evidence with the prosecutor any sooner than she had to because that would only give the other side more time to blow up her defense. But she wanted to plant a seed of doubt in Kalena's mind, especially about Rossi's investigation.

"Here's what Rossi missed. Someone was looking out for Joanie Sutherland, someone she'd known for a long time. This person was giving her money but not for sex, probably because he thought he could turn her life around. He even paid for a private drug rehab stay."

"And then decided to kill her? Really? That's the best you can do? Why would he do that?"

"Because Professor Henry Higgins didn't like it when Eliza Doolittle turned out to be a blackmailer."

Kalena smirked. "And who's Henry Higgins in this fairy tale?"

Alex's attention was drawn away from Kalena when she saw Judge West and Judge Steele and a blond woman she didn't recognize emerge from Judge West's chambers.

"I'll let you know."

Alex wound her way through the crowd. Judge West saw her coming and motioned for her to join them.

"Alex Stone, say hello to Judge Anthony Steele and his bride, Sonia. Alex is one of the public defender's best and brightest."

Alex shook both their hands.

"I was at the state bar convention last spring when you presented a service award to Robin," she said to Judge Steele, not mentioning the photograph of them Robin had kept in her office.

"She deserved it," he said. "Her death is a terrible loss. She was a good friend."

"Our dearest friend," Sonia added.

"Alex was almost the last person to talk with Robin," Judge West said.

"Almost?" Sonia asked.

"Your Honor," Alex said, "I'm not sure we should be talking about that since there's an ongoing investigation."

The judge dismissed her hesitation. "Nonsense. Tony and I are judges, and Sonia, like all judicial wives, is an even higher authority. One of the few perks we get is being able to talk about things no one else can. According to the police, Robin called Alex's cell phone a second or two before her accident, but Alex didn't hear the phone ring."

"Oh, my," Sonia said, her hand covering her mouth. "Did Robin leave you a message?"

"I'd rather not talk about it, if you don't mind."

"Hell," West said, "she didn't even tell me what was in the message, so it must be pretty important."

Sonia squeezed Alex's arm. "You're absolutely right not to say anything. Don't let him bully you. Let the police do their job without us gossiping about it. Robin deserves at least that much." She glanced past Alex and turned to her husband. "That's Paul Levine standing all by himself in a corner. I've got to talk with him. He's stalling on an agreement my client needs signed."

"And I've got to find my bailiff," Judge West said, both of them walking away, leaving Alex alone with Judge Steele.

"Despite what my good friend Bill West says, you're right not to discuss that phone call. Not when there's a pending investigation."

"Thank you, Your Honor. When in doubt, keep your mouth shut, right?"

He laughed, and when he did, Alex saw the same twinkle in his eye that she'd seen in the photograph of him and Robin. He had an easygoing manner that invited you in, nothing like the stiff, aloof style of so many who wore a black robe.

"It's funny, you and I running into each other," Alex said.

"And why's that?"

"Your name came up earlier today in one of my cases."

"Do you have an appeal pending?"

"No. This goes back to when you were on the trial bench in Clay County."

"So it's an appeal of one my old cases?"

"No, but it does involve one of your cases from more than ten years ago. A young woman was arraigned in your court and pled guilty, and you put her in a diversion program."

Judge Steele smiled. "That happened more times than I can remember. Used to drive the prosecutors crazy that I gave kids a second chance, but it made the defense lawyers pretty happy."

Alex chuckled. "And not too many judges are known for doing that. Only this young woman didn't have a lawyer."

Steele's eyes clouded for a moment. "Well, that's a bit unusual, but I imagine it happened from time to time. That's all so long ago, I'm afraid I don't remember the case."

"Don't worry. It's probably more interesting than it is important. Unfortunately, she didn't take advantage of the second chance you gave her, because a couple of years later she was turning tricks on Independence Avenue and last week she was murdered. I'm defending the man accused of raping and killing her."

Steele arched his eyebrows. "Is that the woman whose body was found in the creek? I read about that in the paper."

"Yes, that's the woman. I was going over her arrest records this morning and saw the case you had with her."

"Well, it's a small world. And a sad one at times, like today."

"At least there are people like you who give people like her second chances. In fact, you weren't the only one who did. She had a drug problem and someone paid for her to go to Fresh Start, you know, that private rehab facility up north."

He cleared his throat. "That was very generous."

"We've subpoenaed her medical records from Fresh Start. I imagine the name of whoever paid for her treatment will be in her file."

Alex was fishing, not knowing whether Steele would bite.

"Is that relevant to your case?"

"It could be."

"How?"

"I shouldn't say. If my client is convicted, you may be one of the judges to hear his appeal, and I'd hate for you to have to recuse yourself because of our conversation."

"I wish all lawyers exercised as much discretion. It was nice talking to you."

Alex shook his hand, holding him there for a moment, looking him in the eye. "The woman's name was Joanie Sutherland, if that means anything to you."

He pulled his hand away, pressing his lips together, opening them just enough to answer.

"No. Nothing at all."

FORTY-FIVE

Rossi met Wheeler on the window side of the two-way mirror into the interrogation room where Ted Norris was sitting, rolling a soda can between his hands, a wadded-up sandwich wrapper from Subway and an empty bag of chips strewn on the table. He put the can down, fingered his nose, and stuck his hand down his pants, rearranging his package.

Wheeler said, "I talked to the detective who brought him lunch. He told me Norris bitched and moaned until he got something to eat. Since then, he quit complaining but he's been doing a lot of squirming."

"You think he's more worried about us or Richie the Vig?" Rossi said.

"We still need to find out if Norris is blowing smoke about Richie, but if he's telling the truth, he's more worried about us if he's got a lick of sense. Richie might break his legs, but he could get the needle for killing his ex."

"Was it his car?"

"The damage to the front end of the Camry matches up nice and neat to the back end of Robin's car."

"You're sure about it, even with the damage from when Norris hit Robin's car in the parking lot?"

"Yeah. The nature and extent of the damage depends on how much force there was and what part of the vehicle absorbed the impact. The parking lot hit was low speed and the impact was bumper to bumper. The collision on Barry Road was at a high speed. The Camry had a license plate on the front end and one of the bolts holding it in place gouged the rear of Robin's car above the bumper. I found traces of paint on the bolt that matched the paint from Robin's car. So, yeah, it was the Camry. No doubt about that."

"Proving it was his car isn't the same as proving he was driving it."

"Why, did you see something on the airport video makes you think it wasn't him?"

"Nothing conclusive. Whoever was behind the wheel was careful not to look at any of the cameras," Rossi said, summarizing what was on the video. "Look at Norris sitting in there, picking his nose and scratching his nuts, and tell me he's smart enough to pull off that disappearing act."

"Man could be putting on the dummy act."

"Let's go find out."

Norris was slouched in his chair but bolted upright when Rossi and Wheeler breezed into the interrogation room.

"Did you talk to Richie? Is everything cool with him? 'Cause if it isn't, I'll turn state's evidence on his ass and you guys can put me in witness relocation."

"It's called witness protection and I couldn't tell you," Rossi said.

Norris came out of his chair. "Whaddaya mean?"

"Sit down." Rossi stayed on his feet, glaring at him until Norris did what he was told. "We haven't talked to Richie."

Norris started to get up again but caught himself. "Why not? What the hell have you been doing all this time?"

Rossi and Wheeler took their seats.

"Taking a look at your car."

"My car? You found my car? Damn! That's great!"

Norris thumped his hand on the table and sat back, grinning.

"Actually," Wheeler said, "not so great, at least not for you. The damage to the front end of your car fits like a jigsaw puzzle to the damage on the back of your ex-wife's car."

"Hey, I told you what happened in that parking lot. I wasn't paying attention and she stopped short."

Rossi said, "We're not talking about the parking lot."

"Then what are you…" Norris's voice trailed off and his eyes bugged out as he realized what they meant. He raised his hands. "Hey, no way, man! No fucking way did I run Robin off that road!"

"Where were you between ten p.m. and midnight last Tuesday night?"

Norris's eyes fluttered, his mouth hanging half open. "Uh, uh…I was home."

"Anybody with you?"

Norris shuddered. "No, man. I was alone, but c'mon, you gotta be kidding if you think I'd do that."

Wheeler started to say something, but Rossi put his hand out, stopping him. He wanted to see how far Norris would go and how real it would look. Norris pulled his chair back to the table, propping his head on his fist, eyes closed, pinching the bridge of his nose, staying like that for a moment, until he took a deep breath and slumped in his chair.

"Look, she and I, we had our share of fights over the years, but she was my kids' mother. I'd never do something like that. You got to believe me."

"No, you look, Ted," Rossi said, ticking the evidence off. "She got a restraining order against you during the divorce because you threatened her, and she got another one last week after what happened in the parking lot. You were out of a job and so broke you borrowed money you couldn't pay back from a loan shark. You asked Robin for money and she turned you down. Now you're totally fucked because Richie the Vig is going to take your car and break your legs, so you call Robin, beg her to bring money to you at your apartment. She shows up and tells you no means no. You have a fight. She runs out of the apartment and jumps in her car. You go after her in your car. She doesn't know her way around your neighborhood and she's so scared she turns the wrong way on Barry Road and ends up out in the country. By now, you're so pissed you can't see straight, and when you catch up to her, it's full speed ahead and bam. So, yeah, I think you could do something like that and I think you did."

Norris gripped the edge of the table with both hands. "No, I'm telling you, man. It wasn't me. Yeah, I asked her for the money and she said no just like she'd always done, but that was all over the phone. And she wouldn't set foot in my apartment on a bet. No way, no how."

"Then who stole your car, ran Robin off the road, and dumped your car at the airport?"

Norris let go of the table. "The airport? That where you found my car?"

"Yeah. Economy Lot B. Ever since 9/11, the airport's been blanketed with cameras. You can't fart without it being recorded. We've got you on videotape, Ted, parking the car, getting out, and taking the shuttle bus to the terminal."

Norris sat back, arms folded against his chest. "Okay, you don't believe me, then show me the fucking video, because there's no fucking way that's me."

"The camera doesn't lie."

"Yeah, but cops do, and you aren't gonna scare me into admitting something I didn't do, so take your fucking videotape and shove it up your ass."

Rossi stood, lunging toward Norris, who scooted backward, his chair toppling over, leaving him sprawled on the floor. Wheeler grabbed Rossi's arm, but Rossi shook him off and stormed out of the room, slamming the door behind him. Norris got to his knees, keeping his chair in front of him.

"What the fuck is the matter with that guy?"

Wheeler said, "I'm sorry about that. He gets wound up. You're lucky it wasn't just the two of you in here."

"I oughta file a complaint against the son of a bitch."

Wheeler nodded. "That's your right. I can give you the number for the Office of Community Complaints or the website where you can download the complaint form and e-mail it in. There'll be an investigation and you'll have to provide a formal statement. After that, there'll be a mediation and conciliation process."

Norris rubbed his chin. "You let me outta here and I'll forget the whole thing."

"You're going to have to help me before I can do that."

"What do you want from me? I didn't do it and I don't know who did."

"Can you think of anyone who might want to harm Robin?"

He rolled his eyes. "Are you kidding? The woman was a saint. Her only sin was marrying me."

"You only get to be a saint after you're dead. What about someone she'd defended who wasn't happy with the job she did?"

"I don't know. We've been divorced a long time and we didn't talk much. When we did, it wasn't about her job. It was mostly about me fucking something up."

"What about Robin's social life? Was she seeing anyone?"

"Maybe. My youngest, Kimmy—she's the only one that talks to me—a few months back she told me her mom had a new boyfriend but she was keeping it a secret."

"How did Kim find out about it?"

"I don't know, but Kimmy's smart—scary smart. Not much gets past that girl. If she says Robin was seeing someone, you can bet on it."

"Did she say who it was?"

"When I asked her, she said she didn't know, but I got the feeling she did but didn't want to tell me, so I didn't push. I wasn't looking to stir anything up, and if Robin had something going on, then good for her."

Wheeler had asked Robin's children whether she was seeing anyone and they'd said that their mother dated occasionally but hadn't had a boyfriend in a long time. Except for Kim. She hadn't commented. Wheeler didn't think much of it at the time since Kim had said very little in response to any of his questions. He attributed her sullen demeanor and dismissive body language to a combination of angry grief and teenage angst.

Wheeler tried a different tack. "Did you have a spare key to your car?"

Norris brightened. "Yeah. I kept it in one of those magnetic hide-a-key things inside the wheel well, driver's side, rear."

"Who knew that?"

Norris threw his hands up. "Hell, I don't know. It's not like I advertised it. Wait a second. I told Richie so he wouldn't break a window if he repossessed the car."

"Anybody else?"

Norris thought for a moment. "Just Robin. She was always forgetting where she left her keys, so she hid a key like that. She got me to do it in case she needed the key to my car. After we split up, I kept doing it. Habit, you know."

Wheeler got up. "Okay. Sit tight. I'll see what I can do about getting you out of here."

FORTY-SIX

Rossi was waiting for him outside the interrogation room. They retreated to a safe distance to make certain Norris couldn't overhear them.

"Did you catch all of that?" Wheeler asked.

"Yeah. I thought you were going to help him fill out the complaint."

"Don't worry. My good cop isn't that good. But your bad cop was so good I thought Norris was going to piss himself. You want to let him take a look at the airport video?"

"Not until I get the video from the shuttle stops outside the terminal and the airport police tell me if they found any discarded clothes or the duffel bag."

"What do you want to do with him in the meantime?"

"We can hold him for twenty-four hours without charging him, so let's make good use of the time. Robin Norris had a reason to be up north. If she wasn't meeting her ex-husband, she was meeting someone else. Since she wasn't familiar with the area, she probably took I-29 north from downtown to the Barry Road exit. There are plenty of restaurants that would have still been open that time of night. Send some uniforms up there with pictures of Robin and have them canvass the area, see if anyone remembers seeing her."

"So you think Norris may be telling the truth, that somebody really did steal his car and is setting him up for Robin's murder?"

"Since we know the killer used his car, it's the only other possible explanation." Rossi looked away for a moment, brow furrowed. "In the video from the Economy parking lot, the driver of the Camry stayed in the car until the shuttle bus got close. When he got out of the car, he bent down like he'd dropped something, which took him outside the camera's view. If he used the spare key to steal the car, he could have been putting it back."

Wheeler grinned. "So it would look like the driver had used Norris's key, not the spare. I'll check the Camry to see if the spare is still there and if there are any prints we can use."

"And check Robin's car to see if she kept a spare in the wheel well too."

"That would confirm one part of Norris's story."

"It might be more important than that. If Norris is innocent, the killer had to know about his spare key. Who would have known that?"

"Norris said he told Richie the Vig."

"Yeah, but Richie had no reason to kill Robin."

Wheeler thought for a moment. "Norris said he and Robin had always hidden a key in the wheel wells of their cars, so it makes sense that their kids would have known, but I didn't pick up anything that would make me suspicious of them."

"Except for the daughter, Kim. The other night when we were at their house, she was the only one who didn't cry when I told them their mother had been murdered."

"Now that you mention it, she was more angry than anything else. In fact, she hit me as more angry that she was stuck there with us than that her mom was dead."

"Norris said she's the only one of the kids that still talked to him. He called her 'my little Kimmy.' He didn't talk about the other kids like that."

"You had to stop him from smacking Donny."

"And Kim was the only one who looked like her father. The other four were all Robin."

"Kim sided with her dad after the divorce but she's forced to live with her mom and four siblings that take her side," Wheeler said.

"She doesn't just side with him; she looks like him, and her brothers and sisters look like their mom. Which leaves her alone, outnumbered, and on the losing side. That'll buy you a whole lot of anger."

Wheeler nodded. "Kim knew her mom was seeing someone on the sly. Maybe Kim found out who it was and that was all she could take."

"Kids have killed their parents for less. Talk to Sonia Steele. Robin may have confided in her about the affair and any problems she was having with Kim."

"I don't know. A sixteen-year-old kid, a girl. You think she could do something like that? Lure her mother someplace and kill her? Then cool as cool can be, drop the car at the airport and make it back home?"

"You're right. That's a lot for any sixteen-year-old girl, unless she had help. Get a warrant for her e-mail and texts. We need to find out who her friends are."

"You want to talk to Kim?"

Rossi shook his head. "Not until we know more about her relationship with Robin. Did you recover any hair or fibers from the Camry?"

"CSI is handling that. Maybe we'll find something that ties to Kim and one of her buddies. What's next for you?"

Rossi checked his watch. "I'm meeting someone at five."

"That's in twenty minutes. Is it on this case?"

"No. Something else."

Wheeler raised his eyebrows. "That thing with Alex Stone?"

"Yeah."

"You're like a dog with a bone."

"And I'm about to finish gnawing on it."

FORTY-SEVEN

Rossi pulled into the driveway at Alex and Bonnie's house, sitting in his car for a moment wondering what Bonnie had in mind. Instead of telling him what he wanted to know, she might have some crazy idea of putting him in a room with Alex, demanding that they make peace, like a parent mediating between warring kids. Or maybe Bonnie had convinced Alex to confess and Bonnie was going to be there for moral support. Or maybe they were going to offer him a glass of elderberry wine laced with poison like the spinster aunts in *Arsenic and Old Lace*, a movie he'd fallen asleep watching the night before after downing a bottle of wine. He got out of the car, chuckling and jazzed at the prospect of proving he was right about Alex all along.

Bonnie greeted him at the door, apologizing for her dog, which kept rising on his hind legs, planting his front paws on Rossi.

"Quincy! Down! I'm sorry. He's trained to stop jumping up on people as soon as he's too tired."

Rossi ruffled the dog's fur. "I don't mind."

They stood in the entry hall, Bonnie in taupe slacks and a navy blouse, alternately clasping her hands and letting her arms dangle at her sides, Rossi waiting for his cue.

"Well," Bonnie said. "You're here, aren't you? Thanks for coming."

"Thanks for asking, but I'm still not clear on why you did."

She cleared her throat and wiped her palms on her thighs. "This isn't easy for me."

He smiled. "Then take your time. Maybe we should sit down somewhere."

"Of course. The kitchen. We can sit in the kitchen."

He followed her through the house, admiring a photographed portrait of Bonnie, Alex, and their dog, struck by the joy in their faces. He glanced at the den, noting the matching easy chairs with crocheted throws on the ottomans and the stack of books and magazines on a table between the chairs.

Though the kitchen blinds were drawn, the room was still bright and cheery, with artsy knickknacks adorning shelves, painted plates mounted on the walls, wineglasses hung from a rack above an island, and a red-framed sign handwritten in shades of red and blue on one wall that read:

> WELCOME
> If your shoes are real dirty—
> Please remove them.
> If your socks are real dirty—
> Please take them off.
> If your feet are real dirty—
> Please leave.

Rossi sat at the table, pointing to the sign. "I like that."

"So do we."

Bonnie sat across from him, forearms on the table, rubbing her hands together. Quincy trotted to Rossi, sniffed, turned around, and lay down at Bonnie's feet. Rossi waited for Bonnie to take the lead, but she didn't.

"Why am I here, Dr. Long?"

Bonnie took a deep breath, letting it out. "I want you to leave us alone."

Rossi cocked his head to one side. "I'm sorry?"

Bonnie straightened, shoulders back. "I want you to leave us alone. I want you to quit coming to the hospital to ask me about

Alex. I want you to quit harassing Alex, trying to make her out to be some kind of criminal when all she was doing was protecting herself and me." She paused, drew another breath. "I want you out of our lives forever."

Rossi sat back in his chair. Bonnie had set him up, only not in the way he had imagined, taking advantage of his cockiness, letting him think this was going to be his big breakthrough. But she had to know he wasn't going to go away, which meant he still had a play to make.

"You know I can't do that."

Bonnie smacked her hand on the table. "Why not? Alex told me she can't be retried even if she were guilty."

"Then what do either of you have to be afraid of? Why not just tell me the truth?"

Bonnie paused, nodding. "What if we told you that you were right? What then? What would you do?"

It was a question Rossi had asked himself many times. The answer varied. Sometimes it was that he'd take it to the U.S. attorney's office and the Missouri Bar Ethics Commission and let them sort it out. Other times, he wasn't so certain, thinking just knowing he'd been right would be enough. That was before he suspected that something was going on between Alex and Judge West, raising the possibility that Alex could go to jail for obstruction of justice if nothing else.

"That depends on how much both of you tell me."

"What do you mean?"

"I don't know what Alex has told you, but she may have done more than kill Dwayne Reed. She may have also obstructed justice in order to get acquitted. And, if she did, she can go to jail for that even if she can't go to jail for murder."

"You would destroy our lives for that?"

"It's not me who would destroy your lives. It's Alex and you, if you helped her in any way."

Bonnie rose, went to the small desk in the kitchen, and took a sheet of paper from a drawer, reading from it.

"Marcus Ramsey. Julio Estevez. Rolando Chism. Frankie Meadows. I assume you recognize those names, Detective, since you killed each of them. Shot them to death, from what I understand."

Rossi blanched. He knew those names by heart and couldn't forget them if he tried. The better question was how Bonnie knew them.

"What's your point? Each of those shootings was in the line of duty. And where did you get those names?"

"From a lawsuit."

Rossi planted his hands on the table, leaning in at her. "What lawsuit?"

"The lawsuit that the families of those men are going to file against you and the police department and the city."

"That's not happening. Those incidents go back fifteen years. The statute of limitations ran a long time ago."

"Except for Frankie Meadows. You gunned him down less than two years ago. His wife consulted a lawyer I recommended to her who thinks she's got a pretty good case. Now, I don't understand the law, but it has something to do with you and the department engaging in a persistent pattern of denying the civil rights of minorities through the use of excessive force and intimidation. All the men you killed were either black or Hispanic, but you knew that."

"Every one of those shootings was investigated by Internal Affairs and the county prosecutor and each one was found to be justified."

Bonnie pursed her lips. "Well, you know how some people are, Detective. They're just never satisfied until things turn out the way they want them to. Especially when they suspect that you planted incriminating evidence to cover up what really happened."

Rossi sat back. "So that's what this is about. You're trying to blackmail me with the threat of a bullshit lawsuit so I'll lay off Alex."

"Every night for the last year, Alex wakes up, sweating and shaking. The nightmares are always the same. Dwayne Reed coming after us. Raping us. Murdering us. And even when Alex kills him again and again in her dreams, it's just as terrifying. I hold her and tell her everything is going to be all right, that she did the right thing, but it doesn't do any good. Tell me, Detective, is it like that for you? Do you see those men in your nightmares? Is that why you spend so much time in bars at night drinking alone?"

Rossi stiffened, trying to keep a lid on his anger, knowing if he blew up, he'd only make things worse.

"You don't know what you're talking about."

"Oh, I think I do. You see, I hired a private detective, a woman named Lucy Trent. She's very good at what she does. She found out a lot about you and she found the families of the men you killed."

"If you think you can scare me off, you don't have any idea who you're dealing with."

"Actually, Detective, I think I do. I think I'm dealing with a fundamentally decent man who did his best under impossibly difficult circumstances and who genuinely regrets taking the lives of those men. If you were anyone else, you wouldn't drink so much."

Rossi threw up his hands. "Why do you think coming after me is going to change anything for Alex?"

"Maybe it won't. But at least you'll know what it's like to spend your life defending yourself for having done what you knew was right."

Rossi set his jaw. "Then have at it."

He rose and turned to go.

"Before you leave, Detective, come over to the window and look out in my backyard for a minute. There's something I want you to see."

Bonnie opened the blinds. Rossi hesitated but joined her. Looking out, he saw four women, three of them black, one Hispanic, along with a dozen others ranging from newborns to young adults. They were on the patio, a few talking in hushed tones, most of them silent.

"Who are they?"

"Those are your widows and their children and their grandchildren. The men you killed were drug dealers and thugs, no better or worse than Dwayne Reed. Maybe their wives and children knew all about them and maybe they didn't. Either way, they haven't forgotten that you killed their husbands and fathers and grandfathers. They want justice and peace. Go talk to them. Tell them that they're wrong. Tell them that you have no regrets. Tell them that the men they loved got what they deserved."

Rossi stared at them, swallowing hard. He looked at Bonnie.

"I was exonerated."

"And so was Alex."

Bonnie waited until Rossi drove away before opening the door to the patio.

"I want to thank you for coming over this afternoon. It's so nice to get together outside of the hospital and see how all the kids are doing. The pizzas will be here in about twenty minutes. Who wants a soda?"

FORTY-EIGHT

Alex drifted to the back of the courtroom, tuning out Judge Steele's eulogy for Robin, focusing instead on their brief conversation. He'd been every bit as charming as she had imagined him until she mentioned Joanie Sutherland's name and the light went out of his eyes. There had to be more behind his reaction than his decision years ago to put Joanie into a diversion program instead of sentencing her for shoplifting. He could have stayed in contact with her, using his position to take advantage of her only for her to turn the tables and blackmail him.

The friendship between Judge West and Judge Steele added another tantalizing element to her speculation. If Steele had killed Joanie, he'd have been ecstatic when Jared Bell was arrested for her murder. He might have talked to West about the case, nudging him to get the right public defender appointed to represent Bell. She discounted that possibility because Robin assigned the cases, not Judge West, leaving her to wonder whether West had somehow pressured Robin to assign Jared's case to her. She decided that while there were too many moving parts for that to have happened, she had to dig deeper into the relationship between Judge Steele and Joanie.

Alex left the memorial for Robin, brooding about what Bonnie had said, that she didn't have to go through this alone and that no matter what happened, Bonnie would be there. It was the kind of promise that lovers often made but less often kept because what ended up happening was more awful than either could have imagined. But she wanted to believe that Bonnie was different, that they were different, and that together they were stronger than either could be on her own.

She drove around, aimlessly at first, then purposefully, past the places that had meant so much to them. Where they first met, where they had their first date, where they were when Alex told Bonnie for the first time that she loved her and where they had first made love. Each stop along the way restored her faith in herself and in them until there was no place else to go but home.

She turned onto their street, bright-eyed and singing one of their favorite love songs, the words catching in her throat when she saw Rossi's car in their driveway. She folded onto the steering wheel as if she'd been kicked in the gut, stopping in the middle of the street, staring at her house, the life gone out of her, body and soul.

At first Alex thought Rossi was there to harass Bonnie once again. She hoped Bonnie would tell Rossi that they'd broken up so that Rossi would leave Bonnie alone. Any chance of that happening would be lost if she walked in on them. And then she realized that it might be something worse. Convinced that Alex was going to destroy herself, Bonnie might have invited Rossi in an attempt to broker a deal to save her. It was just the sort of thing Bonnie would do: diagnose the patient's condition and do the best she could to treat it, unaware that this time the cure was worse than the disease.

Crying, feeling like she'd been cut open from the inside out, Alex drove back to the Residence Inn and crawled into bed. She woke up at nine o'clock, not remembering falling asleep. She was groggy, her limbs felt rubbery, and though she wasn't hungry, she knew she needed to eat, but first she needed to move, get her body working again, and that meant going for a run. Putting in five miles would perk her up. She changed into her running gear, laced up her shoes, tucked her cell phone and room key into a fanny pack, and went out into the night.

The temperature was perfect, in the low fifties. Standing on Main Street, she looked across at Penn Valley Park. Bonnie was right. The park was one of her favorite places, 176 acres of rolling hills with an off-leash dog park, baseball diamonds and tennis courts, the World War I Liberty Memorial, and, her favorite, the Scout, a ten-foot-tall statue of a Sioux Indian on horseback mounted on a limestone base and overlooking downtown Kansas City. She loved the simple majesty and power of the sculpture and the amazing view.

Alex didn't share Bonnie's concerns about running in Penn Valley Park at night but, nonetheless, stuck to Main, trotting north and taking advantage of the long descent down to Pershing Road to loosen up. She turned west onto Pershing, staying with it until she reached West Pennway, where she turned again, heading back south, the uphill grade payback for her downhill start on Main.

She was running easily as she started the climb, her arms and legs working together in a steady, fluid motion, her head upright, her chin level, her core holding everything together. There had been a lot of traffic on Main and on Pershing, but only a few cars passed her on West Pennway. South of Twenty-Sixth, the name of the street changed to Penn Valley Drive, signaling the beginning of its route through the park. She told herself that she wasn't breaking her promise to Bonnie because, technically, she was running through the park, not in the park. The thought made her smile until she realized it would be a while before they'd have that conversation, if they ever had it.

Passing a small lake on her right, Alex forgot her promise and left the road, cutting across a wide grassy expanse enveloped in darkness, strong, sure strides carrying her up the gradual slope leading to the Scout. Her lungs swelled with each breath in, contracting with each breath out, in perfect rhythm with the beat of her heart. Sweat poured off her, cooled by the crisp night, her body in perfect harmony with earth and air, joyful at their union.

Alex could see the Scout a hundred yards ahead. It was illuminated at its base, the lights making the bronze shine in the dark. She sprinted as she got closer, the horse and rider looming larger and larger, her breath coming in deeper gulps, her heart pounding. An arm's length away, she reached out to touch the limestone pedestal like she was breaking the tape at the finish line of a race, at once aware of furious footsteps behind her, coming out of nowhere, gaining on her, another runner's labored breathing causing her to turn her head, but she was too late. She caught a glimpse of a black runner's face mask, gasping at a flurry of quick, sharp pains in her back and something warm running down her legs, which had somehow given out on her. She dropped to her knees, collapsing facedown at the base of the statue, bewildered and bleeding.

She tried to cry out, but the sound died in her throat as her assailant pressed a knee into the base of her spine, tugging at her fanny pack and unzipping it. From the corner of her eye, she saw an object sail through the air, knowing it was her cell phone, feeling as helpless and untethered as if she'd been cast adrift in outer space. And then she was alone.

One hand braced against the stone base of the statue, she pulled herself up to her knees, clawing with both hands to get to her feet. Gingerly, she reached behind her, wincing as she found two wounds, uncertain whether there were more. Wiping blood on her leg, she staggered away from the statue, aiming herself toward where she thought her phone had landed, knowing she had little chance of finding it and even less chance of not bleeding to death if she didn't.

She counted her steps as a way of maintaining her focus, telling herself that it was only a little farther, just another step, anyone can take one more step. Anyone. And then she couldn't, her legs crumbling beneath her, the cool wet grass coming up to meet her. She lay still for a moment, eyes closed, opening them when she heard her phone ringing. Lifting her head, she saw it glowing ten feet away. She dragged herself to her knees, crawling to the phone, throwing herself the final distance and pulling it toward her. She rolled onto her back, fumbling with the touch screen until it opened.

"Alex? Alex? Are you there?" Bonnie asked.

Staring at the starlit sky, she said, "I'm sorry," and then the world went black.

When she woke up, she was on a gurney surrounded by people wearing hospital scrubs as they rolled her into the emergency room at Truman Medical Center. She smiled when she heard Bonnie shout orders and closed her eyes again.

Four hours later, she was sitting up in bed, Bonnie at her side.

"How did you find me?"

"I called 911 and they traced your cell phone."

She ran her tongue around the inside of her mouth and Bonnie gave her glass of water. She took a sip, marveling at how good it tasted.

"I was stabbed. Twice, I think."

"Three times. You were very lucky. The wounds weren't deep. Just soft tissue and some muscle damage. You've got enough stitches for some very lovely scars, and you're going to be pretty sore for a while, but that's it."

Neither said anything, the silence awkward until Alex broke it.

"I was going to come home today."

"Why didn't you?"

"I got as far as our street and I saw Rossi's car in the driveway. I didn't know what to think."

"So now you know. We're having an affair and he was fucking my brains out."

Alex laughed, flinching at the pain. "Don't do that. It hurts. What was I supposed to think?"

"What did you think?"

Alex looked away, her face flushed. "That either he was harassing you or that you were giving me up."

"You know I would never do that. And he wasn't harassing me. If anything, it was the other way around."

Bonnie explained the scam she'd run on Rossi, threatening him with a lawsuit.

"I don't think a lawsuit is going to scare Rossi. You think it will work?"

"We'll see, but it wasn't so much about the lawsuit. I gave him credit for being human and feeling guiltier about the men he'd killed than he'd like to admit. I wanted him to walk in your shoes and think about spending the next five years having people call him a murderer."

Alex nodded, studying her, feeling badly that she'd so underestimated Bonnie, whose face was drawn and lined with worry. Her scrubs were splattered with bloodstains. Alex reached out, touching one.

"Mine?"

Bonnie took her hand, pressing it against her. "Yeah."

They sniffled in unison until a nurse came in the room.

"There's a Detective Rossi wanting to speak to your patient."

Bonnie said to Alex, "Maybe we're about to find out if he bought it." Then to the nurse, "Send him in."

Rossi stood in the doorway. "I hear you had a close call."

Alex shrugged. "Yeah, but I'm okay."

"That right, Dr. Long?"

"Yes. She'll be fine as long as she's left alone."

Rossi eyed Bonnie, ducking his chin for an instant, not taking the bait. "Alex, I need to ask you a few questions."

"I'll make it easy on both of us. I left my room at the Residence Inn a little after nine and went for a run. I did a loop down Main, onto Pershing, and back south on West Pennway. I cut across the park heading toward the Scout, and just as I got there, I heard someone coming up behind me. I don't know if he followed me or was just hiding in the dark waiting for someone to come by. I turned to look behind me, saw someone wearing a runner's mask, and the next thing I knew I'd been stabbed and was on the ground. It had to have been some random asshole."

Rossi nodded. "Or not."

Bonnie stood, squeezing Alex's hand, looking back and forth at the two of them. She guessed Rossi's meaning.

"Oh my God! This is about Robin's phone call."

Rossi looked at Alex. "You told her about that?"

"I told her everything."

"And you still think it was some random asshole who just happened to follow you into the park, stab you, and throw your cell phone away so you'd bleed to death before anyone could find you?"

"Until you can prove it wasn't."

"Who knew about the phone call?"

Alex thought for a moment. "I mentioned it to Judge West last week. And yesterday, at the memorial for Robin, he said something about it to Judge Steele and his wife. But I didn't tell any of them what was on the message."

Rossi shook his head and sighed. "Perfect. I'll arrest all three of them and see which one flips first. When can she go home, Doc?"

"You know hospitals these days. No one stays overnight unless they're never leaving. I'll take her home."

"There'll be a patrol car outside your house the rest of the night just in case the random asshole shows up again."

"Thank you, Detective."

Rossi turned to go, stopping for a moment. "One last thing, Alex. You said you left your room at the Residence Inn a little after nine to go for a run. What were you doing staying at a hotel fifteen minutes from your house?"

Alex looked at Bonnie. "Nothing. Nothing at all."

FORTY-NINE

Late Wednesday morning, Alex sat in bed, thinking about Meg Adler's proposal that she take over the Kansas City public defender's office. Though she loved being in the courtroom, she felt tainted by everything that had happened. Running the office might be a welcome change. She'd never managed people before, never run anything that wasn't a race, but she thought she could learn. She wouldn't decide without talking to Bonnie.

Her cell phone rang, the sound jangling her frayed nerves. Between the pain from her wounds and worrying about whether the attack had been random or intentional, she'd hardly slept. She'd put on a brave face for Bonnie, insisting that she was fine and that there was no cause for concern, empty assurances that didn't make either of them feel any better.

The call was from an unidentified private number. The last anonymous call she'd gotten had been from Judge West. He'd called her burner phone, but this call was to her regular cell phone. That didn't make her any more willing to answer it without knowing who was calling. She let it ring, waiting to see if the caller would leave a message.

The ringing stopped, and a moment later, the phone chirped, announcing that she had a message. She opened the phone and played it.

"Ms. Stone, this is Judge Steele. After we spoke yesterday I remembered the young woman you asked me about. I'd be happy to visit with you if you'd like to stop by my chambers this morning. No need to return my call."

Before Bonnie left for the hospital, she gave Alex strict instructions to take it easy for the next few days. Alex promised to do as she was told, but she couldn't ignore Judge Steele's message, certain why he had called. It was one thing to deny remembering Joanie. It was another to deny it knowing that Alex was going to get medical records that identified him as the one who'd paid for Joanie's treatment at Fresh Start. Better to come clean than to invite more questions. And volunteering would buy him credibility for any other denials. Alex could have called him back and let him tell her over the phone, but she wanted to hear it in person to better evaluate whether he was telling the truth.

She had another reason for going. Staying in bed, cooped up in the house, made her feel more trapped than safe. If someone wanted to kill her, she liked her chances better in Judge Steele's chambers than as a sitting duck at home.

She eased herself out of bed and into her clothes, each movement launching a jolt of pain through her midback. She dug through her T-shirt drawer, slipping into one with a favorite marines saying on the front—*Pain is only weakness leaving the body*. Repeating it out loud made her feel better already.

Judge Steele sat on the Missouri Court of Appeals for the Western District of Missouri. It was the only intermediate appellate court in Missouri that had its own courthouse. Located at Thirteenth and Oak in the shadow of the Sprint Center, it was the southernmost of the trio of courthouses on Oak that included the Federal Courthouse at Ninth and the Jackson County Courthouse at Twelfth.

The judge's secretary ushered Alex into his chambers. It was twice the size of Judge West's, a beautiful Oriental rug covering the center of the hardwood floor, two chandeliers hanging from the ceiling, and walls lined with mahogany bookshelves jammed with case reporters and statutes. State and federal flags stood behind the judge's desk, draped floor-to-ceiling windows completing the backdrop.

Judge Steele sat at an oval table on one side of the room, wearing khakis, a long-sleeved polo shirt, and deck shoes without socks, one shoe off and dangling from his toes. He looked up from the brief he was reading, his glasses partway down his nose.

"Come on in, Alex. You're awfully pale. Are you all right? Have a seat, please."

She held one hand over her wounds, grimacing as she slid onto the chair, not wanting to talk about what happened.

"Sort of threw my back out yesterday."

"Believe me, I've been there with the way my wife makes me work out. She's a fitness buff and I suffer for it."

Alex was surprised at his informality, since formality was one of a judge's strongest assets. Lawyers called them by their honorific title as if using their given names was forbidden. Rules against ex parte communications stifled casual conversation. Their black robes and elevated courtroom benches were a reminder of their exalted status. On the few occasions she'd run into judges on a weekend, dressed like civilians and running errands like ordinary folks, she'd almost failed to recognize them. But here was Judge Steele, dressed down and kicking back.

"I didn't know the Court of Appeals had adopted a casual dress code."

"If you had gotten here an hour ago, you'd have caught me in my workout clothes," he said, chuckling and pointing to the duffel bag on the floor. "One of the little-known perks of being an appellate judge is that I can wear whatever I want as long as we don't have any oral arguments scheduled. And if there's an emergency hearing of some kind, I just put on my robe and no one can tell what I'm wearing underneath. It's kind of like the TV anchorman who reads the news wearing a shirt, jacket, tie, boxers, and nothing else."

Alex smiled. Not taking himself too seriously was part of the judge's charm.

"Your message said that you remembered Joanie Sutherland."

"Yes, but not at first. You mentioned something about Fresh Start, and later on, when I was telling my wife, she said that Joanie was probably one of the people whose treatment we had paid for over the years. I went back and checked our records, and, sure enough, that's what happened."

Alex arched her eyebrows. "You and your wife pay for other people's treatment at Fresh Start?"

"Well, not personally. My parents were wealthy—quite wealthy, actually. That's why I can afford to be a judge. They set up the Steele Family Foundation for their charitable work. I had an older brother who died of a drug overdose when he was only twenty-five. My parents blamed themselves for not recognizing what bad shape he was in and doing something to save him. So, they made prevention and treatment of substance abuse one of the foundation's priorities, including paying for the treatment of low-income people who wouldn't otherwise get the quality of care that Fresh Start provides."

"How did Joanie Sutherland get on that list?"

"COMBAT, Jackson County's drug abuse prevention program, referred her."

"We're you personally involved in approving payment for her?"

"I'm certain I was. Since my parents died, I'm in charge of the foundation, and those applications come across my desk for approval."

Alex was deflated. She'd thought she'd gotten lucky with a long shot. Judge Steele's explanation made sense, and since it was easily verifiable, he had no reason to lie. Still, she decided to press.

"Did you or the foundation provide any other financial support to Joanie?"

"Not that I'm aware of, at least not directly. We don't make grants to people like Joanie because there's too much risk that the money won't be well spent. We support organizations and programs that help people like her and she may have benefited from one of those, though the foundation doesn't keep records of the people who use those services."

It was the answer Alex expected. "Well, that explains that. Thank you for your time, Your Honor."

"If you don't mind my asking, why were you so interested in knowing who paid her medical bills?"

"Because lending a helping hand can get pretty expensive if someone asks for too much help."

"Ah, I see. And you think Ms. Sutherland may have been such a person and that may have gotten her killed."

"It's possible."

He leaned back in his chair, hands clasped in his lap and smiled. "Which means you thought, to be blunt, that I might have killed her because she was blackmailing me."

Alex blushed. "I'm sorry, Your Honor, I…"

He waved her off. "You were just doing your job, and in a way, I'm flattered that anyone might think that someone as boring as I am could be caught up in something so dramatic. Thank you for helping me hold up my end of the dinner table conversation tonight when Sonia asks me about my day."

Alex returned home, worn-out. She poured herself into her easy chair in the den and took a nap. After lunch she stayed at the kitchen table, using her laptop to catch up on her e-mail. Late in the afternoon, Grace Canfield called her.

"Where've you been all day?"

Alex didn't want Grace worrying and asking too many questions.

"Home with a cold."

"Drink plenty of liquids."

"I promise."

"I got Joanie's records from Fresh Start."

"Let me guess. The Steele Family Foundation paid for her treatment."

"If you knew that, why did you run my butt around to get these records?"

Alex laughed. "I just found out this morning," she said, filling Grace in on her conversation with Judge Steele.

"So you were well enough to go see the judge but too sick to tell me what he said so I wouldn't spend my day hollering at some poor medical records clerk at Fresh Start?"

"Sorry, but we needed the records anyway to confirm what the judge said."

"Those records may be more important than that. Didn't you say that Charlotte was Bethany Sutherland's daughter?"

"That's what Bethany told me."

"Well, according to these records, Joanie told the doctors at Fresh Start that she was Charlotte's mother."

"Really? Did she say who the father was?"

"Said she didn't know, which I can believe, given her chosen occupation. Anyway, I checked the city's birth records and Joanie is listed as the mother on Charlotte's birth certificate. The father isn't listed. She was born at Truman Medical Center. I'm going to subpoena the hospital's records to see if there's anything in them about the father and who paid the bill."

"Lean on them like you did with Fresh Start. I wonder why Bethany told me that Charlotte was her daughter."

"Probably because she's the one that was raising her."

"Okay, but here's something else that doesn't make sense. Bethany also told me that she didn't know who paid for Joanie's treatment at Fresh Start. Since Judge Steele's foundation paid for it, Joanie would have had to jump through who knows how many hoops to get that free ride. There's no way Bethany couldn't have known about that."

"And then there's the money, the five thousand dollars. Where's Bethany or Joanie gonna get that kind of money? Maybe it's all tied together. Maybe they were blackmailing the judge and he was using his foundation to pay her off. We'd have to subpoena the foundation's records to trace the five grand."

"Yeah, and you can bet Steele would fight that subpoena to the death, and without more proof, Judge West will quash it." Alex looked at her watch. "Bethany has to be at work in about an hour. If I leave now, I can catch her and get some answers."

"I thought you were sick."

"Not that sick. Get that subpoena over to Truman and ask Bonnie to help you cut through the red tape."

Alex was relieved when she saw Bethany's Impala parked in front of her trailer. She climbed the single step to the open door. The lights were off, strands of daylight leaking through the lowered blinds on the trailer's windows, casting shadows and stirring dust mites. The television was playing in the background, Meredith Vieira asking *Who wants to be a millionaire?* Bethany was slumped over the dinette table as if she was dozing. Alex called to her.

"Bethany."

When she didn't wake up, Alex rapped on the side of the trailer.

"Bethany!"

Then Alex caught the rank, sickly-sweet scent of decomposing flesh and knew that Bethany was dead. She stepped inside. Charlotte wasn't there. Back outside, she flung open the door to the storage shed. Not finding her, she ran around the trailer, shouting.

"Charlotte! Where are you?"

FIFTY

Wednesday morning, Rossi and Kalena Greene sat in front of the computer on Rossi's desk playing the airport security video over and over, using freeze-frame and slow motion to break the action down. Kalena drained her cup of coffee and pushed away from the screen.

"This is hopeless," she said. "If you and I can't identify Norris in the video, there's no way a jury can."

"What about having some video geek enhance it?"

Kalena shrugged. "We can try that, but your twenty-four-hour hold on Norris expired two hours ago. We've got to charge him or let him go."

"So charge him. We know his car was used, and his alibi is for shit."

"So is our case if we can't put him in the car. You got a warrant to search his apartment last night and you didn't find the duffel bag or anything else to link him to the murder. And your canvass of around Barry Road and I-29 didn't turn up anything."

"There's still his daughter Kim. She may have been in on it with him. If Norris thinks we can prove that, he'll confess if we agree to treat her as a juvenile."

"What do you have on her?"

"Wheeler talked to Sonia Steele, who was Robin's best friend. According to Sonia, mother and daughter have fought for years."

"Fought about what?"

"Whatever moms and teenage daughters fight about, which I guess for them was everything. Things got worse in the last six months or so. Kim started staying out all night and Robin was afraid she'd graduated from smoking dope to using meth. And a few weeks ago, Kim was expelled from school when she was caught with a box cutter in her purse."

"How did Kim explain the box cutter?"

"She said she was going to use it to cut a bitch."

"Damn, that white girl went ghetto in a hurry."

"Not hard when you take the meth express. Sonia said that Robin was trying to get Kim into an alternative high school but that Kim refused to go."

"Have you gotten into Kim's computer and phone yet?"

"Wheeler is getting a search warrant for the computer and is going to serve the phone company with a subpoena today."

"What about the hidden car keys? Any luck with that?"

"The one for the Camry was right where it was supposed to be, but there were no prints. Not even partials, smudges, or swirls. And nothing on the metal box it was kept in."

"So," Kalena said, "the killer wiped the key and the box clean, which supports Norris's story. If he'd been behind the wheel, he'd have used his own key."

"Unless he used the spare and wiped it clean to make it look like someone stole his car."

"Which is a theory in search of proof. I hate to say it, but you've got to let him go. Whoever did this did a pretty good job of hiding his tracks, but you'll find him."

"What makes you so sure?"

"Aren't you sure?"

"You know that I am."

Kalena grinned. "Then, that's good enough for me."

Rossi gave instructions for Norris to be released and headed to the City Diner at Third and Grand, taking a window booth at the back, ordering coffee and telling the waitress to keep his cup full. He needed the caffeine to weed out the cobwebs from the night before and figure out what to do next.

He'd let Bonnie Long get to him, taking it out on a bottle of scotch he'd meant to save for a better occasion. He was halfway through the bottle before he decided he didn't give a rat's ass about the lawsuit. The lawyers for the department and the city would tie the case up in knots that would take years to untangle. When he finished the bottle he fell asleep, waking in the middle of the night and looking out the window, seeing the women and children from Bonnie's patio standing outside, staring at him, then waking a second time, realizing the first time had been a dream.

He'd killed four men in the twenty years he'd been a cop. The department's shrink had to clear him before letting him return to duty after each shooting, which meant giving him tests to find out how fucked-up he was, never telling him he was too fucked-up to go back. He figured they knew he was lying when he told them the nightmares never lasted more than a week or two and that his drinking wasn't a problem but looked the other way because they needed a guy like him who wasn't afraid to put a bad guy down. Their unspoken deal had worked for both sides for a long time.

Stirring his coffee, he chided himself for letting Bonnie Long knock him on his ass. She'd called him out, and for the first time in a long time he had to admit that there wasn't as much of a difference between him and Alex Stone as he wanted—needed—to believe. They'd both worked the system.

Bonnie had proved tougher than he'd expected. Instead of getting scared and folding, she'd gotten angry and fought back. Walking through their house, seeing their family portrait and the home they'd created, he understood why. And if he had any doubts, seeing them together in the hospital took care of that. Their life together was worth fighting for, and he was no longer certain he had the stomach to take it away from them.

He sipped his coffee. It had gone cold with all the stirring. The waitress came by to freshen it, but he told her, "No, thanks," and left. It was his day off. If he went back, Mitch Fowler would tell him there was no money in the budget for overtime and to get lost.

He stood in the parking lot, the day cool and crisp for late September. He clasped his hands together behind his neck, stretching the kinks out of his muscles. A day off. What the hell was he going to do with that? He knew the answer. He'd work the case on his own time.

The neighborhood canvass had been a bust. But a lot of those businesses had their own video surveillance systems that might have captured Robin and her killer. The cops doing the canvass hadn't checked for that.

I-29 and Barry Road was a major intersection in the northland. There were shopping centers on three corners and two motels on the fourth. Continuing west of the intersection, the direction Robin Norris had chosen, there were a couple of churches, a high school, a park, and several residential neighborhoods, after which development thinned out, turning Barry Road into a little-traveled, unlit country lane by the time it reached the curve five miles farther west where Robin had been killed.

Rossi was confident that his basic premise was correct. While there were many different routes to the intersection, because Robin was unfamiliar with the area, she would have used I-29 to bring her to the junction with Barry Road. She placed her last-second call to Alex at ten fifteen p.m. She could have been anywhere on either side of I-29 prior to that. The timeline he had established for her movements had a gap of seven hours from the time she left the office to the time of the phone call. But the most important part of that period was the fifteen to thirty minutes before she called Alex. Something happened in that time frame to send her racing into the unknown darkness.

He started on the east side of I-29, working his way west, limiting himself to the places that would have been open that late in the evening, like the Hooters, Boston Market, and Starbucks. There was nothing on their videos.

There were more places to check on the west side of I-29, and the going was slow. Some managers refused to allow him to see their videos without a warrant and without authorization from someone higher up in the company food chain. Others confessed that their video cameras didn't work. And still others told him that they recorded over their videos so that they had only the most recent twenty-four hours.

It was late afternoon when Rossi got to the motels. The manager on duty at the first one cited company policy requiring a subpoena or court order before allowing anyone to look at their security videos. Rossi told him that he'd be back the next day with a subpoena and warned him not to let anything happen to the video.

The manager at the second motel, an overweight, middle-aged man named Milton with a comb-over and beer breath, was more helpful, taking Rossi to his office and pulling up the video from the night of the murder. After watching for ten minutes, Rossi turned to the manager.

"Why are we only seeing three sides of the motel? What about the west side?"

Milton shrugged. "No cameras on that side."

"Why not?"

"Can't afford 'em."

"Then why did I see cameras on the west side when I drove through the parking lot?"

Milton stuttered. "Uh, uh…what I meant to say is that we got cameras but they don't work."

"Let me ask you a question, Milton. Suppose I get a search warrant and bring the department's video crew up to take a look at those cameras. You suppose they'd work then?"

Milton paled. "Well…I don't know…"

"Oh, Milton. I think we both know."

"I could get in a lot of trouble."

"More trouble than with a search warrant? More trouble than you being charged with obstructing justice?"

"If I tell you, can we keep it just between the two of us?"

"I'll do the best I can to help you out, but one way or the other, I'm going to find out, and when I do, you'll be a lot better off if I can tell the prosecutor that you were very cooperative."

Milton swallowed. "Okay. The rooms on the west side are private."

"Aren't all the rooms private?"

"Not like these. They're more like apartments, really. Paid up a year in advance."

Rossi nodded, getting the picture. "For men who are cheating on their wives and don't want to check in at the front desk and tell you if they need one key or two."

"Yeah, like that."

"Show me the names of the men renting those rooms."

Milton shook his head. "I…I…"

"We've been down this road, Milton. Show me the names or get ready for turning this place into a cop convention with twenty-four/seven media coverage."

"Okay, okay. I get it."

He pulled up a spreadsheet with names and room numbers. Rossi dropped one of his business cards on the manager's desk.

"E-mail the list to me."

Rossi waited for the e-mail to pop up on his phone and forwarded it to Wheeler, telling him to call immediately.

"A Detective Wheeler is going to be here in the next hour with a search warrant for this computer. If you alter or delete this file, if you do anything at all to it, if you so much as sneeze on the screen, you'll go to jail for obstruction of justice. Are we clear?"

Milton's eyes fluttered and his jowls quivered. "We had a deal! No search warrant if I gave you what you wanted."

"I told you I'd do my best, and that's as good as it gets."

Rossi's phone rang. It was Wheeler. He took the call as he walked to his car.

"Why are working on your day off?"

"My bowling league doesn't start until seven."

"What's on the file you sent me?"

Rossi explained, Wheeler whistling when he finished. "Get a search warrant and get up here. I want the computer and I want to know who was using those rooms on the west side the night Robin Norris was killed. Let's find out if someone saw Robin or Ted Norris's car."

"On it. By the way, we can cross the daughter off our list unless all the kids were in on it. They were all at home the night Robin was killed."

"I don't mind the list getting shorter as long as we end up with the right person still on it." Rossi's phone beeped with a waiting call. "Gotta go. I've got another call."

It was from Gardiner Harris, a burly veteran homicide detective who'd worked the Dwayne Reed case with Rossi.

"Hey, Rossi, I hear it's your day off."

"So they tell me."

"Hope I'm not interrupting your golf game."

"I had to cancel my tee time when I remembered that I left my driver up your ass. What's up?"

"I got a dead body you're gonna wanna meet."

FIFTY-ONE

By the time Rossi arrived at the Blue Ridge Mobile Home Park, a perimeter marked off with yellow crime scene tape had been established, interviews of neighbors had begun, and an assistant coroner had completed a preliminary examination of the body.

"You're going to love this," Gardiner Harris said when Rossi got out of his car.

"A dead body on my day off. What's not to love?"

"Guess who called it in."

"Who?"

Harris pointed to a uniformed cop standing next to a patrol car. "Hey, Travis!"

The officer opened the rear car door and Alex Stone stepped out.

"Fuck me," Rossi said.

"She found the body, a woman named Bethany Sutherland. Stone says she's the sister of Joanie Sutherland, who's the vic in one of your cases. And she says Joanie Sutherland's daughter was living in the trailer. Name is Charlotte. Ten years old and autistic. Doesn't say a word and likes to wander off. I got teams out looking for her, but so far, we got nothing."

"I arrested a homeless guy named Jared Bell for raping and murdering Joanie Sutherland. She's his PD. So what's the connection to the sister getting killed?"

"Beats me. Stone says she'll tell me when she tells you."

"What can you tell me about the sister?"

"White female, thirty-three years old. Killed sometime last night by a blow to the left temple from a sharp, heavy object. CSI is about done inside the trailer. Thought you might want to get a look before we remove the body."

"Thanks. I'll do that first, then talk to Alex."

"Alex, huh? You two on a first-name basis these days?"

"Trying not to be."

Alex caught up to Rossi and Harris as they walked to the trailer.

"Aren't you supposed to be home taking it easy or something?" Rossi asked her.

"I tried that. Didn't work for me."

"And finding dead bodies does?"

"It's not like I was on a scavenger hunt and that was the next thing on the list."

They reached the trailer, Rossi holding his hand up to Alex.

"Wait out here."

"Look, I was here on Monday. Bethany is dead and Charlotte is missing, and even if she weren't she doesn't talk. I'm the only one who can tell you if something is missing."

"She's got you there," Harris said.

Rossi sighed, shaking his head, and motioned for her to follow them. Alex stayed by the door as Rossi examined Bethany's body and did a quick tour of the trailer.

"Okay, Counselor, what's missing?"

Alex studied the layout, stopping at the ironing board leaning against the dishwasher. "There was an iron on the floor, but it's gone."

Harris said, "I didn't see an iron. That fits with what the coroner told me. Sharp, heavy object. The killer could have clocked her with the pointed end of the iron."

"The blow was to her left temple, so the killer was probably facing her, which means he was right-handed and strong enough to swing an iron weighing three or four pounds with enough force to kill her. Anything else missing, Alex?"

"Check the stack of mail on the counter. There should be five thousand dollars in an envelope underneath Bethany's bank statement."

Harris put on a pair of latex gloves and picked up each piece of mail by the corners.

"No cash."

"Which," Rossi said, "means Bethany stashed the money somewhere else or this was a robbery gone wrong that has nothing to do with Joanie Sutherland's murder."

"I think you're wrong," Alex said.

Rossi directed her outside. "And now I get to hear you tell me why I'm wrong."

"I think Joanie and Bethany were killed by someone they were blackmailing."

Rossi rolled his eyes. "Is that what this is about? You're trying to use the sister's murder to get your client off? Give me a break."

He turned away. Alex grabbed his arm.

"Hey! Hear me out. There's no way Joanie or Bethany could come up with that much cash."

"So you're saying Joanie got her hooks into a john with more money than sense and raised her rates in return for not telling his wife."

"It was about sex in the beginning, but it turned into something more."

"More than sex?" Harris asked. "What's more than sex?"

"A child," Alex said.

"Charlotte?" Rossi asked.

"Yeah. A wife might forgive her husband for going to a prostitute, but having a child with the prostitute is a lot harder to forgive and a lot more expensive if you throw in child support and treatment for autism. We find Charlotte's father, we might find who killed Joanie and Bethany."

Rossi looked back inside the trailer and then at Alex. "Okay. It's possible."

"You got any candidates for this father of the year?" Harris asked.

Alex hesitated, taking a deep breath. "It has to be someone with money or power or both, someone with more to lose than the average john."

Rossi said, "That makes for a long list. Can you shorten it up?"

"I tried to but I struck out."

"Who?" Rossi asked.

"Anthony Steele."

"The judge? Christ! You've got to be kidding. What possible connection does he have to either one of them?"

"Joanie's first arrest was in Clay County for shoplifting. Steele was the judge and he put her in diversion before she even had an attorney. Fast-forward to five years ago and Joanie is a hooker with a drug problem and Steele pays for her to go to Fresh Start for rehab."

Rossi raised an eyebrow. "Out of his own pocket?"

"No. His family has a foundation, the Steele Family Foundation. They paid for it."

"How do you know that?"

"Steele told me. When I saw him at Robin's memorial yesterday I said that his name had come up when I reviewed Joanie's arrest record. He said he didn't remember her but he gave me a Voldemort look when I mentioned her name."

"A Voldemort look?"

"Yeah, Voldemort is the bad guy in the Harry Potter books. He's so scary that just saying his name out loud will ruin your day, and Steele acted like I ruined his. And then he calls me this morning and says he remembered Joanie and would I come to his chambers so he can tell me all about her."

"And I'm guessing that instead of thanking him for taking the time to help you out, you accused him of murdering Joanie?"

Alex shrugged. "It sort of came up."

"How'd he take that?"

"He laughed it off, said I was just doing my job and he thanked me for giving him something to talk about at dinner."

"I'll bet," Rossi said, dipping his chin for a moment, his eyes narrowed in concentration. "Wait a second. Back up. What did you say the name of the foundation was?"

"The Steele Family Foundation, why?"

Rossi opened his phone and pulled up the spreadsheet Milton had e-mailed him, scrolling down until he found the entry that read *SFF*.

"Motherfucker."

"What?"

"Tell me about your conversation with Judge Steele in his chambers and don't leave anything out."

Alex grimaced, suddenly woozy, her wounds throbbing. She grabbed a patio chair and eased herself into it.

"You should have stayed in bed. You okay?"

"Peachy. Let me think for a minute." She took a breath. "Okay, I walked into his chambers, we said hello, he told me I looked like shit and I said I threw my back out. He said he'd been there because of how much his wife makes him work out. He was dressed down, khakis, no socks, that kind of thing. I asked him if the court had adopted a casual dress code and he said he could always put on his robe and that if I'd been there an hour earlier I'd have caught him in his workout clothes. His gear was in a bag on the floor—"

Rossi interrupted. "The bag. Tell me about the bag."

Alex furrowed her brow. "I don't know. It was a bag, you know, some kind of duffel."

Rossi pulled up the airport video on his phone, freezing it on a close-up of the duffel bag. "Did it look like this?"

Alex took the phone, playing with the image, making it larger, then smaller. "Who's that in the video?"

"We don't know yet. Just focus on the bag. Does it look like the one you saw in Steele's chambers?"

Alex played with the image some more, wrinkling her nose. "Could be. What's that word on the bag? This image is too fuzzy for me to make it out."

"*Solutioneering*, all lowercase."

Alex nodded. "Yeah. There was something printed on his bag. That could have been it."

Rossi's face lit up, his eyes dancing. "How well did you know Robin Norris?"

"Like I told you before. We were good friends but in a professional way. I didn't know much about her private life."

"What about her and Judge Steele? Was there anything going on between them?"

"Not that I knew…Wait, let me show you something. Meg Adler packed up Robin's personal stuff from her office and I offered to drop it off at Robin's house. It's in my car. I'll get it."

Alex started to get up, but Rossi put his hand out.

"Keys."

He brought her the box from her car, putting it at her feet.

"Show me."

She retrieved the framed photograph of Robin and Judge Steele, handing it to Rossi.

"That was taken at the state bar convention earlier this year. The judge presented Robin with a service award. Later that night, I saw them having a drink, and they looked so cozy that I kidded Robin about it the next morning. She told me I was being ridiculous because he was married and she was close friends with both the judge and his wife."

"Hmm. But she kept a picture of the two of them in her office." Rossi turned the frame over, raising the clips holding the photograph in place, sliding it out, and turning it over. "I think she was a little closer to him than she was to his wife."

He handed the photograph to Alex. There was an inscription on the back. *This will have to do until the next time we can be alone.*

"Is that Robin's handwriting?" Rossi asked.

Alex shook her head. "No. It must be Judge Steele's. Wow. Who's that in the video?"

"Robin Norris's killer."

Rossi opened his phone and called Wheeler.

"Did you find out who was using the rooms on the west side of the motel?"

"Yeah," Wheeler said. "Only one room was occupied. It belongs to someone with the initials *SFF*, but your buddy Milton swears on his life that he doesn't know who that is."

"I do. Meet me at the court of appeals."

FIFTY-TWO

Alex stayed in the patio chair while Bethany's body was bagged and carried out of the trailer. The wooziness she'd felt had passed. Harris approached her.

"You okay to drive yourself home? I can have an officer take you and another one drive your car."

"Thanks, but I think I can handle it."

"Okay, then. We're pretty much wrapped up here."

"What about Charlotte?"

"We're combing the area. If she's on her own, she's probably fairly close by. If the killer took her, it's anybody's guess. We don't have much to go on."

"I guess Rossi thinks Judge Steele killed Robin."

"Yeah, lover's quarrel and all of that. They'll have him in custody before you get home."

She shook her head. "The whole thing is unbelievable. Robin and Judge Steele. How could he do it? How could he kill her?"

"C'mon, Counselor. You spend enough years doing what you and I do and there's nothing we can't believe. Look on the bright side. You may not have found the killer you're looking for, but because of you, Rossi got his guy."

"Swell."

Alex took her time going to her car, slow steps less painful than rapid ones. If Rossi was right about Judge Steele, then the judge must have also tried to kill her. But if he had, why invite her to his chambers the next morning? She slid into the driver's seat, grunting at a flash of pain, and sent Rossi a text, asking him to let her know when he arrested Judge Steele.

As upset as she was about Robin and Judge Steele, she was more worried about Charlotte, ten years old and alone in the world. Had she been home when Bethany was killed and somehow escaped? Was the killer hunting for her because she was a witness? Or had she been out wandering only to discover Bethany's body when she came home, leaving again because she was afraid and didn't know what else to do? And if she was on her own, where would she go? Alex could think of only one place: Liberty Park.

She left her car at the north end, just as she had before, making her way south, taking her time, zigzagging from side to side to cover as much ground as possible, calling Charlotte's name as she went, hearing nothing in reply. The sun was beginning to set, shadows washing in from the west and climbing up the eastern bluff. The ground was covered with a tangle of weeds that grabbed at her ankles, tagging her with burrs and thorns. She caught her foot in a rut, falling to her knees, groaning, her wounds burning.

As Alex neared where Joanie's body had been found, she hugged the creek bank, hoping to find Charlotte at the water's edge, but she wasn't there. The campground was deserted. Even Gladys Knight's tent was gone. That left the thick woods at the south end, a trek she wasn't certain she could make. She sat on a tree stump to catch her breath, peering into the creeping dusk for a sign of the girl, a flickering light at the base of the bluff catching her eye.

Taking a deep breath, she made her way toward the light. The closer she got, the more the light danced, and then she realized it was flames coming from a campfire shielded by a low rock wall. A moment later, a voice called out from behind it.

"That's close enough."

Alex stopped. "Gladys? Is that you?"

"Who else would I be? The question is who the hell are you?"

"Alex Stone. I talked to you the other day. How are the Pips?"

"Just dandy. Now, go away."

"What happened to your tent?"

"Blew away. Got me a nice little hollowed-out cave instead. Suits me just fine."

"I'm looking for the little girl I told you about. Her name is Charlotte."

"Get lost. Don't know anybody named Charlotte."

Alex heard someone rustling around in the cave, then the sound of something being scraped against the rocks and a child humming, though it sounded more like a closed-mouth whine.

Alex scrambled over the wall, finding Gladys sitting cross-legged in front of the fire and Charlotte banging her spatula against the cave. Gladys jumped to her feet, putting herself between Alex and Charlotte.

The hollowed-out cave was exactly that, extending no more than five feet into the base of the bluff, as if it had been carved out with a giant ice cream scoop, the ceiling just high enough for Alex to stand. The campfire was at the mouth of the cave. Gladys's belongings, including a stack of milk crates filled to the rims, were piled against the back wall.

"You got no right," Gladys said.

"How long has Charlotte been here?"

"Hmph. Her name's Charlotte? Never knew what to call her, so I didn't call her anything. She showed up in the middle of the night last night, same as usual."

"She can't stay here. The police are looking for her."

"Who said anything about staying? She'll go home when she's ready like she always does."

"She can't, not anymore."

Gladys scratched her cheek, looking over her shoulder at Charlotte, who was tracing an invisible pattern on the cave wall, oblivious to them. She motioned to Alex to follow her. They walked around the mound of rocks, Gladys leaning against them.

"Why not?"

"Charlotte was living with her mother and aunt in a mobile home park not far from here, and now they're both dead. Her mother was the woman whose body was found in the creek. Her aunt was murdered last night. Charlotte might have seen who killed both of them."

Gladys squeezed her eyes tight, shaking her head. "What's gonna happen to that poor child?"

"I don't know, but she can't stay here. I have to call the police and tell them I found her. Someone from Child Protective Services will pick her up, and they'll probably put her in foster care for the time being."

"I don't want no goddamn police coming around here."

"Then I'll take her."

"Like she'd go anywhere with you! She don't know you. You try and make her and she'll just run off, sure as hell."

"Can't be helped. It's either me or the cops."

Gladys tugged at her hair. "Ah, hell! She'll go with me, so you'll have to take both of us, but we ain't goin' to no goddamn police station."

"Where else would we go?"

"You got a house, don't you? Child could use a bath."

Alex smiled. "Sure. That'll work."

They went back into the cave. Charlotte had knocked over the stack of milk crates and was sitting on one of them, hugging a black dress. Alex stepped toward her, but Charlotte retreated, swiveling around on the crate, giving her back to Alex.

"Gladys, where did she—where did you—get that dress?"

Gladys spit in the fire, cocking her head at Charlotte. "She brung it."

"When?"

"What difference does it make?"

"A lot, maybe. Charlotte's mother was wearing a black dress the night she was murdered."

Gladys cocked her head, her rheumy eyes fluttering. "I wouldn't know nothing about that."

"I'm not saying you do, but that dress could help us find whoever murdered Charlotte's mother and aunt."

Gladys circled the fire, muttering.

"Okay, goddamn it. I mind my own business and see what it gets me! That child showed up in my tent last week with that dress, and when I heard about the body they found in the creek, well, I ain't stupid."

"The killer probably stripped the body in the woods and while he was dumping it in the creek, Charlotte must have taken the dress. Which means she could have seen her mother die."

"Way I figured it."

A wave of dizziness came over Alex. She pressed a hand against the cave wall to steady herself, the other hand to her forehead.

"What's the matter with you? You look feverish."

Alex couldn't think of a reason not to tell Gladys the truth.

"Somebody stabbed me last night."

"And people say being homeless is dangerous." Gladys put her hand on Alex's cheek. "You're burning up."

Alex turned away from her. "I'll be okay."

"Not if you keep bleeding like that."

"What?" Alex reached behind her, feeling her back. Some of her stitches had given way and she was oozing blood.

"You better see a doctor."

"I've got one waiting for me when we get home."

"Well, ain't you the lucky one. She know you're gallivantin' around?"

"No. She's called me half a dozen times today and I told her that I was watching television."

"Well, if she's waitin' for you at home, that story ain't gonna get you too far, but it might be fun to watch you give it a try." Gladys reached out to Charlotte. "Let's go, child."

Holding on to the dress, Charlotte took her hand.

FIFTY-THREE

Alex pulled into their garage just as Bonnie drove in behind her. Bonnie's expression morphed from stony-eyed anger to wide-eyed worry when she saw Alex, pale and dripping with sweat, swaying as she stood in the garage, holding on to the car door.

"Holy crap, Alex!"

Bonnie rushed to her, throwing Alex's arm across her back, using her shoulder to support her, doing a double take when Gladys took Alex's other side and recoiling at Gladys's odor.

"Who are you?"

"Gladys Knight. The Pips got lost on the way over. The little girl is Charlotte."

Bonnie swung her head around. "What little girl?"

"That one." Gladys pointed to Charlotte, who was standing in the corner of the garage, drawing air circles with her spatula.

"I can explain," Alex said.

"Not until I stop the bleeding," Bonnie answered.

While Bonnie cleaned and stitched her wounds, Alex told her about Judge Steele and Robin and about Bethany, Charlotte, and Gladys and the black dress.

"Put that dress in a plastic bag. I've got to preserve some kind of chain of evidence for it. And put it where Charlotte can't find it. By the way, she's autistic. She doesn't talk and you can't touch her, but she loves her spatula."

"Noted."

"I need to call Detective Harris and tell him that I found Charlotte."

"Fine, but if you get out of that bed before tomorrow morning for any reason except to pee or poop, I'm going strap you down."

"Promise me you'll use the fake-fur straps you got at Erotic City."

Bonnie grinned. "What am I going to do with you?"

Alex smiled. "Love me."

"I might as well. Hate for the toys to go to waste. I'll check on Gladys and Charlotte."

Alex left Harris a message when he didn't answer, then sank into her pillow and fell asleep.

Charlotte took a bath and Bonnie put her clothes in the washing machine, giving Charlotte a pair of sweatpants and a T-shirt left over from when her niece visited a year ago, not objecting when Charlotte took her spatula into the tub.

After a lengthy argument with Gladys that ended when Bonnie promised to let Gladys pick a clean outfit from her closet, Gladys agreed to take a shower. Bonnie didn't bother to wash Gladys's clothes, burying them in the bottom of the barrel of trash that would be picked up the next day. Quincy followed her into the garage, sniffing and whining at the barrel until Bonnie made him come back in the house.

Satisfied that a semblance of order had been restored, Bonnie poured herself a glass of wine and settled into her easy chair, Quincy curled up beside her. The doorbell rang before she could take her first sip. Quincy raced her to the door, barking, sticking his head out as soon as Bonnie opened it, not recognizing the middle-aged blond woman who had rung the bell.

"Hello. I'm Sonia Steele. May I come in?"

It took a moment for Bonnie to register her name, making the connection to what Alex had told her, wondering why Sonia was standing on her doorstep instead of trying to get her husband out of jail. Not knowing what to say to someone whose spouse is an accused murderer, she decided to act like she didn't know.

"Of course, of course. Forgive me. I wasn't expecting anyone."

Sonia walked through the entry hall, glancing in every room until she found the kitchen. Bonnie hurried to catch up.

"You must be Bonnie."

"Yes. I'm sorry, but do we know each other?"

Sonia smiled. "No. Alex is a friend of mine. I was hoping to talk with her. Is she home?"

Alex hadn't described Sonia as a friend and Bonnie didn't like the way she'd swept into the house, both of which made her uneasy.

"She's asleep. I'll tell her you stopped by. I'm sure she'll call you tomorrow."

"It's important. I'd rather not wait until then."

Bonnie stiffened. "I'm sorry, but she's not feeling well."

Sonia drew a gun from her purse. "That's the least of her troubles."

Alex stirred, hearing Quincy bark, murmuring.

"Shut up, dog."

She smiled when Quincy quieted.

"Good doggie."

A moment later, Gladys opened the bedroom door. "Pssst. You got company."

Alex propped herself up on her elbow, rubbing her eyes. Gladys, her hair wet and pulled back in a bun, was wearing a pair of Bonnie's Juicy Couture velour pants, a Free People pullover Alex had given Bonnie for Christmas, and a pair of Alex's boots.

"What on earth are you doing wearing Bonnie's clothes and my shoes?"

"That doctor of yours drives a hard bargain."

Alex sat up in bed. "I can only imagine. What did you say about having company?"

"There's a woman in the kitchen with the doc."

"Who?"

Gladys put her hands on her hips. "Like I'm supposed to know."

"Then why did you wake me?"

"On account of your dog."

"Don't worry. He's harmless."

"But she ain't."

Alex rubbed her face with both hands, staring at Gladys, wondering if the woman was an escapee from *Alice's Adventures in Wonderland*. "Who isn't?"

"The woman in the kitchen."

Alex swung her legs off the bed. "How do you know that?"

"I told you, the dog. I heard the bell and the dog and then I heard voices. So I took a peek. All I could see was that dog of yours. His hair is up and he's holding still as a statue."

"You're crazy, you know that, don't you?"

Gladys glared at Alex, arms crossed over her chest. Alex's phone chirped with a text message from Rossi. *It's not the judge. Call me ASAP.*

Rossi answered on the first ring.

"Where are you?"

"Home and in bed. What do you mean it's not the judge?"

"He's got an alibi that checks out. He was at something called the Inns of Court. It's a lawyers and judges thing."

"I know what it is. What about the affair with Robin?"

"He admitted it. Said his wife found out and she wasn't happy. But that's not all. You were right about him and Joanie. They had a thing after she got out of diversion, but it didn't last.

Then she told him she was pregnant and asked him to pay the bills."

"So he's Charlotte's father?"

"Not according to him. He says Joanie told him it was someone else. He says he paid her medical bills anyway because he had a soft spot for her. He says the next time he heard from her was when the sister, Bethany, pressed him to get her into Fresh Start."

"That was Bethany's idea?"

"So he says. Makes sense. Not too many addicts get to rehab on their own, and she knew what Steele had already done for Joanie."

"What about the five grand?"

"His money, not the foundation's. He said Bethany called him a couple of weeks ago and told him that Joanie had lied about the kid not being his and demanding money."

"Or she'd go public."

"Right, but here's the kicker. Bethany told him the kid is autistic and she needed the money to pay for the kid's therapy."

"But Bethany told me she didn't have money to pay for therapy. She must have been planning to keep it for herself."

"She may have planned on using the money for Charlotte at first, but she got greedy and told Steele that the five grand was just for starters and that she wanted ten thousand a month."

"What did Steele say?"

"He said that if Charlotte was his kid, he'd take care of her but he wanted DNA testing to confirm that he was the father."

"So how did it all get sideways?"

"When Steele's wife found out about him and Robin, he decided to come clean about the kid, and then she went ballistic, told him they weren't going to pay a dime and that she would take care of it."

"You think Sonia killed Robin?"

"Had to be her. Steele had a permanent reservation at a motel on Barry Road that he and Robin used. The motel manager confirmed that someone used it the night Robin was killed. My guess is Sonia met Robin there, they argued, and the rest is history."

"I think I may have found the dress Joanie Sutherland was wearing when she was killed. If there's any of Sonia's DNA on it, that could tie her to Joanie's murder."

"And Bethany's if she decided to get rid of both blackmailers. We're looking for Sonia but she's in the wind."

Alex looked at Gladys, who was listening to Alex's side of the conversation, giving her a wide-eyed, now-do-you-believe-me look.

"I think the wind just blew her into my kitchen."

"Don't do anything stupid. I'm on my way."

Alex went to the top of the stairs, surprised to see Charlotte sitting on the bottom step, tapping the carpet with her spatula. Charlotte got up, went down the hall into the kitchen, and began screaming, a piercing, terrified wail. Alex hustled after her, Gladys on her heels, both rushing into the kitchen.

Bonnie was standing by the sink, pale and bracing herself with one hand on the counter. Charlotte was balled up on the floor next to a small desk opposite Bonnie, screaming so loud it was difficult to hear. Sonia stood next to the kitchen table, holding a gun, the three of them forming a triangle, Alex and Gladys falling into the line between Bonnie and Charlotte. Quincy was on all fours, hugging Bonnie's side.

The veins in Sonia's neck swelled, her eyes blazing, her jaw set. She aimed the gun at Charlotte. "Somebody shut that little bitch up before I do it for her."

Quincy went to Charlotte, licking her face. Instead of shrinking from the dog, she stopped crying and stroked his fur. Quincy kept himself in front of Charlotte, shielding her, his ears back and his eyes locked on Sonia.

Alex's heart was racing, pounding against her ribs, making her wounds throb with pain. Light-headed, she glanced at

Gladys, whose arms were locked at her sides, her fists balled as she raised her heels up and down like she was winding herself up to launch at Sonia. Certain that Sonia would shoot Gladys at the slightest move, Alex put her hand on Gladys's arm, holding both of them in place. She wanted to keep Sonia talking, hoping Rossi would get there in time.

"Her name is Charlotte. She's ten years old and she's autistic. She was screaming because you frightened her."

"Why would I frighten the bitch?"

"Well, the gun is scary enough. But when the woman holding the gun is the same person Charlotte saw murder her mother and her aunt, that's really scary."

Sonia kept her gun on Charlotte. "You know, I could have lived with Tony having an affair. After all, what man hasn't? I could have even gotten over him fucking my best friend. But having a bastard child with a prostitute? This…this pathetic little thing." She bared her teeth. "That was too much, and her whore mother and her vulgar aunt demanding my money to save my husband's reputation!" She shook her head. "I told Tony that I wouldn't stand for it!"

Alex said, "So you strangled Joanie Sutherland in the woods at Liberty Park and threw her body in the creek, and then you crushed her sister Bethany's skull with an iron."

Sonia's face reddened, her lips quivering. She turned her gun on Alex. "Well, I wasn't going to put them on the fucking payroll. And you! You made it worse refusing to tell me what Robin said in her message. How could I risk not knowing if she said something about me?"

"She didn't but if she had, the police would have already talked to you so you stabbed me for nothing."

Sonia's face slackened. "You don't know that."

"Of course I do but you're like some other killers I've represented. You got so caught up in killing that you couldn't think of anything else."

"But don't you see, that's the point. Stabbing you wasn't my fault! You could have told me there was nothing on that message about me. And if Tony had kept his dick in his pants, Robin would be alive! They'd all be alive! None of this is my fault! None of it!"

"I know the people you cared about didn't just let you down; they betrayed you. But none of us had a hand in that. Charlotte didn't ask to be born. Bonnie and Gladys never met you before. And I am so sorry I didn't tell you about the message. But there's no reason to make things any worse. We can find a way out of this."

Sonia's mouth turned down, her face sagging with resignation. "Don't kid yourself. We both know there's only one way this can end."

She swung her gun in an arc, pointing at them one at a time like she was deciding whom to kill first, settling on Bonnie, who looked at Alex, stricken.

"I love you, Alex Stone."

"Sonia! Please! You don't have to do this."

"But it will feel so good."

Quincy sprang at Sonia as she pulled the trigger, barreling her to the floor and throwing her aim off so the bullet missed Bonnie. He clamped his jaws on her gun hand, shaking it like it was a rag doll.

"Get him off! Get him off!"

Sonia battered Quincy with her free hand until Gladys kicked her in the head, knocking her out. She straddled Sonia, brushing her hands together.

"Can't stand a person what would hurt a dog."

FIFTY-FOUR

Alex got to work early Monday morning. She stood in the doorway of Robin's office looking at the desk and the credenza behind it, at the chairs and at the bare walls. There was no trace of Robin, no way to know that she had lived within those walls for so many years.

She crossed to the windows looking down at the street below, at the people and cars passing by, small and distant, caught up in their own lives, as they should be. She raised her gaze to the eastern horizon, smiling at the rising sun, grateful for a new day, a new beginning.

Bonnie had encouraged her to take the interim director position, telling her it was a great career move and assuring her that she had the right skills for the job. What went unspoken was Bonnie's relief that Alex would be one step further removed from the violence and death that had so haunted them. Alex shared her relief, knowing that she'd no longer have to wrestle with her duty to her clients and that she would put welcome space between her and Judge West. Though in her private moments over the last few days, she found it hard to imagine herself so far removed from the battle, she told herself that she'd get used to it and if sitting behind a desk all day allowed Bonnie to sleep better at night, she'd happily do it.

Any doubt that she could leave the past behind was erased the night before while they were enjoying a glass of wine, the television on in the background. The screen flashed with a bulletin about breaking news followed by a reporter standing outside a farmhouse that Alex recognized. She put her glass down and turned the sound on, listening to the reporter.

I'm standing outside the home of Jackson County Circuit Court Judge William West, where police tell me they found the bodies of both Judge West and his wife, Millie. According to police, Mrs. West shot her husband and then committed suicide. We'll have more details as they become available.

Dumbstruck, they had remained glued to the television, absorbing the news. Millie West's mental illness had claimed both her and her husband, her paranoia swamping reason. Their deaths hadn't wiped away Alex's sins, but they had buried them, and she promised herself that she wouldn't look back.

Meg Adler rapped on the door. "You're going to do great things."

Alex smiled. "Thanks."

"You know, when I first moved from the courtroom into management, I was sure I'd miss it, you know, the jousting, the killer closings and cross-examinations."

"Didn't you?"

"For a while, until I realized that I could accomplish more by making sure my lawyers did their jobs well than I could ever accomplish on my own."

Alex nodded. "I hadn't thought of it that way."

"You will, but there will be days when you're overwhelmed with budgets, bureaucracy, and politics and you'll go home at night cursing my name."

They both laughed.

"I guess there's no such thing as a perfect job."

Meg gave her a final hug and left. Alex tried Robin's desk chair but couldn't get comfortable. She swapped it with the one from her old office, smiling and beginning to feel like she was in the right place. Grace Canfield helped her hang her pictures and diplomas, telling her to go get them both coffee while she organized Alex's desk. When Alex returned, there were flowers from Bonnie and a stack of files and assorted paperwork to review.

The day passed quickly, work interrupted by a steady flow of well-wishing colleagues and congratulatory e-mails and phone calls. Late in the afternoon, the receptionist called her.

"Detective Rossi to see you."

"Bring him back."

By the time Rossi had arrived at her house last week, Sonia was conscious, Bonnie was bandaging her tattered hand, and Alex was holding a cold compress to her head while Gladys toyed with Sonia's gun, telling Sonia to sit real still because there was no telling if the gun might accidentally go off and shoot right her between the eyes.

The next day, Alex went downtown to give a detailed statement to Rossi and to work out Jared Bell's release with Kalena Greene. She hadn't talked to Rossi since and wondered what was on his mind.

"Nice digs," Rossi said when the receptionist delivered him.

"Yeah, but it still feels weird. Have a seat."

He set a large envelope on her desk and pulled up a chair. There was no name on the envelope, but Alex was certain it was for her. Though curious, she'd let him get to it in his own time.

"So how are you feeling? Wounds healing okay?"

"Pretty good. I've graduated from sore to itchy."

Rossi looked around the office. "I think this suits you."

"You think?"

"Yeah. Someone like you will live a lot longer behind a desk."

Alex chuckled. "Bonnie would agree, especially since she wants us to have a baby."

"No kidding."

Alex was surprised that she told Rossi, given their history, but she was getting a different vibe from him, like maybe he was ready for a cease-fire.

"Yeah. We're going to do the whole turkey-baster thing as soon as we find a donor."

"Speaking of kids, how's Charlotte doing?"

"Child Protective Services was going to put her in foster care until Bonnie convinced them that the three of us could take care of her for now."

"The three of you?"

"Bonnie, Gladys, and me."

"That crazy old lady? You sure that's a good idea?"

"No, but it's working out so far. Gladys is the only person left that Charlotte has any kind of relationship with. The county sent a social worker to our house to observe them and said they've got a bond that she doesn't want to screw up. So they're both staying with us. Plus, Charlotte loves Quincy and it turns out that having a pet can help an autistic child develop some social skills."

"What about Judge Steele? You going to find out if he's Charlotte's father?"

"He says he'll agree to DNA testing, but we'll see. He's got his hands full right now. You heard he resigned from the bench so he could help with his wife's defense?"

Rossi nodded. "Which is interesting since she set him up as her second option to take the fall for Robin's murder."

"Second option?"

"Robin's ex, Ted Norris, was her first choice. She knew Ted kept a spare key hidden in the wheel well of his car. That's how she stole it and used it to run Robin off the road. She left the car at the airport, and when she got out of the car, she was carrying her husband's duffel bag, the one you saw in his chambers. She made sure it would be picked up on the airport security cameras. If we gave up on Ted, the duffel was going to be the first bread crumb leading us to the judge."

"So why would he want to help with her defense?"

"Because he says he loves her and doesn't believe she'd do that to him or that she's guilty of anything except justifiable jealousy."

Rossi reached for the envelope. "Listen, there's something I need to show you."

He opened the envelope, removing a photograph encased in a plastic sleeve showing her kneeling over Dwayne Reed's body. Alex gasped, her stomach grinding. She stared at the photograph, unable to speak or look at Rossi, her hands clenched in her lap.

"It came in the mail last Friday, addressed to me, no note, no explanation, just the photograph."

Alex forced herself to look at him. "I…I…I can explain."

"You don't have to. It's a fake."

Alex blinked, slumping against the back of her chair. "How do you know that?"

"I gotta admit, when I first saw it, I thought I was gonna bust the buttons on my jeans. But you know what they say about things that are too good to be true. I had one of our forensic photographers check it out, and he said it had been Photoshopped. He pulled the photographs from Dwayne Reed's file and showed me how it was done."

"Wow."

"Wow is right. So naturally I was curious about who sent the photograph to me and why, so I had it and the envelope it came in checked for prints."

Alex swallowed. "And I take it you found some."

"Big fat ones, one on the envelope and one on the picture. They were so clear and distinct, it was like somebody went out of their way to make sure we'd find them."

"Could you identify them?"

Rossi nodded. "Yep. Ran them through the system and got a match."

Alex was afraid to ask but knew Rossi wanted her to. "Whose are they?"

Rossi leaned back in his chair. "Millie West. Turns out she was arrested for disorderly conduct a few years ago and that's how her prints got in the system."

Alex's chin dropped, her mouth hanging open. "What?"

"Nuts, right? So Friday night, I go see her. She and the judge are out at their horse farm, and man, that horseshit is nasty stuff. But I guess you know that from helping that friend of yours clean out their stables."

Alex straightened, her relief ebbing away. "Go on."

"So, like I was saying, I go out there to talk to Millie, and right away the judge is on my case, what's this all about, and I tell him I need to talk to his wife and he says what for and I say that's between her and me and he says if I think he's going to let her talk to me alone, I'm out of my mind, so the three of us sit down at the dining room table and I put the photograph on the table. Don't say a word. Just put it out there."

Rossi's eyes were dancing, a grin creeping out of the corners of his mouth. Alex didn't know how to read him.

"What happened?"

"He about shit a brick and she started laughing, I mean cackling like a witch with a new broomstick on Halloween, and wouldn't stop. He finally had to take her into another a room and give her a pill to calm her down. Then he comes back and tells me that she made the picture and sent it to me. I asked him why she'd do something like that and he said she's bipolar and doesn't always take her meds and when she doesn't she goes kind of crazy."

"Maybe that explains the disorderly conduct thing."

"It does. But it doesn't explain why she'd jack around with this photograph or how she even got ahold of the file photographs in the first place."

"How did Judge West explain that?"

"He said there were copies of the pictures in the court file. He had the file at the ranch during the trial and that's when she must have done it. I told him that explains the how but not the why, and you won't believe what he said."

"Try me."

"He said that being bipolar and not taking her meds makes his wife paranoid and she became convinced that you and the judge were having an affair and that this was her way of getting even with both of you. She made sure her prints would be found so that he'd know what she'd done."

Alex shook her head. "I'm stunned."

"I know. It's crazy. But here's the really crazy part. How'd Millie know to put you in that picture in just the right way to prove that you murdered Dwayne Reed? I mean, if she wanted to embarrass you and the judge, why not doctor up some naked pictures of the two of you?"

Alex took a deep breath, letting it out. "I don't know. I guess you'd have to ask her."

"Kind of hard now that she blew her brains out. Besides, I don't think she could tell me how your fingerprints also ended up on the photograph."

There it was. Rossi wasn't going to leave her alone. No matter that she'd helped him solve three murders. No matter that she and Bonnie had nearly been killed. No matter anything. Weariness swept over her. She couldn't do this anymore. She couldn't keep running from Dwayne Reed while she slept and from Rossi while she was awake.

"Go ahead. Ask me."

"Did you shoot Dwayne Reed in self-defense?"

Alex flattened her hands on her desk and looked him in the eye. "No. I shot him and put his gun in his hand and pulled the trigger to make it look like he fired first."

"What was going on between you and Judge West?"

Alex took another deep breath. "West had been shading cases in favor of the prosecution for years but doing it in ways that would stand up on appeal. He saw how upset I was after I got Dwayne acquitted and he murdered that family and he recruited me to throw my really awful clients under the bus without doing a bad enough job to give them grounds to appeal based on ineffective assistance of counsel. That night I ran into you at the Zoo, I'd been at his horse farm. I told him I was out, that I wasn't going to do it anymore. He handed me that photograph in an envelope just like you did. That's how my prints got on it. He told me he'd ruin me if I backed out. Then he told me Jared Bell would be my next case and that he'd use the photograph if I didn't make sure Jared was convicted. I still don't know how he knew about Jared."

"Interesting thing about that. Kalena told me about Robin getting Jared's file ahead of schedule. She said no one in her office was responsible. West could have done it but we couldn't figure out why he would, so I asked him. He admitted giving the file to Robin but said she asked him for it."

"And you believed that?"

"Until Judge Steele told me different. When he heard on the news that a prostitute's body had been found in Liberty Park, he was afraid it was Joanie even though her identity hadn't been released. The only good news was that we'd arrested Jared. Steele was scared that Sonia might have killed Joanie and he called Judge West and asked him about the case."

"He must have known what West was doing."

"He did. They were hunting buddies, and West got drunk one night on a hunting trip and told Steele enough that he figured it out."

"Did Steele tell him about Sonia?"

"Not directly. He just made it clear that this was one case that needed to go away in a hurry, and West said he'd take care of it. I don't know if or how he made sure you were assigned to the case. West might have been telling the truth about that or he might have had something on Robin. We may never know for certain. What we do know is that you didn't go along with West."

"No. I didn't."

"Why not?"

Alex pursed her lips. "I hated what I'd become and I didn't want to be that person anymore, and I was willing to let whatever was going to happen, happen."

Rossi nodded and then stared out the window, lost in thought for a minute. "I guess you know what Bonnie pulled on me, that thing with the lawsuit?"

"Don't blame her. She was just trying to help me. You don't have anything to worry about. It was total bullshit. There isn't going to be a lawsuit."

"I know that. I checked up on the family members of those men. I don't know who she had at your house, but they definitely weren't who she said they were."

"Now what?"

He picked up the photograph. "Nothing. This thing between you and me, it's over."

Alex was wide-eyed. "Why?"

"Bonnie was right. I probably didn't have to kill those men, but I did. And the cops who investigated the shootings, well, let's just say they take care of their own. After I left your house that day, I went home and got drunk, and when I sobered up, I realized something."

"What's that?"

"All this time I was chasing after you, I was really chasing the dead, and I'm done doing that."

Alex went home. Bonnie was waiting for her with a bottle of their favorite wine, ready to toast Alex's first day in her new job, until Alex's cell phone chirped with a text. It was from Claire Mason, her law school mentor and the lawyer who had defended her when she was charged with murdering Dwayne Reed. Alex opened her phone and read the text.

"Who texted you?"

"Claire."

"What did she want?"

"You know she's part of that national group of defense lawyers who've volunteered to defend the detainees at Guantanamo?"

"Yes."

"Here." She handed Bonnie the phone. "Read it."

Bonnie read the text aloud.

"I need you. Come to Guantanamo as soon as you can. And bring Bonnie."

NEWSLETTER SIGNUP

If you'd like to receive an email letting you know when Joel's next book will be released, sign up at www.joelgoldman.com/newsletter/. Your email address will never be shared and you can unsubscribe at any time.

REVIEW THIS BOOK

Thanks for adding *Chasing The Dead* to your library. Readers depend on readers to recommend good books and authors depend on readers to generate positive word-of-mouth for their books. If you liked *Chasing The Dead*, please leave a review on Goodreads or any other online platform of your choosing, even if it's only a few words. It will make a big difference and Joel will be very thankful.

LET'S CONNECT

Joel enjoys engaging with his readers. Drop by his website, www.joelgoldman.com, to find out more about him and his books. Read what he has to say about the writer's life on his blog, www.joelgoldman.com/blog and join him on Twitter at www.twitter.com/joelgoldman1 and on Facebook at www.facebook.com/joelgoldmanauthor. And watch videos about Joel and his books at www.youtube.com/user/joelgoldmanwriter.

ABOUT THE AUTHOR

Joel Goldman is the bestselling author of the Edgar and Shamus nominated Lou Mason thrillers, the Jack Davis thrillers and the Alex Stone thrillers. He is also the co-author of the Carter & Ireland Caper Series with Lisa Klink. Together with Lee Goldberg, he founded Brash Books where they publish the best crime novels in existence. He lives with his wife and two dogs in Leawood, KS. He was a trial lawyer for twenty-eight years. He wrote his first novel after one of his partners complained about another partner, prompting him to write his first thriller, kill the son-of-a-bitch off in the first chapter and spend the rest of the book figuring out who did it. And he never looked back.

Made in United States
Orlando, FL
28 April 2023